THE COMPANY
OF
STRANGERS

Eileen Campbell was born in 1947 in Inverness, where she has lived all her life apart from a few years spent in Louisiana. She now works in the Highlands, alongside her husband in his security business, and is a committed member of the Scottish National Party. *The Company of Strangers* is her first novel; she is working on her second.

THE COMPANY OF STRANGERS

Eileen Campbell

FOURTH ESTATE • London

First published in Great Britain in 1998 by
Fourth Estate Limited
6 Salem Road
London W2 4BU

Copyright © 1998 by Eileen Campbell

1 3 5 7 9 10 8 6 4 2

The right of Eileen Campbell to be identified as the
author of this work has been asserted by her in
accordance with the Copyright, Designs and
Patents Act 1988.

A catalogue record for this book is available from
the British Library.

ISBN 1–85702–767–1

Typeset in Palatino by
Avon Dataset Ltd, Bidford on Avon B50 4JH

Printed and bound in Great Britain by
Clays Ltd, St Ives plc, Bungay, Suffolk

This book is dedicated to my parents.

For my late father
Alex Campbell
who lived loudly, with music and laughter, and
with great joy.

And for my mother, and my friend
Ina Campbell
who should be the pattern for all mums,
everywhere.

Acknowledgements

Thank you to *Writers News* and *Writing Magazine* for their excellent articles and interviews, one of which resulted in the publication of this book.

Thank you to my brilliant editors, Caroline Upcher and Jan Boxshall. They showed me how to turn a manuscript into a novel, and gave me the courage, and encouragement, to keep going.

Thank you to my 'reading committee', my mum and sister Liz, who read everything chapter by chapter and refused to let me dwell on rejections, or countenance failure. (Special thanks to Liz, for putting up with the midnight phone calls.)

Thank you to my beautiful daughter, Laura, for her unflinching faith, and for always being able to make me laugh. Her pride in me could never equal my pride in her.

Thank you to my husband, Robert, who got fed up listening to me threatening to 'write a book', and bought me a word-processor for Christmas. Thanks, also, for foraging for 'victuals' on too many occasions, so I could get on with my writing. And thanks, most of all, for coming into my life, and for always being there. In case I forgot to tell you, you are the best thing that's ever happened to me.

Finally, my grateful thanks to you – whoever you are – for investing your time (and, hopefully, your money) in this book. I hope you enjoy it, for without readers, there would be damn few writers.

PROLOGUE

They say that when you look back on the summers of your childhood, you remember only the sunshine.

Not me.

My summers were filled with days born of grey skies – waiting, ever watchful, for the rain; watchful, ever waiting, for my mother's descent into leaden despair.

There were, of course, brighter moments, even in Kilmoran; snatched hours spent in the company of my best, and only, friend, Janet. These hours, too, were often fraught with fear; for the rapturous anticipation of becoming 'teenagers' brought with it all manner of dangers with which we would have to contend.

That summer, the summer of 1959, began as always with the rain; the rain which ruined Dad's shirts – and washed away my childhood. And, for the two weeks which followed, as my eleventh year came to a close, I discovered a world beyond Kilmoran – a world called Inchbrae.

It was Inchbrae, a tiny Highland village, which

1

became my place of exile – a strange and formidable place, populated by strange and formidable people; none more so than my grandmother, Dot Fairbairn. Yet it was in Inchbrae I was to find shelter; in the arms and the wisdom of Dot. It was in Inchbrae I set out to find Johnny Starling. And it was in Inchbrae I walked in the sunshine – with a dog called Hooligan.

CHAPTER 1

'Can I go to Janet's now?'

Dad laid down his fork and knife, and looked at me over praying hands. (I always thought of them as praying – they were long and thin, and he always clasped them together whenever he had to correct me.)

I was getting better at beating him to it. 'Sorry. *May* I go to Janet's now?'

He nodded. 'You're quite finished?'

'Yes thank you.' I shifted my own fork slightly to cover what was left of my HP sauce. I'd taken more than I needed, as usual. I could never judge it quite right.

'Mother?' Dad looked across at Mam.

She nodded. 'Home by nine,' she said. Her voice was too quiet for me to hear the words, but I knew them anyway. It was what she usually said.

'Do you need some help before she leaves?' Dad asked.

I held my breath. Helping Mam could take all night.

She shook her head. 'No, thank you, Adam.' She

was thanking him for something that *I* might have to do. It wasn't fair, but you got used to it. I slid from my chair. Even though I would soon be twelve, I was still the smallest in my class, but I was the youngest as well, so it was quite wrong to say I was stunted. It was only ignorant people who called you stunted, and that was a fact.

There were a lot of ignorant people in Kilmoran. Dad said it came from being a small Highland town, but we were nearly as big as Inverness now, and they'd built a new school two years ago, which meant we didn't have to go away to the Academy any more. Janet and I had both passed our eleven-plus, and we'd be in the big school after the summer. We couldn't wait – but we were a bit scared too.

'Take your jacket, it looks like rain,' Mam said.

'Pessimism, Sylvia,' Dad said, chiding her like he did me sometimes. He was smiling, and she shouldn't have taken it the wrong way. She was always doing that, and you could get a sore head from not saying things to upset her. I tried to say the right things as often as I could. Sometimes it made no difference.

'It's not pessimism, Adam. I don't want her catching a cold. She's delicate.'

Dad's face went like cement, and I got back on my chair. It often started like this, and you had to watch their faces for clues. I might not be going to Janet's after all.

'Unless you happen to be wasting away in a

4

hospital bed, being delicate is a state of mind, Sylvia,' Dad said. 'Eleanor is not delicate.'

He was right. I wasn't. But Mam kept saying how we were all so delicate in her family, which wasn't strictly correct. My gran, Mam's mam, wasn't a bit delicate. She couldn't have been. She'd been married three times, and went off to New Zealand when Mam was nineteen 'without so much as a by-your-leave'. Nineteen seemed quite old to me, but Mam said it was far too young to be abandoned. Mam didn't want to go to New Zealand, and went into digs instead.

'She catches cold very easily.' I hadn't had a cold since Christmas, but Mam wouldn't leave it. 'She's not as robust as you'd like to believe, Adam – not like your side at all.'

Dad wasn't that robust. He caught far more colds than me *or* Mam. But he never missed his work, not once. I nearly got perfect attendance at school from his example, but Mam kept me off with the Christmas cold, and spoiled it. She always said my other gran was a robust woman.

We hadn't been to see my other gran since I was five, and she'd never been to our house as far as I knew. I didn't really remember going to see her. Mam said there had been a 'commotion' and Dad and his mam had fallen out. Mam never said *she'd* fallen out with my Granny Fairbairn. In fact, she smiled when she spoke of her – and Mam didn't smile too often. Still, Granny Fairbairn always sent me a card for my birthday, even though she didn't

5

send Dad one for his. It was usually a few days early, or sometimes late, but it was nice to get. It made me feel just like the other kids, knowing that at least I had a granny of my own.

When I showed Janet my last birthday card, she asked me why it wasn't from my granny and grandad. It hadn't occurred to me before, but I started to think about it all, and I decided to ask Mam. I could see she was getting in a state almost as soon as I opened my mouth, but I felt I *should* know. It wasn't fair not having any grandad at all, considering everyone else had at least one.

At that point, Mam's whole body started to shake, which I hated, and she said I was never, never to mention 'that man' to Dad, and if anyone asked I was to say my grandad died a long time ago – before I was even born. I didn't know why it would have put Dad in a bad temper to ask about my grandad, but being responsible for putting Dad in a bad temper was the worst thing you could do in our house, so I agreed not to ask any more about it. It didn't stop me wondering, though.

I imagined it was all to do with the 'commotion'. Maybe my grandad had been sent to jail for committing a terrible crime, or had run away to a desert island somewhere, and was living with the natives as their white God, and had a Man Friday and dusky maidens fanning him with palm leaves. You were always reading about such things, though not often in the *Kilmoran Courier*.

'Have it your own way, Sylvia,' Dad said,

interrupting my thoughts of desert islands. He looked tired, and it was only Thursday. He didn't mind admitting he was tired on Fridays. 'I'd just like to recuperate, Sylvia,' he'd say on Friday nights. Nearly every Friday he'd say it.

I got off my chair again. So did Mam. She gathered the dishes, and stumbled into the kitchen. Our kitchen was always cold, even in July. Dad had paid a man to box in the sink with blue Formica to match our table and chairs. It was very tasteful and bright, but all that blue hurt your eyes, and it was very cold to touch. I liked it better when we had the old pipes showing. At least when the hot water went through, you could warm your hands on them.

'I'll help you with the dishes before I go,' I offered.

'No, Ellie. You just go . . . Go on to your friends.' Mam sighed. 'I'll manage.'

Dad had switched on the wireless. I could have gone out the back door, but I went back through to the living room, so he would know I had tried to help before I left.

'I'll be home sharp,' I promised.

He looked at me, but I was invisible again. I didn't want to go to Janet's any more, but I didn't want to stay, either. It was cloudy and smelled of rain outside, and I was sorry I hadn't taken my jacket.

Our house was on the corner, a semi-detached. We

had a wrought-iron gate at the front, and a wall on either side which Dad was really proud of, as he'd paid the brickie a lot of money to get it right. It was a good enough wall, but it looked a bit daft, with everyone else having fences and wooden gates. We had lovely flower-beds, though. They were perfect diamonds, in the centre of the grass on each side of the path. Even though Dad said it was awkward to mow around them, they looked very sophisticated, and he loved the look of them when he'd finished with the edging shears. Mam liked them too, and spent a lot of time lifting things and moving them about, and making bands of colour with the flowers – purple, white, red – at least, that's what they were this year. I loved it when Mam and Dad talked about the flower-beds. They were so pleased with each other.

The back wasn't very exciting; just grass, and the path leading to the shed, and the washing-lines on both sides. Still, the shed was important. Mam often remarked on how neat Dad kept the shed. (I wasn't allowed inside it, in case I got near the turps or caused untidiness. It didn't bother me at all. It was a very neat shed, you had to agree.)

Mrs Anderson, our next-door neighbour, didn't even have a shed, but she didn't need one. She went to her sister's for the summer every year, and Mam and Dad looked after her house when she was away. Dad cut her grass for her. He always did, anyway, on account of her rheumatics and being old. Mam liked Mrs Anderson, because she was very quiet and didn't interfere. Sometimes, she'd come in and talk to Mam over a 'strupach' (it's what Mrs Anderson called tea, being a west-coaster). You could tell she didn't like children much, but she tried to hide it in front of Mam. I hated her being in the house.

Another thing I didn't like – she was always saying 'You have my sympathies' to Mam, and Mam would just be more upset when she left; even though she insisted Mrs Anderson was an understanding person, having no family to rely on herself. I thought she was an old bitch, but I only told Janet that. We liked to swear sometimes, Janet more than me.

All of our street was semi-detached, which was better than Janet's. Her house was terraced. Dad said we were saving to get out of the council estate, and that was the reason he had to work so hard. There were new houses going up beside the big school, and Dad said he'd 'earmarked' one for us. He hardly ever used slang, but he was so proud when he told us that that he probably forgot.

Mam cried. She said it would be like moving to another town. Dad carried on saving anyway. You couldn't blame him for wanting to see something for his hard work. That's what he said when he got her to stop crying, and it sounded reasonable enough to me. Course, she didn't stop for long.

It was nearly half past six by the time I got to Janet's. She was three streets over, and across the park (which was only four swings and a paddling-pool that never had any water in it).

We always had our supper when Dad came in at quarter past five, but in Janet's house they could still be eating at seven. You never knew. I loved going to her house. It was a midden – not clean like ours – and there was always loads of noise. Janet's dad was just a porter at the railway, but they had a television set already, and they all had bikes.

I thought I would be getting a new bike for my birthday on July 23rd. It would be something big for passing the eleven-plus, and would be well worth waiting for. I hoped it would, anyway.

Janet had already been given a new watch.

'D'you want a pie?' Mrs Cuthbert asked as soon as I went in. 'There's one going spare.' As soon as she said it, Craig, Janet's youngest brother, swiped it off the plate and ran outside.

'Y'wee bugger. The lassie could've had that,' Mrs Cuthbert called after him.

'I had my supper, thanks,' I assured her, but she was back in the kitchen and didn't seem to care who had it.

'Upstairs,' Janet said, pulling my arm.

We ran up to the room she shared with her sister, Marie. Marie was nearly fourteen, and out most of the time. Mr Cuthbert was always warning her about 'behaving herself', but she'd just laugh and kiss him on his bristly cheeks and go. Mrs Cuthbert often kissed him too. They were quite strange, but very nice.

Janet and I had the bed to ourselves, but we weren't allowed to get up on it with our shoes on, and we had to straighten the quilt and make a nice crease under the bolster when we got off. That was one of 'the laws of the jungle', and all of the Cuthberts pretty much obeyed each other's rules and got on very well – with the exception of Craig. Mrs Cuthbert often said he was 'a hell of a mistake to go to yir grave with'.

Janet closed the bedroom door, and threw herself on the bed. 'Marie's got her period,' she whispered. She was very excited. 'Mam gave her a book.' She reached into the top shelf of their wardrobe, and brought it down. 'Marie says we can look at it. She says she already knew everything in it, but I don't think she did. She nearly spewed when she looked at the pictures.'

I couldn't wait, but Janet rummaged in the wardrobe some more. 'Look,' she said. She had a brown packet of sanitary towels, and a wee envelope. Inside it was an elastic belt with two suspender hooks hanging from it. Kathy Munro was the only girl in our class who had her period. She was a year older than us, but had had to repeat primary seven when her family moved back here from Kenya. We only got to know about it because she'd brought two letters excusing her from gym, and she sat next to Janet, who naturally guessed the reason. Besides, Janet wasn't a clipe, and Kathy knew that she wouldn't tell anyone – except me, of course. We *were* best friends. Eventually Kathy agreed to show Janet and me a towel. We waited for her in the toilets, but she was really embarrassed when Janet asked her for it. Janet was like that, though. You would always give in, even if you didn't want to.

'They're spares,' Janet informed me, placing her finds on the quilt. 'You have to have spares.' We marvelled at this for a while, and Janet said Marie had told her that you needed quite big safety-pins to keep the towels on the suspender hooks. 'Marie wouldn't take the pins from the sewing-box. She bought new ones,' Janet said.

When we couldn't wait any longer, we opened the book. The pictures were marvellous. You could see the baby inside the mother's stomach and everything. This was referred to as the 'womb'. We said it out loud. 'Womb.' 'Woo-oomb.'

Over the page there was another diagram showing how a baby's born, which was something we knew, except we weren't sure how it actually got out. It didn't look real, though. We thought maybe somebody who couldn't draw made up the pictures. The chapter on the man's part was horrible and disgusting. We were laughing so much we were nearly sick, but it scared you – a bit.

Janet admitted she was scared before I did, and we agreed we would never have S-E-X, and even if we did (if we got married and *had* to) we'd definitely not have any babies. Janet said you had to use 'French letters' not to have babies, but we

12

weren't sure if you got them at the post office, or maybe sent away for them.

'Nancy Mackillop couldn't have known about them, which goes to show how grown-up *we* are,' Janet said. 'At least we know you can get them.' We still didn't know where, though.

Nancy Mackillop had had a baby without getting married, and you weren't allowed to talk about that either, even though she was pushing a pram into Lipton's every other day. Some people didn't mind stopping to speak to her. I'd seen her myself with the pram and her wee boy sitting up in it. He was bonny enough, but I'd be scared to talk to her, just in case. Janet had heard her mother warning Marie you could catch a baby without being married – like polio or something. Janet promised to ask Marie for more details, but Marie hadn't passed the eleven-plus and was in the Domestic course, so it was unlikely she'd be smart enough to know.

Mrs Cuthbert burst in with Vimto and Rich Tea biscuits. Janet shoved the book under her skirt, but the packet of towels was still on the bed. 'You'd better put them back where you found them,' Mrs Cuthbert warned. 'Marie'll be flaming if she finds yis examining them.' She put the tray down, and closed the door behind her. We put the towels and the belt back in the wardrobe.

'Are you coming over tomorrow?' Janet asked me, between mouthfuls.

'I'm going up the town with Mam in the afternoon,' I answered. It was the first Friday of my summer holidays and I was looking forward to it. 'I'll probably be over at night though.'

'I could meet yis in the town.'

'No. Eh, no, Janet. Mam's no' in very good form. She'd be . . .'

'God, is she ever anything else? What's wrong with her anyway? And why can't I come to your house sometimes?'

'I'm sorry,' I apologised, for the umpteenth time. Maybe Janet would be allowed if I asked, but I didn't want her to come over. I didn't want anyone in the house, and I didn't really know why, except it was maybe just a bad habit I'd formed. Dad said it was very easy to form bad habits.

We weren't quite right with each other for a few minutes, but then Janet forgot about it. She was a great friend to have. She was my only friend, but you didn't need more than one – not really.

I left at ten to nine so I'd be home sharp like I'd promised. Mam had been right. It had started to rain. I wished we lived in a country like Hawaii, where you'd have a lot of sunshine, and wear sarongs like Dorothy Lamour, or even where Doris Day lived in America. She always wore summer dresses, and mostly short sleeves.

I opened the back door quietly, as Dad didn't like to be interrupted with noise when the news was on. I was never even allowed to say goodnight until it was finished. Then he'd kiss the top of my head, and I had to lean forward to let him, which was baby behaviour, but I couldn't help it yet. I would be glad when I was tall enough for him to kiss me on the cheek.

The thought of Marie's book came into my head as I walked through the door. It was kissing that started it – everyone knew that. I didn't want to think about Mam and Dad maybe kissing, and doing those other disgusting things, but I was sure they didn't. I was sure there was a way round it all.

Dad wasn't listening to the news. He was in the kitchen, drying the dishes and putting them away, which Mam should have done hours ago. I shivered from the rain, and from feeling scared again.

'Where's Mam?'

'She's in bed, Eleanor. She was too tired to clear up, but we can't have a dirty house, can we?' He was smiling at me, but he looked more tired than Mam ever did.

'I'd have done it, Dad. I wouldn't have gone . . .'

He shook his head. 'No, Eleanor. You're too young to be taking on this . . . responsibility.'

I couldn't believe my ears. Dad was always saying how we had to learn responsibility. It was one of his favourite things – responsibility.

'We're going up the town tomorrow,' I said. 'Mam promised.'

'She'll be fine tomorrow. She just needs some rest.'

Mam had had rest before. Sometimes I had to wait for hours for her to get up, especially on my holidays. 'It's good you're home with me,' she'd say, climbing the stairs. 'I'll just rest for a while.'

Mam was always taking to her bed, and her room was so dark, I didn't like going in there. She liked the dark. When she was feeling well, she'd take me to the pictures, and we'd sit together in the dark. Mam and I had a lot in common there. We loved the pictures.

I helped Dad to finish clearing up, and went upstairs. I didn't feel like going through all the palaver of washing myself. I hated taking my clothes off in the bathroom. Somehow it made you feel more naked than when you undressed in your own bedroom. But I wasn't allowed to wash myself with them on, in case I got wet stains on them, and no matter how carefully I laid them across the bath, something always fell on the floor. Tonight it was my slip. I picked it up.

It was always the same. Brush teeth, wash face, neck, behind ears, arms up to elbows, dry thoroughly, put on pyjamas. Check for mess. I didn't check too hard. I couldn't be bothered. I went to my room, and climbed into bed. I pulled up the covers, and lay listening to the rain. I hoped it would stop by the morning, and it did.

But then, when it started again, everything in my whole life changed – and all because of the black washing.

CHAPTER 2

'It's not my fault!' Mam sobbed.

She was sitting on the back step with her arms over her head. I kept agreeing that it wasn't her fault, but she didn't seem to hear me. That was always the scariest bit – being invisible.

We'd been all ready to go to the town. Mam was even wearing her new dress which had red roses all over it and big black buttons down the front, like the liquorice wheels you got at McColl's. There was a long-sleeved bolero to go with it, and I adored it.

Just as we were about to leave the house and walk up to Sutherland Street to catch the bus, Mam realised it had started raining again. She ran to the back window, and sure enough there they were; two big bikes propped against the fence between us and the Murchisons, who were our next-door neighbours on the other side. The bikes belonged to Peter the Lum and his son (who was also called Peter the Lum), and they'd been sweeping the Murchisons' chimney for the summer. They swept ours in August before I went back to school. Dad

17

said it was a more sensible approach.

Dad had four white shirts, and three of them were on the line; except they weren't that white any more, and the rain was spreading the sooty bits all over them. I thought I could maybe get them inside before they got any worse, but when I ran out with the basket and pulled down the pole they were already soaked. I pushed the pole back up again, and went to sit beside Mam. It was a fact that there's no point in taking in wet washing.

'It's not my fault,' Mam said. Over and over. 'It's not my fault.' Then she'd cry again. The rain went off, and came back on, and we spent the afternoon right there – on the back step. No matter what I said, Mam wouldn't move. After a while I just gave up.

I saw Mrs Murchison at her kitchen window once. She knew I'd seen her, and she moved back. She had two boys and three girls, and Dad was always saying what a hard-working woman she was, and how immaculate she kept her bairns. I knew they got just as dirty as everyone else, but Dad would be at work at the time so he wasn't around to see it.

Mam didn't speak much to Mrs Murchison, and I could tell she didn't like it when Dad made admiring comments about her. Once, Mam was in the kitchen when Dad was going on, and she called Mrs Murchison 'a sleekit cow' under her breath. She didn't know I heard her.

Dad would be home soon. I made myself think

18

about Gene Kelly. I knew all the words to 'Singing in the Rain'. They weren't hard to remember. I imagined Dad with a big umbrella, singing and dancing his way up the road, and Mam would start singing with him and we'd dance about in the puddles, the three of us. Mam might have known I was thinking that, because she was sort of rocking like she could hear the music.

'Sylvia?'

I jumped. He had an umbrella right enough, but he was snapping it closed and not looking a bit like Gene Kelly.

'Sylvia!'

'The washing's black. Your shirts . . .' Mam whispered. Then she made a sound, like when you choked with something in your mouth that was too big to swallow.

'Get inside, Eleanor,' he said, not looking at me when he said it. I got up. My bum was sore and cold from the step, and my skirt was wet enough to stick to it. I tried to pull it straight, but then I didn't care. Dad took Mam by the arm, and they came inside too.

I didn't like it when the doctor came to the house. For a start he looked like Charles Laughton, and he wasn't pleased when he had to climb the stairs to see anyone. I didn't think he was very nice to Mam. The last time he came, he made her worse, and she couldn't make up her mind about anything for ages afterwards. It was two whole weeks before she took me to the pictures. Dad seemed to like Doctor Stewart though. They would whisper a lot, and shake hands.

Dad saw Doctor Stewart out, and came into the living-room. I wanted to cry from all the waiting and the whispering, but I sat up straight and waited for Dad to speak.

'Your mother's going to need a lot of peace and quiet, Eleanor,' he began.

'What's wrong with her?'

'Nothing a little rest won't cure.' Dad always said that. He never said Mam had 'the nerves'. It was Iona Murchison who told me that, one day at the fence. She said it like she was sorry for me. She was nearly fifteen and I hated her, but she was quite nice really. She said she didn't like her brothers and sisters, and that she was a slave to her mother, so she understood what I was going through. I told her I wasn't going through anything except the fence if she had any more to say about Mam.

Iona laughed and told Tommy, who was the youngest of the Murchisons, and younger than me, and happened to be about that day. They ended up making me cry between the pair of them, but I went back into our house before I'd let them see me.

'She's to stay in her bed for a while, and take things easy,' Dad said.

'I can look after her when you're at work, Dad. And I won't make any noise at all. You'll hardly know I'm here.' He wouldn't put up with noise. He liked a quiet house, and I knew that. I said it to let him know I understood the situation. It was something we'd been learning in school – to be aware of situations, like Hitler wasn't.

Dad smiled. He had lovely teeth, all in a row, square and straight – except they were a bit small. I had big teeth, not really big, but obvious – like Mam's. She didn't like having obvious teeth. She covered her mouth a lot with her hands. I did too, when I remembered.

'No, Eleanor. That wouldn't be possible. You're too young to be here all day on your own, I'm afraid.'

'But I wouldn't be on my own! Mam . . .'

'No buts!' His voice went quieter. It was something he did to make you realise he meant what he said. He didn't have to do it. He always meant what he said.

'Fortunately, I'll be at home over the weekend, and during the week I can attend to your mother before I go to work. I'm sure you can appreciate that I can't stay here with you all day . . . and we can't have your mother worrying about you while she's recuperating.'

That was something else; he never, ever called her Mam. We'd be talking sometimes, and he'd nearly say it. But between 'M—' and '—am' it would turn to 'Mother'. Usually, though, he called her Sylvia. That's her name, so I shouldn't have minded him calling her that, but there was always a feeling of . . . something. It's hard to explain, like the way he always called me Eleanor, even though everyone else called me Ellie, ever since I was small.

Once, just to try it on, I called her Sylvia too. 'Do you feel like a bite to eat, Ellie?' I was helping her do the dusting. It had been a good day; she'd baked earlier, which she hardly ever did, and there was a lovely smell coming from the oven. I didn't care what she baked; it was the smell I really liked. 'I wouldn't mind a scone when they're ready . . . Sylvia,' I answered.

She smiled to herself, but she looked sort of uncomfortable. That made me feel embarrassed, so I never said it again – not out loud. But she wasn't angry, or upset – like she sometimes was if Dad said 'Sylvia' the wrong way, – even though he didn't know he was saying it the wrong way.

Dad was still talking. 'Taking care of you is our main concern right now, Eleanor, so I'm going to arrange for you to stay with your grandmother for a couple of weeks.' He was trying to make me feel that Mam didn't need me with her, that I was being sent away to make them *both* feel better.

For a minute, I thought he meant my gran in New Zealand. I might as well have been a spaceman. They could send me to the moon, and I wouldn't have anything to say about it.

'I don't want to go to New Zealand,' I said. It came out a whisper.

Dad frowned as though I was being deliberately stupid. It was a look I really, really hated.

'Inchbrae, Eleanor. Not New Zealand.'

22

My Granny Fairbairn lived in Inchbrae (I knew it wasn't a big place, because I'd heard Mam refer to it as a 'backwater') and I certainly did *not* want to go and stay with her – leaving Mam when she needed me, and Dad not even realising that, and me by myself with a granny I hardly knew.

'I'll contact your grandmother,' he said, walking to the lobby. We had a telephone on a table across from the hall-stand. Hardly anybody else I knew had one. Dad was a civil servant, which was very important and kept him very busy, and having the telephone was all to do with his work. Nobody called much though, and me and Mam weren't allowed to use it, except for emergencies.

Once, Tommy Murchison threw himself off the roof of their shed and nearly brained himself, and Mrs Murchison went all the way to the phone-box at the Green Street shops to call an ambulance. Mam waited with Tommy. She had blood all over her good camel skirt but she never said we had a phone for emergencies. Tommy was OK, as it turned out, but I thought we should have mentioned that we had the phone.

I followed Dad to the lobby. 'Back inside, Eleanor.' He pointed to the living room. I went. It was past our dinner-time and I was really hungry now. Dad finished his call and went through to the kitchen. He made omelettes, which I hate. I was cutting mine into equal squares when the telephone rang and gave me a fright. It always did that.

'That'll be your grandmother,' Dad announced.

She didn't have a telephone. Dad said he had called a neighbour who would have delivered the message. I don't know how she got the message, or how Dad knew her neighbours when we had only been there once that I knew of, but she was his mother, so I supposed he had taken the time to find out these things.

The phone call was quite a short one, and the only thing I heard was when Dad raised his voice a bit – he was never loud-spoken. 'I wouldn't ask if there was someone else . . .'

So! It was quite clear that my gran didn't want me in Inchbrae. My throat was sore from trying not to cry, and eating the horrible omelette at the same time.

'It's all arranged,' Dad said, coming back into the kitchen. He stopped to straighten a corner of the carpet where it had curled against the surround at the living-room door. You could see your face in the surround, and the kitchen lino too. Mam paid me to polish them every Saturday. Who would polish them now?

'We'll get your things together in the morning,' Dad said, sitting back down at the table. He rubbed his forehead as though he had a headache. 'The bus leaves at noon on Saturdays. You'll be there by two.'

'I'd like to take my hula-hoop.' I don't know why I said it. I didn't even know where it was.

'I didn't realise you still had that. You never play with it any more.'

It was true. I didn't. 'I'd like to take it.'

He shook his head. 'I don't think so, Eleanor. It would take up too much room. Take some books.' He looked at the clock on the window-sill. 'It's just about bedtime.'

'Can I go in and see Mam?'

He drew in his breath, and I thought he was going to say no.

'Please?'

He nodded. 'Just for a minute. She's . . . tired.'

I pushed the door all the way open. I didn't like seeing her in bed, especially from the door which was quite far. All I could see was her hair, black on the white pillow. It was scary, and I closed my eyes for a moment. I didn't want to keep a picture of it in my mind, and maybe give myself nightmares. I hated nightmares. Then I opened my eyes, but I couldn't see her moving, so I thought she must be asleep. I started to tiptoe to the bed, but then I thought that I wanted her to wake up and see me, so I made a bit more noise, pressing heavy to make the floorboards squeak.

Sometimes they did it and sometimes they didn't. One squeaked, so I pressed it again. Mam turned her head and lifted herself up a bit.

'Come over, Ellie. I'm OK.' Her voice was like he said – tired.

'You're going to your Gran's?' She lay back down. 'It'll be a holiday for you.'

'No it won't.'

'Please, Ellie. She's . . . fine. Honest . . . I like her.'

'Dad said two weeks.'

'At the most . . . It's not that long,' she said. Her eyes were funny, a bit wet but not crying, and not really seeing either. I realised that she must be going blind.

'Can you see me, Mam?' I felt a bit breathless, like when you went to the baths with the school, and someone was always walking along the edge saying it was time to take your water-wings off, and they'd talk to your teacher and decide what was best for you, and you never wanted them to do it, but they were going to take them off anyway. It was that kind of feeling, but I didn't want her to know that I'd guessed she was going blind, so I tried to say it quite natural.

'Of course, Ellie. I can see you fine.' She sort of shook her head, without hardly moving it. 'Don't worry about me. Doctor Stewart gave me some-thing . . . something to make me sleepy. I can hardly keep my eyes open.'

'Oh,' I said. It was such a relief. 'I'd better let you sleep then.'

'Come here. Give me a lovey.'

I tried. I laid my head against her, but all I could do was put my arms over the quilt and squeeze. It wasn't like a real cuddle, and she didn't squeeze back. 'You be a good girl for your gran, and remember to say your prayers.'

I didn't always remember, even at home, but, I said I would. I used to do the whole thing. 'Our Father' all the way through and bless everyone as well, and all the animals who couldn't say prayers

26

for themselves. But now that I was older I'd shortened it a lot. I read a book with a prayer in it that I liked, and mostly that was the one I used.

I said it that night before I slept.

'Keep me loving.

'Keep me safe.

'Keep me here.'

I said it over and over.

I meant it. It didn't work, though.

CHAPTER 3

Dad packed my clothes and left the case open for me to put in a few things, but I couldn't decide what to take, so he closed up the straps and fastened the buckles. It was pouring rain all morning. I wanted to wear my good coat which was blue and had a wide skirt.

Once, Mam gave me some empty Max Factor things – a compact and a lipstick which still had a bit right at the bottom, enough to get your creeny in. She had some perfume in a lovely bottle and she put a wee drop behind my ears. It was called 'Evening in Paris'. If I ever decided against going to Hollywood, I was going to go to Paris. I put on my blue gingham blouse which was just like one I'd seen Doris Day wearing on a *Photoplay* cover, and folded my good coat in half, with the sleeves tied round my waist. From the front it stuck out enough to look very like a ballgown.

Mam was listening to 'Mrs Dale's Diary' (Mrs Dale always seemed to be terribly worried about Jim, who I think was her husband) and pretending to ignore me, but it wasn't the kind of ignoring that frightened me. I spent a long time going up and down our stairs, making entrances and things. I did Bette Davis and Joan Crawford and a few others. They were all good. I couldn't choose the best.

Dad said I couldn't wear it though, my good coat. I had to wear my raincoat, which had an evil hood that let the rain in the sides and made your neck wet, and sometimes your back. I put two Famous Five books in my vanity case which had my Max Factor stuff in it, and my autograph book from school. Also a banana and an apple, and a Fry's Cream which was my favourite.

Then Dad took me up to say cheerio to Mam, but she was sleeping again. Even trying not to be, I was really angry with her for letting me go, so I was glad I didn't have to talk to her.

Dad kept me under the umbrella and held my hand, which was a bit babyish, but nice. We had to get off our bus before the Town Hall and go down Northgate to the bus station. I was thinking maybe there wouldn't be a bus there, and we could go home. I wasn't mad at Mam any more.

Even though it was pouring, I tried to slow up a bit so I wouldn't have to go so soon. 'I don't even know her!' I said, looking up at Dad. He was pulling me along. 'Dad, I don't even know my gran.'

'Well then, this will be a good opportunity to correct that, Eleanor. Perhaps it's time you had a ... little more contact with her.'

'Why didn't I have contact with her before, Dad?'

He was going faster, and nearly making me trip.

'We had a difference of opinion, Eleanor. Your grandmother . . . drinks a little. You know it's something I disapprove of.'

I hadn't thought about it, but now that he'd mentioned it, I realised that I'd never seen my Dad drink, except for a glass of Glenfiddich at Christmas and on Hogmanay. Mam wouldn't take one even then. We always had raspberry cordial, me and Mam.

Mam didn't disapprove of drink though. Not long ago, Janet and I got an awful fright when a drunk man bawled after us because we'd bumped into him in Boots' doorway. We thought he must have been a wino, as there were quite a few of them in Kilmoran, but they usually sat together behind the gasworks, and we never went near there. When I told Mam about it, she'd said that taking a drink once in a while didn't mean you were a wino, so I knew Mam didn't disapprove of drinking. She probably just preferred raspberry cordial.

'Does she get drunk?' My heart was hammering from running to keep up with Dad, and being scared of going to stay with an old woman who liked to drink, and trying to shout up at Dad with the rain soaking my face and getting in my mouth.

'No . . . of course she — Come *on*, Eleanor!'

I should have known that Dad wouldn't send me to his mother's if she couldn't look after me. It would have been most irresponsible.

'Maybe your father taught her to drink.'

Dad whirled me to a stop so quickly, I nearly left the pavement.

'I don't ever, *ever* want to hear you talk about my ... that person again, Eleanor. Is that abso-*lute*-ly clear?'

I nodded. I was going to cry. I didn't know why I had said that, or even what made me think about any of this. Sometimes, you just thought things and spoke things, and got yourself in trouble with your own stupidity. This had been pointed out to me before. I'd been getting better at not saying things, being older and wiser (Mam often said I was too old for my years, but I think she was glad that I was), and now I'd gone and spoiled everything – as if they weren't spoiled enough.

I *was* crying now. I couldn't help it, and I knew some of it was because I was angry with Dad. It was only natural to ask about your grandad, and nobody would ever tell me *anything*. I made up my mind then. I would ask my granny, and I'd keep asking until I found out what the big secret was. And Dad wouldn't know I was asking, and it would serve him right – for everything!

I really didn't want to go away.

There were four different buses. They were all single-deckers. We went to the second one. The driver was standing on the front of the bus turning a handle at the top of the windscreen so the people would know where the bus was going. He had on a navy blue coat, and wasn't happy with the rain.

Dad put me on the bus, and I wiped my face on

31

my sleeve, which was so wet it didn't make any difference. Dad stepped up after me, turning to shake off his umbrella. He stuck it under the stairs, and pointed to a double seat about half way down. I sat beside the window, and Dad put my case beside me. He said I was to take it on my knee if anyone needed the seat, and if the bus got full to remember to stand for my elders. I would have done that anyway.

Dad went back up to speak to the driver who was also the conductor (it being a country bus), and I stopped crying. It felt quite grown-up to be sitting by myself, waiting to go on a journey. I would make the most of it. It would be an adventure. Then the driver turned the motor over, and my stomach lurched. What if I missed my stop – or got off at the wrong place and got stranded miles from nowhere? What if my granny wasn't there when I arrived? What if she was? How would I know her?

Dad was making his way back down the aisle, his purse still in his hand. He handed me two half-crowns, which was more than two weeks' pocket money. I usually only got two shillings on a Friday; one-and-six for pocket money, and sixpence for helping Mam. Dad reminded me every week that this was more than a lot of people got. I'd already saved my florin from last week for going to the town with Mam, so now I had seven shillings.

'It's extra, for your holidays,' Dad said. 'Don't lose it.' I put it in my skirt pocket under my coat. 'The driver knows where to let you off. Your grandmother will be waiting for you.' Then he bent and kissed the top of my head.

'Be good, Eleanor. I'll see you soon.' When he got off the bus he started running, which is something he never did. I could hardly see him, with the rain pouring down the windows. I wanted to run after him.

The bus stopped a lot. People got on and off. Most of them knew each other, and they were all girning about the weather. A farmer and his wife sat in front of me. He was the only one happy about the rain, but the driver shouted back at him that he never knew a farmer who was happy for long. The farmer told him to 'Bugger off', and his wife said, 'Mind yir language, there's a bairn behind you.' She turned and smiled at me. She looked nice, except she had a moustache.

I didn't need to move my case. Nobody wanted to sit beside me. We waited at one stop quite a while. It was outside a town, and the driver took his paper out of one pocket and a plum from another. He was eating the plum while he read the paper, and I was thinking I'd have my sweetie, but I'd just opened it when the driver folded his paper and put it back in his pocket. He spat the stone out of the window. Someone at the back shouted, 'Come on, Archie man, there's no-one travelling in this weather except us fools that's here.'

The driver started the bus. 'You're right enough by the looks o' things, Bob.' We didn't go through

33

the town, just kind of round it. I ate all the chocolate off each section before I ate the cream. It was the best way to do it.

The rain stopped, and it was getting hot on the bus. There was a horrible smell from the steam coming off everyone, and the farmer must have had dog's dirt or manure or something on his shoes, which made everything worse. I tried breathing through my mouth, but I could still smell it. You couldn't see out of the windows at all. I drew a few pictures on my window; hearts and Donald Duck (which I was very good at), and my name twice, printing and joined. Then I wiped it off, and waited till the window steamed over again. I played one game of noughts and crosses, but it's no good by yourself, because you know what you're going to do.

I licked the window. It tasted the same as the town buses when they were wet, except there was more taste of tin in it. The sun was coming out, but there wasn't much to see; just some fields, and cows by a river. We went along beside the river for quite a while, and I saw two swans. They were beautiful. I thought of myself at Sadler's Wells, dancing 'The Dying Swan'; as good as Markova probably. It made me sad, and I usually got sleepy when I was sad.

'Right, hen. This is your stop,' the driver called. I wasn't really sleeping, just enough to have to wake up. I had a sore bit on my head where I'd been learning against the metal on the corner of the seat.

Archie stopped the bus, and came back for my case. It wasn't that big, and I wanted to carry it myself.

Maybe my grandmother would look at me wet, with a case, and think I resembled an orphan, and take pity on me and send me home to my wonderful parents who were already broken-hearted from missing me. Archie pulled the case away, and took my arm. The farmer's wife said, 'Cheerio, hen,' when I passed.

Archie went down the step in front of me and put the case on the ground. Then he reached up and swung me down beside it, which made me a bit dizzy. When I looked up, there was no-one there. Not exactly there. There were people close, but no-one waiting. Then a wifie leaned her bike against the window of a butcher's shop and came over. Archie got back on the bus and waved. 'She's all yours,' he shouted, and drove off.

'You're Eleanor,' the woman said. I nodded, even though it wasn't a question. She was wearing green corduroy trousers and a green jumper, and she had a red chiffon turban round her hair, which was mostly grey. She nipped out her cigarette and stuck it behind her ear. She must have done this a lot, as there were quite a few holes in the chiffon.

Her face was brown, and quite wrinkly, and her eyes were the same blue as my favourite egg-cup. I was just thinking they were a bit scary-looking when she smiled. She had the same teeth as Dad, but hers were lovelier. Maybe it was the way she smiled, like she meant it. I smiled back. I expected her to say how big I'd got since she saw me last.

'Can you ride a bike?' she asked.

'Aye.'

'Good. We're a couple of miles down the road, so I've got you a len of an old bike that the Cameron boys had. It's in the shed for you. We'll walk it today . . . unless you don't mind the bar?'

I looked at her bike. It was a man's, with a bar and a big basket at the front. I shook my head, meaning I didn't mind, but I didn't fancy it much.

'You can put your coat in the basket. It's fine an' dry now.'

I took off my coat. She didn't try to help me, but when I started to fold it, she took it off me and slung it over her arm. We walked over to the bike and she just threw my coat in the basket. I tried to sort it while she got my case. The basket smelled sweet and woody and warm all at the same time.

'Well, now that you're here, we better show you off a bit,' she said. I was pleased at that. At least I wasn't to be ignored. She looked at me, and her hand shot out and grabbed my face. The fright went all the way down to my knees.

She turned my head from side to side. 'You're a bonny bairn. You take to my side.' I shivered when she let me go. She roared and laughed. Her laugh was like a man's too – loud; what Mam would call vulgar.

'I didn't mean to frighten you, hen. I'm no' used to bairns.'

'It's all right . . .' I couldn't say it – Gran.

'Call me Dot,' she said, not a bit embarrassed with it.

I tried it. 'Right-oh . . . Dot.' It felt a bit awkward, but it was better than 'Gran'.

'And I'll call you Ellie,' Dot said. 'Eleanor sounds too formal for the likes o' us, don't you think?'

I smiled. I hadn't imagined we'd be on such good terms already. The door of the butcher's shop opened, and a woman came out. She kept her head down, and didn't look at us, but when she passed she sort of nodded at Dot. 'Goot day, Miss Fairbairn.'

Dot nodded back. 'That's the rain off, Mrs Fishbein.'

Mrs Fishbein ran into the grocer's. 'Poor wifie,' Dot said, but didn't explain. I looked around. There was only one street and a few houses. You could see how everyone would know each other here. We went next door. There was a sign hanging outside with a man in a kilt waving a sword. The sign said 'The Jacobite'.

It was dark inside. There was a staircase ahead of us with a sofa at the bottom, almost round the corner, and a big plant beside it that looked a bit withered. In front of the couch was a table with a couple of magazines on it, and on the other side of the staircase there was a kind of alcove with a counter, extending out to a bar.

We walked over. There were three stools at the bar, and four small tables with two chairs each in front of it, but hidden by the wall of the lobby. The most light was from the door, which Dot had left open. I'd hardly set foot in Inchbrae and Dot had me inside a bar already. I thought it was quite interesting and wasn't scared a bit. That would have made Dad very upset if he knew.

I'd always thought you had to be quite old, and not very wise in the head, to go into bars; and that there would be people half-dead from the drink lying all over the place. But the Jacobite wasn't like that at all. I mean, there was the smell of Pledge and floor-polish, and anyone would have felt quite respectable sitting at one of the tables. It was all quite . . . ordinary.

Dot hit a brass bell on the counter, and a man appeared in the alcove almost at once. I'd been looking back at the door, so the light was in my eyes and I couldn't see him for a minute or two. He sounded irritable.

'I might've known. Lil said you were coming in the day.'

'And here I am, Eck,' Dot said. 'A large one, and one for yirself.'

'I'm shut,' he answered.

'Y' are not,' Dot said.

He grunted and shook his head. I could see him now. He had big red eyebrows and he looked as irritable as he sounded.

'You'll have the bobbies after me,' he complained.

'There's no' a bobby this side o' Locheirnan,' Dot said. She turned and nodded her head for me to come closer. She was smiling again. 'This is Ellie – Adam's lassie.'

Eck put a tumbler in front of Dot, and poured one for himself. Then he was ready to look at me. 'I hope you haven't much of an appetite, Ellie,' he warned. 'She doesn't cook, y'know.'

'Never mind him, Ellie,' Dot said. 'I can cook as well as the next one – when I feel like it.' She took the cigarette from behind her ear and struck a match on the underneath of the counter.

'That's the size o' you, Dot. Everything's when *you* feel like it. Would you like a lemonade, Ellie?' he asked. He didn't look so grumpy any more.

I nodded.

'What's your poison?' he asked.

'D' you have tangerine?'

'Yir in Inchbrae! There's orangeade or still. Which?'

'Orangeade, please.' There was plenty of fizz in it. I let it settle for a minute as I didn't want it going up my nose.

'Where's Lil?' Dot asked.

'Taking a lie down. She had a morning of it wi' Hugh, and we've a busy night in front o' us. Wullie Mackenzie's lassie got married in Locheirnan an' there'll be a rake o' them back here afterwards to finish it off.'

'I hear you've got one o' your rooms let.'

'Aye. We'll be half-full, or half-empty, depending on how you look at it.'

'How long for?'

'Just Monday night, and back again on Wednesday; no' enough to retire on. Some bloke from Newcastle, taking pictures for a calendar.'

'It's all business, Eck. How much do I owe you?'

'Nah. It's on me. I'll make up for it wi' the wedding party. Buggers'll spend their last penny on drink.'

'Lucky for you.' Dot laughed.

'We'll see you again, hen,' Eck said, gathering the glasses. 'Don't let her get the best o' yis.'

We came back out into the sunshine. There weren't many people about, and only the one car. It was up the street a bit, in front of a clothes shop. There was an awning pulled out above the window for the sun, the same as the one at the butcher's, though this side of the street was darker.

'Cross over,' Dot said, 'to the sunny side of the street.' She sang the words. We were in front of a newsagent's. The bell rang when Dot opened the door, and there was a lady behind the counter who looked quite old. She had white hair, and glasses that came halfway down her nose, but she was nice-looking; like how you imagined a granny to look. Not a bit like Dot.

'Come away in,' the lady called.

The shop smelled like the red polish Mam put on the doorsteps, and it was nice and warm. You could see bits of dust in the sunshine that came through the window, but it wasn't a dirty shop. It was very clean. The woman was sitting on a chair, knitting, with her ankles sticking out from the end of the counter. Her stockings were thick, and her shoes were shiny brown, with a small heel and laces. I looked down to see what Dot had on her feet. She was wearing black sandshoes, which looked worn out.

'You're quiet, Jessie?' Dot asked.

'Aye. A lot o' them at the wedding, and then the weather – you never know what it's going to do.' She put her knitting into a paisley bag with wooden handles, and stood up.

'Who's this bonny wee lass you've brought to see me?' She smiled, her arms folded across her chest.

'I'm Ellie,' I said, not waiting for Dot to introduce us, which was a bit rude.

'Pleased to meet you, Ellie. I'm Mrs Alexander. You come in any time you want. There's hardly a bairn left in the place.' She turned to Dot. 'She has a good look o' Adam,' she said, 'as well as I can mind o' him.'

Dot nodded. She was tapping one of her feet. 'I'm bursting, Jessie. Could I use your . . . ?'

'Help yourself,' Mrs Alexander interrupted. Dot went through a door on the right behind the post office bit, and I could see what looked like a small kitchen. I was needing the toilet too, but I didn't know whether to follow Dot or not.

'On you go, pet,' Mrs Alexander said, reading my mind.

Dot had closed the door after her, and I'd just got behind the post office counter when the shop bell jangled again and a body came hurtling through the door. I froze.

The man was roaring something and his head

was lolling from side to side. He pushed his face up against the glass. His head was bald and he was grinning and slavering at me. He looked like a spastic, and his face was funny, like young and old at the same time.

'Hugh, Hugh, you're frightening the poor cratur!' Mrs Alexander was taking his arm, pulling him back from the glass. 'C' mon now. Come on. You shouldn't be out in the sun without a hat. Where's your hat, Hugh?'

Hugh began waving an arm in the direction of the bar we'd just left. 'Come on then. We'll go and get your hat. Come on, darlin'.' Mrs Alexander was leading him out of the shop. He was still making a lot of noise, but happy with it.

Dot came out. 'You've met Hugh then?' she asked, as though it was the most natural thing in the world to be frightened to death by a slavering madman. 'D'you need the toilet, or d'you want to wait till we get home?'

Home ... I was going to cry again. Dot looked at me for a minute. Then she bent down and put her arm around me. There wasn't much room.

'It's no easy, hen, being in the company of strangers. But we'll make the best of it ... I promise.' This close she smelled of whisky and cigarettes and bicycle oil.

I went through the kitchen, and into the toilet. I locked the door. Then I cried.

CHAPTER 4

'We'll look in on Rita, then we'll head up the road. You'll be getting hungry.' Dot didn't appear to notice that I'd been crying. We walked out of the newsagent's, leaving it empty, even though Mrs Alexander was nowhere to be seen.

The door of the clothes shop was open, pushed against the wall with a heavy iron cockerel. A woman was sorting through a rail of frocks. Her hair was short, with two big kiss-curls on her cheeks. She hardly looked at us. She was wearing a black and white checked blouse, and round her waist was a black elastic belt with a big clasp that made the blouse frill out below it. Tight red trousers came halfway down her legs, and she had matching red high heels. She looked like a film star.

She turned back to the dresses. 'I'll have to reduce the lot,' she said. 'There's not a woman in the place with a bit o' style to her. I'd be better off selling knitting patterns.' She sounded annoyed. 'Is that your grand-daughter?' she asked. I could've been anyone.

'Aye, Rita, and she'd appreciate a minute of your time – *if* you can spare it.'

'Sorry, Dot. I've that much on my mind . . .' She took a look at me. 'What's your name?'

'Ellie.'

'Would you like to buy a dress, Ellie?' She wasn't interested in me at all. She went back to sorting her frocks.

'Right, then, we'll be off,' Dot said, grabbing my arm, and sounding annoyed now too.

Rita sighed, and turned again. 'Keep yir drawers on, Dot. Look, if you're going to be around for a wee while, I'll give the bairn a lift when I close.'

'We'd no' want to be a burden to you. I'll see you tomorrow, and I hope you'll be in better tune . . . don't bother coming by if not,' Dot warned. We walked back over to her bicycle. 'D'you like sausages?' she asked.

'Aye,' I replied. I loved them.

'We'll get some at Pat's. His boy might be around. He's about your age.' On the window above Dot's bike there was a semi-circle of big gold letters outlined in black. 'P. Conroy, Purveyor of Choice Meats.'

'What's a purveyor?'

'In this case, a chancer. He's got decent meat, though.' She pushed open the door. The smell of fresh sawdust hit you before you even stepped inside. It made me feel even more homesick, though I don't know why.

'Two beautiful ladies at once – a sight for sore

eyes, so y'are,' the butcher said. He had black hair and lovely eyes. He was as handsome as anything. I smiled at him.

'Don't give us your patter,' Dot said. 'Sausages is all I'm in for, Mr Conroy.'

'Then sausages you shall have, my bonny colleen.'

Dot roared. Her laughing made my throat feel sore. 'Don't pay any attention to that blarney, Ellie. He's never seen the shores o' Ireland.'

'Aah, but my heart's there just the same, Dot.'

'In a Glasgow tenement, more like. You're no even a Catholic, Pat.' Dot grinned at him. 'Where's your boy?'

He nodded over his shoulder. 'In the back. Joseph!' he called.

'What?' Joseph came through with a scowl on his face, but he had a look of maybe being shy. He didn't see me at first.

'This is my grand-daughter, Joe. Maybe you'll get to spend a wee bit time together,' Dot said.

'Not with a *girl*!' he said, and started to turn away.

All the smiling left his father's face. 'We wouldn't be forgetting our manners now, would we?' Mr Conroy said. There was a warning in his voice.

'Pleased to meet you,' the boy muttered. He wasn't, though. I could tell by the way he scuffed the sawdust.

'Right pleased,' Mr Conroy added. 'Delighted

we are. Now then, links or sliced?'

Dot looked at me, her eyebrows raised.

'Links,' I said

Dot added black pudding and half-a-dozen eggs to the order, and we left. She pulled her bike from against the wall, and turned it around. 'D'you want to walk or get on the bar?'

'Maybe we can walk a bit . . .'

'No maybes. One thing or the other. We'll walk.' She lifted her hand and stuck two fingers in her mouth. She let out the best whistle I'd ever heard. We just stood there, and I didn't know what we were waiting for. Then I saw him.

He came loping along from the far end of the street. He was about the size of a collie, and mostly black. His ears didn't match; they looked like they were different sizes, but maybe it was the way he kept one down and the other up. The bits of him that were supposed to be white were dirty, and his tail was wagging like mad – a long thick tail that was too big for his body. He cheered you up just looking at him.

'What's his name?' I asked.

'Hooligan. He's no' mine.'

'Whose is he?'

'Well, he doesna really belong to anyone, but he hangs around Dreep most o' the time. Dreep's an old wino hereabouts. He doesna go in for food much, so Hooligan comes home with me most nights. I feed him – and then he leaves. Don't try'n make a pet of him. He's an independent sort.'

46

I was disappointed. I'd been wanting a pet all my life. I got a goldfish at the shows two years running, but they both died; it was a fact that they never lasted long. Dad said it was no surprise because they were half-dead when you got them, but it didn't stop you feeling sad when they died.

Hooligan let Dot ruffle his ears, and I got to clap him. His coat was warm and soft, and he grinned at me, which Dot said was his normal expression. We set off.

The road was dusty and the puddles at the side were already drying up. There was hardly any traffic – two or three tractors, and a couple on a tandem bike. Dot waved as they passed, and they waved back. They were very cheerful looking. The woman reminded me of Mam, except I couldn't imagine Mam and Dad on a tandem, not even in the country.

Hooligan kept disappearing off into the bushes and squeezing himself under barbed wire fences and other hazards. Dot kept her eye on him, but she didn't make him walk beside us. After a while we came alongside a river, and I asked Dot if it was the same river I'd seen from the bus.

'Aye, that's the Eirnan. It goes on out to the firth.'

'D' you live far from the river?'

'No, no' far at all. Close enough for the bloody seagulls to ruin my washing.'

I didn't want to think about dirty washing.

'You're a quiet bairn. Are you this quiet at home?'

'I'm quite quiet. Dad doesn't like noise.'

'He never did. A good laugh would be the death of him. Not me, now. I like my dram and I like my music, and I'm used to having my friends over by. A good ceilidh now and then keeps you going.'

'Is that what you're having? Tomorrow?'

She looked puzzled. 'Tomorrow?'

'You were saying to the lady in the dress shop, about tomorrow . . .'

'Aye well, it's a ceilidh of sorts. Rita and Lil usually come over for a few hours on a Sunday afternoon. Mind, Rita's missed a couple of Sundays lately – with reason, I've no doubt.' This was another of those remarks designed to keep you guessing. Grown-ups were very fond of this type of sentence. They didn't realise how aggravating it was.

'Still,' Dot continued, 'Lil enjoys the break. It's a couple of hours without having to watch Hugh. She needs it.'

'What's the matter with him?'

'No-one's very sure. He was born that way, and they said he wouldn't make it past twelve . . . but our Lil wasn't going to let him go that easy. He's thirty-seven now, and still going strong – as you noticed. He's a handful though, no question.'

Thirty-seven! He was nearly as old as Dad, and older than Mam. It was hard to imagine. 'He gave me an awful fright.'

'Aye, he does that. But he doesna mean it. He just wants to be friends with everyone.'

I didn't imagine he had any friends. I thought

about what it would be like, but I couldn't. 'Poor Hugh,' I said.

'Och, don't feel sorry for him, hen. He lives in the palaces of his mind. He's a happier soul than most of us.'

Dot pushed her bike off the road. There were no fences here, and the ground was rocky, with straggling bits of broom all over. She pushed through a couple of bushes, and I followed. Then we were at the side of the river. It was really a small bay, with shells and driftwood and bits of seaweed. Dot laid the bike down and sat on a biggish rock. I squatted beside her, but she moved over a wee bit so I could share the rock. I didn't feel like getting that close, but I didn't want to hurt her feelings.

She took a packet of Senior Service and a box of Swan Vestas out of her pocket. She tapped the cigarette a couple of times on the back of her hand, and put it in her mouth. She didn't strike the match on the side of the box though; she struck it off the rock. Then she cupped her cigarette in her hand till it was lit, and two streams of smoke came out of her nose. You could tell she was very used to smoking.

'I like it here,' she said. 'You can look at the water and the hills and you know there's no' another place in the world that'll fill your heart like this.' She started humming. Then she sang some words, 'God bless the child, da-duh-duh-duh.'

I wondered if she was drunk. She didn't look drunk. I was beginning to feel a bit scared again.

'Eleanora!' She shouted it. I jumped. I fell off the rock, and nearly murdered my hand on a sharp bit of shell.

'That's her real name – Eleanora. Have you heard her singing?'

'Who?'

'Billie Holiday. Lady Day.'

'Lady who?'

She laughed again, but quieter, thank goodness.

'No, I don't suppose y'have. Best damn jazz singer ever. She can hang a song on a couple of notes, and knock the breath from you. She was born Eleanora, so you've got something in common. I knew I was going to like you, Ellie. I knew it.'

Your granny was supposed to like you. I felt a bit disappointed that she'd thought she might not. But then, when I was thinking it, I remembered that I wasn't going to like her, not unless she liked me. I suppose that made us even, and I was glad to have something in common with a person Dot admired so much.

'That's what my name's going to be when I get to Hollywood.' It was out. I'd never said it before – not to anyone; not even to Janet, far less a granny I had just decided to like. Maybe I had 'the nerves'.

'Which name are you going to have?' She was stubbing out her cigarette. It was a real question, not the kind that grown-ups ask just to make you think they're listening.

'Well, I thought . . . I would drop the "El" and add an "a". That would be "Lenora". And I'd drop the "bairn", definitely. So it would end up "Lenora Fair".'

'That sounds like a Hollywood name all right . . . and it would be close enough to your own name to feel comfortable.'

'That's what I thought,' I agreed.

'Aye, you wouldn't want to be like John Wayne with a real name like Marion, would you? I'm sure he's a helluva lot happier answering to John.'

Dot knew about film stars!

She got up. 'You'll hear my records when we get home. I think you'll appreciate them.'

'I'm sure I will, Dot,' I said. She whistled again. It sounded even better here, with all the space about us, but Hooligan didn't appear till we were well on the road. He was standing at the wayside when we got to him and he let us get in front before following us. He'd been in something wet and smelly, but he still looked stunning.

'There's half a mile yet. D'you want a go on the bar?'

I nodded. Dot helped me to get up, and we wobbled a bit at first. It wasn't comfortable, but I hadn't expected it to be.

We passed a house on its own, quite low and very modern looking. 'That's Rita's,' said Dot. 'She moans a bit, but she's no' short of a bob or two. We've been neighbours a long time.' I was still admiring the house when we turned off on to a track. 'You'd better get off now, hen. It's a bit too bumpy here.'

I got down. We walked, and Hooligan ran ahead for the first time. You could see part of Dot's house from here; it wasn't far off the road. We heard the lorry before we saw it, and Hooligan started barking immediately. Then he stopped and circled back on the lorry, which had bags of coal stacked neatly on the back. We had to move over against some lilac trees to make room for it. A man was leaning out of the window. He was wearing a bonnet with a flap at the back covering his neck, and there was a leather collar on his shoulders that was as black as his face.

'There's a hunnerweight o' shilbottle in yir bunker, Miss Fairbairn. Tommuck couldn't make it yesterday. His wife went into labour, and they had to get the ambulance from Locheirnan. Another boy – ten o'clock this morning. First one born in the hospital . . . tae Tommuck's shame.'

'Ashamed he should be. Five bairns in four years. It's himself that's needing put in the hospital. God, it's no' me that would put up wi' it . . .'

'It's no' you that has to,' the man interrupted her. 'Tommuck'll be back round next week. Mind'n pay him. I'm just helpin' oot.'

'It's himself that knows he'll get paid. You wouldn't be here otherwise.'

'Och, don't start wi' me.' He tapped his cap and drove on.

'Does everyone call you *Miss* Fairbairn?'

Dot looked at me and frowned. 'Why wouldn't they? It's what I am,' she said. 'And if you've been

52

told otherwise, it's myself that'll put you straight.'

'But you're a Miss? You're not ... You weren't ... ?'

'Married? No. I was never married.'

It was Nancy Mackillop all over again. Dot had been pushing a pram about the place, and had never been married! And the baby in the pram had been *Dad*! No wonder I wasn't allowed to talk about my grandad.

I didn't know what to make of it. I realised that this terrible secret had always been there – there in our house, yet Dot was talking as though it was the most natural thing in the world, as though it had never needed to be a secret in the first place.

'What happened to my grandad?'

'Who knows?' Dot said. 'Who cares? And why would we waste our breath on the likes o' him?'

It was my cue to shut up. I was good at taking cues. You had to be if you were going to be a famous actress. But I'd already learned something important, and I knew I could learn more. I would have to be patient. I was good at that too.

CHAPTER 5

Dot's house was two storeys high at one end and all on the level at the other. The windows had wee panes of glass and it was painted brown, like the houses you saw in a pop-up story book. It wasn't what you'd call tidy. There were books and magazines in piles here and there, and old newspapers stuffed in a basket beside the fire. The coal scuttle was full, and the fire was laid, even though it was summer-time.

On the mantelpiece there was a wooden clock very like our own, and beside it was an ornament of a tall lady, bending backwards and holding a round mirror in her arms. She was naked on the top with just a drape of cloth around her legs. Dot saw me looking at her.

'I call her Isadora,' she said. I didn't know who Isadora was. If she was a film star I hadn't heard of her.

There were two armchairs which didn't match, and a card table was folded against the wall, with a kitchen chair on each side of it. A radiogram was centred under the living-room windows, and on either side of the fireplace was an alcove laden with bits of stuff Mam would have called junk.

Hooligan didn't come in. Dot walked through to the kitchen and opened the back door. She passed behind an old wooden table and opened her press. There were two metal bowls at the door, and she tipped out some dog food into one, and put the other under the tap and filled that too. I waited till Hooligan had finished, and then I knelt down beside him. He let me pat him a couple of times, and then he moved back out of the doorway and lifted his leg against Dot's wall.

'Good on you, Hooligan,' Dot said, smiling. 'Nothing ever grew on that wall till he started coming round. Look at it now.' I walked outside. There was a gorgeous purple flower growing up the wall. Hooligan was already round the front and halfway down the lane. I wished he could have stayed.

Dot had the frying pan out, and was cutting off a slice of Cookeen, which sizzled when it hit the pan. I was starving. She put the sausages on first, and went back through to the living room to play a record. A lady started singing about loving her man. She had a strange voice, but nice. Dot shook her head, and stood listening for a minute.

We ate our supper at the kitchen table, which was rather scarred. Dot didn't use a cloth or napkins at all, but the food was delicious. Then she opened a can of peaches and Carnation, and I asked her how she knew it was my favourite. She said it was hers too. I was pleased, knowing that. Then she filled the sink and sprinkled some Omo in the water. She put all the dishes in it, but she didn't wash them; she just left them there.

After that, she showed me the upstairs. The steps were really worn in the middles, and it felt like you might fall, but Dot said they were perfectly safe as long as you held on to the banister. There was a toilet on the landing which didn't have a bath. I remembered then (it was a long time ago), Mam saying, 'She doesn't even have a bath.' I didn't think it was all that important.

There were two bedrooms, which smelled of old clothes, but they were OK. We put my things in a big wooden wardrobe, and I noticed a saucer with Smarties in it on my bedside table. That seemed very thoughtful to me.

When we came back downstairs, Dot put on more records and then went through to the kitchen. She came back with a glass of milk, which she put on my side of the mantelpiece, and a little glass full of whisky for herself. The glass had a blue sailing boat on it. After a while I thought she might have dozed off. I looked at everything on the shelves, but she didn't have any photos up; just shells and bits of wood and different kinds of boxes. I kept watching the clock. I waited till nine o'clock.

'It's time for me to get washed for bed,' I said. I couldn't make out if Dot was sleeping or not.

She got up, and went back to the kitchen. Her glass was full again when she returned.

'Are you dirty?' she asked.

'Of course not,' I said. 'I'm very clean.'

'Are you tired then?'

'No.'

'Well, there's no sense in getting washed and going to bed then. Is there?'

There wasn't. It was a marvellous idea.

Billie Holiday was singing about someone being her thrill. Dot leaned back in her chair. I counted the tiles on the fireplace; up the left side, along the top, and down the right side. Then I did it again, the other way round. Then I multiplied the ones going up by the ones going across.

I wanted to go home.

'I'm tired now.'

'All right, hen. You can wash yourself in the sink if you like.'

I shook my head.

'D'you want me to come up with you?'

'It's OK, I can manage.' I didn't want to cry again.

'See you in the morning, Ellie.'

Keep me safe.

Keep me loving.

Please God. Please, please God, let me go home.

I wasn't sure if Dot had gone to bed. She was still in the chair in the morning. She stood up and lit a cigarette, and coughed for a while.

'I'll get you some breakfast, Ellie. I used the sausages, but you can have peaches and cream.'

They were still good, but they tasted different for breakfast. Dot poured us both some coffee, without me asking. I told her I wasn't allowed it.

'Why not?'

'Dad says it's not good for you, that all the beatniks go to coffee houses, and now they're getting so used to drinking it, it makes them want more.' I couldn't remember his words exactly, but he didn't like beatniks.

'What a load o' shite!'

I was glad I hadn't lifted my cup yet, because I lost my breath when she said that. Dad never swore. He said it proved you had a limited vocabulary. Janet disagreed. She said you could have a good vocabulary, and swear too.

'You're in *my* hoose now,' Dot added. Her eyes were a bit wild, and it sounded as though she was giving me a row – almost, anyway. 'Drink your coffee!'

I didn't like it much, but I was feeling all nervous again, so I finished it as quick as I could.

Dot remembered about the eggs ages after that. I had a boiled egg and toast for dinner. Dot said it was as good then as any other time, but Mam would never have given me a boiled egg for my dinner. I hoped she was feeling better.

Dad would be home all day today. He read a lot on Sundays, and listened to the wireless. Sometimes we went for a walk, if Mam was agreeable to the idea. I didn't like going for walks with Dad, though I was never given a choice. We always had to hurry to keep up with him, and we were home before you knew it.

He took us to the beach once. We went in our car which was kept in a lock-up at the bottom of our street. We didn't use it much. It was a bit like the phone, except not just for emergencies.

There were some stands at the beach, and Mam bought me a blue pail and spade. Dad also bought me a sun visor which had a yellow snoot. I couldn't remember what happened to the pail and spade. I maybe left them there, although I don't think so. I still had the visor though. We had a real picnic and Dad bought us ice cream. Then Mam took me down to the water. Dad paid for a deckchair, and stayed behind. He couldn't even see us from where he was sitting.

We made a magnificent sandcastle, but other people were letting their children run all over the place, and showing no respect, so it got knocked down. I wanted to start a new one, but Mam was getting anxious with it all, so I said it would be nice to go for a paddle. We were just at the water's edge when I saw Dad walking towards the bowling greens, away from us. He was walking like he was going to work, like he didn't know he was at the beach.

Mam was holding my hand, but she was looking after Dad at the same time. I screamed at the cold water to make her stop looking at him. She smiled at me, and I screamed again, and tried laughing really loud, but she looked scared when the waves came on us, and I said I didn't want to paddle any more. I said we should catch up with Dad. I knew it was what Mam wanted.

Dot got the Cameron boys' bike out of her shed, but I didn't know where to go, so I just went up and down the lane a few times. It was a horrible bike, but I thought I'd better get used to it. It was hard to pedal, because I didn't want to stand to get my speed up. I was scared I might miss the saddle when I sat, and come down on the bar. I didn't know why boys had to have bars anyway. They didn't do anything useful, and it might be even worse for a boy to come down on the bar, but I tried not to imagine that.

Luckily, I was back at the house when Rita arrived. I wouldn't have wanted to be in her way, as fast as she'd driven up the lane. There was another lady with her, and that was Lil, mother of Hugh. She was very stout, and had a job getting out of the car. Rita just left her to struggle, and marched on into the house. She smiled at me on the way past, as though I'd always been there. I decided to give her a second chance.

'Can you give me a hand?' Lil called at me.

I rushed over, but she didn't need me to get her out of the car, just to take her messages. She was looking a bit distressed by the time she was all out, but she gave me a hug and said she was Mrs Bryce and she never would have recognised me, I'd got so big. We were nearly at the door when she said

Hugh was looking forward to getting to know me. I nearly dropped her messages.

She was kind, though. She brought me a bag of assorted toffees and a box of Fruit Gums. It's strange how they always tasted better in the box than the tube. There was also a bottle of tangerine lemonade. 'He doesn't know everything,' she said. I didn't question her.

There was a bag of apples too, and she told Dot to be sure I had one every day. Dot was blethering to Rita and didn't answer. Then Mrs Bryce took out a fruit cake and a blue enamel dish with a steak pie in it.

'You'll have that for your supper, Ellie. It's fresh cooked before I left. Be sure to heat it,' she shouted to Dot, and put it in the oven. 'Have you got tatties? I don't suppose so. I said to Eck I should bring you some tatties, and he said surely to God you at least had a tattie in the house.' She was going through Dot's press. Dot and Rita were in the living room.

'Would you look at that?' she said, holding a paper bag in front of me. There were four potatoes in it, and their runners were halfway up the sides. Mrs Bryce took off her coat, and rolled up her sleeves.

'I should have brought my peeny. It's no use getting dressed to come to this house. No use at all.' In no time, she had the tatties peeled and soaking in a bowl. Then she put the kettle on. 'We better go ben and see what they're up to,' she said. It was like she was their mother, the way she said it.

Dot and Rita were sitting at the card table. They both had a whisky, and Rita was talking.

'So what d'you think?'

Dot shrugged and raised her glass.

'What does she think about what?' Mrs Bryce asked.

Rita turned to her. 'The shop. What d'you think?'

Mrs Bryce sat in my chair. Well, it wasn't my chair, but it was the other one, the one Dot didn't sit in. Dot walked over to the radiogram.

'Spare us,' Mrs Bryce said. 'I'm no' in the mood for the wailing o' that Billie Holiday, Dot, and I'm deaved wi' your shop, Rita. I've had a terrible week myself, but do I complain? I do not.'

Rita went cock-eyed at Mrs Bryce's back. I was sitting on the floor with my back to the wall, and Rita saw me watching her, and did it again. I smiled at her, and she winked.

'Well, I've only got till Friday to decide,' Rita said. 'I was hoping I could count on youse two for an opinion.'

Whatever Rita was talking about must have been important. Dot returned to her chair without putting on any records. The kettle whistled, and Mrs Bryce looked over at Dot.

'Help yirselves,' Dot said. 'I'll have coffee, Lil.'

Mrs Bryce pushed herself up. 'Am I your slave? As sure as death, if I wasn't here to do for you all, what would yis do . . . ?' Her voice faded off into the kitchen.

'It's this or ... the other, Dot. I don't know, I really don't,' Rita continued.

'What d'you want the most?' Dot asked. 'If you go, you know what's in front of you. If not ... well ... maybe it's time for you to get married.'

Rita threw her head back. 'I've *been* married. I'm not sure I ... Oh, *Goddd*!'

Dot laughed. I was getting used to it. 'Doesna sound to me like you're ready to do it again.'

'It's not that!' Rita retorted, looking very annoyed. 'And who are you to advise me, Dot Fairbairn? There's never been a wedding-ring on *your* finger that I know of!'

'Thank God for that,' Dot said, not the least put out. You'd think she'd have been embarrassed, but she wasn't. Not a bit.

'Thank God for what?' Mrs Bryce asked, returning with a tray of cups, a plate of fruit cake, and a glass of tangerine. 'Don't be sitting there,' she said, putting the glass beside me on the floor. 'You'll get a draught.'

'For no' having a husband,' Dot answered.

Mrs Bryce stared at Dot for a minute, and Dot looked away. 'Did it ever occur to you that there was a man out there who might have been meant for you?' Mrs Bryce asked.

'It did not,' Dot answered, glaring at Mrs Bryce. 'And did it ever occur to *you* that it's none of your business?'

'Pardon me for living,' Mrs Bryce said, throwing herself back down on the chair, but not before she'd helped herself to some cake. Rita seemed lost in thought, and hadn't seemed to notice anything, but it made me wonder just how much Mrs Bryce knew about my grandad. If he'd been *meant* for Dot, why *weren't* they married?

'If I marry Pat, I'm stuck here for the rest of my life,' Rita complained.

'And if you take the shop? You don't think that'll be a tie?' Mrs Bryce asked.

'It's just . . . I have plans for the shop. It's a good location, and at least Locheirnan has people *living* there. I could move my stock, and develop it . . . like a real business.'

'You *have* a real business,' Mrs Bryce said. She'd eaten two pieces of her own cake already. 'You could keep that going here, and be married too.'

'That's the point, Lil! Nothing would ever CHANGE!'

'I'm no' for change,' Mrs Bryce answered. 'There's far too much change if you ask me. There'll be another war yet!'

Rita spread her right arm in front of her. ' "Bella Donna",' she sighed.

'Bella what?' Mrs Bryce asked. The cake was coming out of her mouth in crumbs, and she wiped them off her chest, but they just landed in her lap.

' "Bella Donna – You'll knock him dead!" It would be a slogan. A name *and* a slogan . . . a marketing strategy.'

'A what?' Mrs Bryce was eating again.

'Marketing. A strategy, like they had in the war. Strategies.'

Dot was nodding. 'Bella Donna ... beautiful lady. Or...'

'*Exactly*,' Rita said. 'Or ... pure poison. Either way, it would knock him dead!'

'I don't get it,' Mrs Bryce said.

Even I got it.

Rita went cock-eyed again. 'Forget it, Lil. Just forget it.'

'Don't take that tone with me, Rita. Can I advise you if I don't understand your "strategies"? I can not.'

Rita's tea was cold. She drained her whisky. 'I'm off,' she said, rising. 'I'll come back for you at five, Lil. Be ready.' She walked towards the kitchen, calling back over her shoulder. 'We're going to talk about it tonight. I'll bring his boy over here, Dot. He can stay with Ellie for a couple of hours. OK?'

'Aye, fine,' Dot answered. 'He can have a bit o' Lil's pie.' She nodded at Lil's back, and I knew to expect a reaction.

Mrs Bryce whirled, or as near as she could, being wedged in the chair. 'That pie's for you, and that poor bairn.' I realised I was the 'poor bairn'. I quite liked that. 'Thon Pat Conroy's got steak enough to choke a horse, an' his boy's no' needing a bit of my pie.' She straightened herself in the chair and pulled up her bosoms. 'No' that I grudge it to him, y'understand.'

'I doubt you'd find a horse that would want to choke on steak,' Dot mused.

Mrs Bryce glared at her.

I wondered where Joseph's mother was. I would ask him when he got here.

Mrs Bryce and Dot blethered back and forth, and I got a bit bored just sitting there. I asked if it was all right for me to go upstairs for one of my books, and Dot nodded. Mrs Bryce gave me a smile when I excused myself. As I left the room I heard her saying, 'She's a wee delight, so she is.'

Dot had put my vanity case in the cupboard of my bedside table. The cupboard smelled damp, but when I opened it, it felt very dry and sort of dusty. My vanity case was sitting on top of a couple of lace doilies which were yellow and stained from being old. It was a shame because they would have been very pretty otherwise.

I sat up on the bed, and opened my Famous Five book. I was on page nine before I realised I didn't know what was going on. I had let my attention wander, and had to go back three pages and read them again. At home my attention never wandered. I loved reading my books, and sometimes got 'too wrapped up in them', Dad said. Maybe I couldn't concentrate because of being in a strange room.

I looked about me, but the room was really quite bare. I ate some Smarties, and tried to read some more, but it was useless, so I got up and opened the wardrobe. There was just my own clothes and an old raincoat in it, and two blankets on the top shelf – nothing at all interesting. I closed it up, and decided to go back downstairs. The doilies got a bit ruffled when I tried to put my vanity case away, and I took them out to smooth them. An envelope as yellow as the doilies fell from their folds.

It was addressed to 'Mr J. Starling, c/o Mrs Parkin, 20 Seaton Street, Newcastle'. It wasn't sealed, and the ink had faded so it was light blue and scratchy looking. Dot must have written it a long time ago.

I put it back where I'd found it, and placed my vanity case carefully on top. Then I went to the toilet before going down to join Dot and Mrs Bryce. It was while I was sitting on the toilet that I began wondering who Mr Starling was. Newcastle was such a long way from Inchbrae. I supposed he must have been a friend of Dot's. Maybe even a boy-friend.

I reached for the chain, and Mrs Bryce's words flashed through my mind. A *boyfriend*! I held my breath while the toilet flushed. It was too much to bear. I scolded myself in the mirror. I could never, *never* read somebody else's letter. It would be a terribly wicked thing to do.

I carried on downstairs, and Mrs Bryce looked up as I came in. 'Was that you at the toilet, hen?' she asked.

'Who else would it be?' Dot said, smiling at me. 'Did you get fed up wi' yir books?'

'A bit,' I answered.

'Well, we're just a couple of boring old farts, I'm afraid,' Dot said. 'But you're right welcome to sit with us till Rita gets back.'

Mrs Bryce's mouth had dropped open. 'Dot!'

'Och, it's true,' Dot said. 'God, Lil, I can't remember the last time we set foot out o' Inchbrae. What could we talk about that would interest a bairn?'

That made me wonder even more. If Dot had hardly ever been out of Inchbrae, why would she be writing to a man in Newcastle? And why hadn't she posted it?

Sometimes Janet and I made up love-letters to famous film stars. We'd written a really great one to Tony Curtis, but we'd never have sent it. We didn't post any of them. Perhaps Dot's letter was a love-letter too. It very likely was. The more I thought about it, the more obvious it became. It was definitely a love-letter.

I waited a while longer, so as not to sound suspicious. 'I think I'll go back upstairs, Dot,' I said, sighing. Sighing *and* stretching.

'D' you feel like a lie-down?' Dot asked.

'I might take a nap,' I suggested. 'Just for a wee while.'

'On you go,' Dot said. 'I'll give you a shout when the troops arrive.'

I sat on the bed for a very long time. I was scared to read the letter, scared in case I was caught. But it wasn't as though it was sealed. I would never have *opened* somebody else's letter. Besides, it was foolish to think it was a love-letter. It was probably an old bill or something which Dot had meant to return to some silly man in Newcastle who'd sent it to the wrong person. Dot surely wouldn't mind me looking at an old bill.

Even though I knew that she wouldn't, my heart was thumping when I pulled it out. There was just one sheet of paper inside, and the lines had faded along with the ink. The writing was neat enough at the beginning, but it was all over the place by the end.

There was no date.

Dear Johnny

You'll be shocked to get this letter. I wouldn't have known where you were, but Jockie Falconer said he'd come across you when he got paid off from the Clyde, and was down there looking for work. He said he'd been in digs at this address with you for a couple of weeks before coming back north (he's still not working, but it's hard with just the one eye now).

Anyway, I've had this envelope ready for quite a while. Maybe you're not even there any more, and you'll never get this letter. Maybe I'll never send it.

Well, Johnny, you'll be happier to know that Lil seems to have forgiven you. That's good, isn't it? Although you broke her heart just taking off like a thief in the night. I'm not going to get angry with you, though. I also (scored out) I too am over you leaving – and Lil doesn't know anything that happened between us.

(Here the writing started wandering off the lines a bit.)

I'm afraid she might know soon, though, as I'm expecting. I hope (scored out) I have nobody to help me if you won't. I'm not begging or anything. I'm not one to beg, as you know. I was just hoping that you'll (scored out) you might
What? (scrawled) WHAT? (again)
GOD HELP ME.

I folded the letter and put it back between the doilies. I put the doilies back in the cupboard, and put my vanity case on top. I was shivering, but not at all cold.

Johnny Starling. He even sounded like a film star. I was sure he must look like Tony Curtis to have had Dot and Mrs Bryce both in love with him, and be very dashing to take off like a thief in the night. It wasn't really a love-letter, though, and I found it a bit hard to understand, so I kept going over it in my head. What what happened between Dot and Mr Starling? And why was Dot afraid Mrs Bryce would find out? And what was it Dot was expecting to happen?

Suddenly it hit me. 'Expecting.' It wasn't some*thing* Dot was expecting to happen, it was some*one* – Dad, MY Dad – which would mean that Mr Starling was my grandad. My head was spinning, and I tried to concentrate really hard. It *had* to be true. Mr Starling had to be my grandad. I'd just made up my mind to ask Dot about it when I remembered that I couldn't do that. She would know then that I'd read her letter.

But wouldn't it be great to have a grandad? And then Dot could have a husband – and Dad could have a dad. We'd be a great family altogether. Perhaps I could write to Mr Starling myself. There must be *something* I could do.

I shook my head, which I realised was getting quite sore with it all. Mr Starling was miles away, *if* he was still there. Maybe Mrs Bryce could help. Maybe she would know how to get hold of him for me. But that wouldn't work either. Even if she did know, she had been Dot's friend for so long that she wouldn't be at all happy at doing something behind her back, and I just knew she wouldn't approve of me having read Dot's letter. I sighed again. Here I was, having found out something this important, and there was nothing in the world I could do about it.

I decided to write down Mr Starling's address anyway, before I forgot it. Perhaps when I got home Janet could suggest a way of finding him. I felt better then. Janet would surely help me. It would be an adventure, just like the famous Five. It could be our mission!

I nearly jumped out of my skin when I heard

Dot's voice. 'Joseph's here,' she called up. 'Come on down, Ellie.'

I waited till she'd moved away from the stairs. I didn't want her to give me that scary look and know I'd read her letter. I hoped it didn't show on my face. Mam always said she could see right through me. I consoled myself with the fact that Dot didn't know me nearly as well as Mam.

At least not yet.

CHAPTER 6

Joseph stood at the back door. Rita gave him a push. 'Get in the house,' she said. He threw her arm off and wouldn't budge. I could tell she was exasperated with him.

'C'mon in, Joe,' Dot said. 'We'll no' eat you.'

He came in, but just as far as the living-room door. Mrs Bryce aimed a farewell kiss at him, but he dodged her and landed beside me on the carpet, shuffling over a bit so he wasn't so close to me. I'd noticed Mrs Bryce rolling her false teeth round her mouth, and tried to avoid her too, but I couldn't. She was very strong, and had very big arms.

Dot saw Lil and Rita off. Rita said she would be back again later, but she didn't say when. Joseph still wouldn't look at me. He was picking at a scab on his knee. 'You shouldn't pick it,' I said. 'Not till it's ready.'

'Bugger off.'

'I'll give you "Bugger off",' Dot said, appearing beside him, but she didn't sound too upset. She put on a record; another song about loving a man. They all were, all the ones I'd heard. Dot must have loved Johnny Starling a lot.

'Well, what d'yis want to do?' she asked.

I wanted to go back upstairs and think about the letter, but I was hoping too that Hooligan might appear. 'Will Hooligan come for his supper?'

Dot shrugged. 'He might. Usually he waits for me to get him.'

'I'm no' going anywhere,' Joe said.

'Please yirself,' Dot answered. 'If you want to sit around here, it's up to you. Pity to waste the day, though.'

'It's no' wasted,' he said. 'I was out wi' Da all day – until we had to go over *there*!' He lurched in the general direction of Rita's house.

'Where did you go wi' your da?' Dot asked him.

'Around.'

'Are you wanting yir supper?' Dot asked me, ignoring Joseph, but not in a rude way.

I was still full from the lemonade and cake. 'I'm not very hungry yet, thank you.'

Dot shrugged again. 'We can go down to the river.'

Joe didn't say anything, which was nearly a 'yes'.

Dot left the radiogram playing and the door open. We could hear Billie Holiday halfway down the lane. There were bees in the lilac trees, so I kept to the middle. Joe was ahead of us. He had a yo-yo in his pocket which he spun while he walked. He was very good at it. I was no use with a yo-yo, not even standing still. Dot was smoking a cigarette. I was the only one not doing anything.

'Is Rita going to marry Joseph's father?'

Dot put her hand on my chest to slow me down a bit, even though we were already going slow. Joe got quite a bit in front, almost to the road.

'What Rita spoke of was in confidence, Ellie. D'you understand?'

I knew about confidences. At school Janet and I always marked our notes 'Highly Confidential', even though we passed them to each other and made sure no-one else could read them. Dot's letter hadn't been marked 'Highly Confidential' or even 'Confidential', but I knew it had been wrong to read it, and I began to feel guilty.

'Aye,' I answered. 'But . . .'

Dot interrupted me. 'If Rita had left her handbag in the house, would you give it to someone else?'

'Of course not!'

'It's the same thing, Ellie. It's her business. It doesn't belong to anyone else.'

I felt myself flush. Did Dot know I'd found her letter? She couldn't have. Besides, it was different. Johnny Starling *was* my business.

Joe was waiting at the roadside. We caught up, and crossed almost together. We went through a fence and across two fields thick with buttercups and daisies, and swarming with butterflies. Dot said it was a shame the fields didn't have a crop in them, but I thought they were beautiful.

One of the butterflies seemed to be keeping

company with us, and I tripped on a stone from watching it. I hit my big toe, and had to count to ten to squeeze back the tears. Dot said it was a very sore thing, stubbing your big toe, and that it always brought the tears to her own eyes.

Joseph laughed at me hopping about. 'Hah! Serves you right,' he shouted. It didn't serve me right. I hadn't done anything to him. I hadn't done anything to anyone.

The pain went off quite quickly. We pushed through a gap in the whins and we were at the river, but further round the bay than yesterday. There were a few dunes behind us, but there wasn't much sand. What there was was grey looking and full of pebbles. Joseph started skiting stones off the water as soon as we got there. That was something else I couldn't do, but to be fair, I'd had no practice, whereas he probably did it all the time.

It was still very hot. Dot lit another cigarette, and you could smell the sulphur from her match long after it was out. She brushed off a big stone and sat down, facing the water and the hills in the distance. She didn't look like she was going to talk much, and I hoped she wouldn't start singing. It would make me embarrassed in front of Joe, even though I didn't think I was going to be friends with him.

I saw a ladybird, all alone among the stones. It was a long way from the bushes, but I didn't try to pick it up. 'Ladybird, ladybird, fly away home. . .' Right then, nothing seemed more important than going home.

I walked down to the water's edge, and watched Joe for a while. He was never going to talk to me. 'Where do you go to school?' I asked.

'Locheirnan.'

'How d'you get there?'

'The bus.'

He picked up a branch and broke it in half across his knee. The scab came with it. 'It's off now,' I pointed.

He looked disappointed. I hated it myself when it fell off and you didn't notice. It was better when you picked it. There were a few drops of blood.

'See, it wasn't ready. You'll get another one,' I assured him.

That seemed to cheer him up. 'I'm going to the big school after the summer,' he volunteered. 'I'll get to stay in the hostel.'

'Me too,' I answered. 'I won't have to stay in the hostel, though.' I quite fancied staying in the hostel, as the girls in my Mallory Towers stories were always having midnight feasts and great adventures. The hostel wasn't quite the same as boarding school, but it might still be an adventure.

'D'you have any friends here?' I asked.

''Course I do. Malc and Ian. They're on their holidays.'

'Like me.'

'They didn't say you were coming for your holidays,' he said. He was looking right at me. 'They said yir ma's sick.'

'She is not. She's just . . . needing some peace and quiet.'

'D'you have brothers and sisters?'

I shook my head.

'Yir an only child,' he said. I hated being called that. Sometimes, the way grown-ups said it, it was like you were something to be pitied. Worse than that, though, sometimes they said it like you were really spoiled and got everything you wanted.

'I don't like being called an only child.'

'Me neither,' Joe said. He handed me half his branch. 'D' you want a throw?'

I shook my head. 'No thanks. I'm not much good. Where did your friends go? On their holidays?'

'Dornoch. They've got a caravan.'

'Are they rich?'

'Nuht. It's their uncle's. They just get a shot of it.'

'Are they in your class?'

'Malc is. Ian's his brother. He's the oldest. He's in the Academy.' He walked on a few steps, and threw the two bits of branch back into the bushes. 'We've got a skiffle group,' he said.

'Are yis any good?'

''Course we are. If we keep practising, we'll be as good as Lonnie Donegan.'

'Is that what you're going to be then? A musician?'

'Prob'ly. I'm no' going to be a bloody butcher!'

I looked to see if Dot had heard, but she was just gazing at the hills.

'I'm going to Hollywood myself.' It's funny; when you'd said it once, it was real, and you didn't mind saying it again.

'Y'are not,' he sneered.

'I am sot.'

'What for?'

'To be a film star.'

He didn't say anything.

'D'you play Film Stars at your school?'

'Sometimes,' he answered. 'Depends.'

'C.G.'

'Gary Cooper,' he shot at me, too quickly to have thought about it.

'That's G.C. I'll give you another try.'

'Get lost.'

'It was Cary Grant,' I said.

'I knew that. I forgot.'

'Are yis hungry yet?' Dot shouted.

'I'm no' eating at her house,' Joe said.

'We're fine,' I called back. 'Why not?' I asked him.

'She gives me the creeps.' I kind of knew what he meant.

'She's been very nice to me.' I felt I should defend her.

''Course. She's yir granny.' He looked at Dot. Then he looked at me. 'Why don't you call her "Granny"?'

'I don't know her well enough.'

'That's daft,' he said. He just said it for something to say. He looked confused.

'D'you want to go for Hooligan?' I asked.

'He might no' be around.' He seemed more interested.

'We could look for him.'

'Aye'

I was pleased. I started to skip back to Dot, but I remembered my toe, and walked instead.

'Can we go for Hooligan now?'

'It's OK wi' me.'

Dot kept mostly to the roadside, but she let me and Joe go through the fields. We had to get out once because there was a big bull. He was lying down, which Dot said meant it would probably rain. I thought he was just tired with the sun. There were flies all over him, in his eyes and everything, but he looked content enough. We were past him before you got the smell, and Dot said it was lucky there wasn't much wind.

Inchbrae looked like a ghost town. I mentioned this fact to Joe. He took two pretend pistols from his pockets and started shooting as we came up the street. One-two. One-two.

'J.W.' I knew he would get it.

'John Wayne. Easy.' Joe kept shooting. 'G.F.'

'Glenn Ford. My turn.'

'I'm no' playing.'

Dot gave him a dunt on the back of his head. 'It's her turn.'

He rubbed his head, but you could tell it wasn't sore. 'I don't want to play it any more,' he insisted; bravely, I thought.

'It's OK,' I said quickly, in case Dot skelped him again. Two men came out of the Jacobite. I stopped.

'Are we going in there?' I asked.

'Aye. I'm dying o' thirst,' Dot said.

I didn't move.

'C'mon,' Joe urged. 'We'll maybe get something.'

'Will Hugh be there?' I whispered to him. Dot was already pushing open the door.

He grinned. 'Prob'ly. He's all right. He's just a mongol. C'mon.'

My heart was beating very hard. I could hear it in my ears. 'What if he attacks us?'

'He doesn't *attack* people! He's harmless. Come *on!*'

'We haven't had any pie.'

'*What*?'

'Mrs Bryce said we had to eat her pie. We haven't, yet.'

'If you don't come in, I'm going to tell Hugh you're out here. He'll come and get you.'

I was through the door before him.

CHAPTER 7

Mr Bryce was leaning on the bar talking to Dot, but there was no sign of his wife – or Hugh. One of the tables was occupied by two men playing dominoes. They looked up when we came in.

'Sit over there.' Dot pointed to the sofa at the bottom of the stairs. 'I'll put a lemonade over to yis.'

'Make mine a large one, Dot,' one of the men called out.

'That'll be right,' she answered. 'D'you remember the last time that bugger bought anyone a drink, Eckie?' she asked, as though the man couldn't hear her.

'No indeed. He's been nursing a half-pint for nigh on an hour as it is. You'd be here till your teeth are black before you'd make a profit out o' Arthur.' The man called Arthur didn't seem to mind being insulted.

I sat on the farthest-away bit and Joe sat the closest. He leaned over the arm, watching what was happening at the bar. I heard someone coming down the stairs, and closed my eyes.

'Look at you,' Mrs Bryce said, swatting at Joe with a duster. 'Don't be leaning on my arms like that. They'll be all shiny with you.' Joe straightened.

She smiled at me. 'Did you eat, pet?'

'We're going to,' I assured her. 'As soon as we get back.' I didn't want her to make a fuss. 'We came for Hooligan.'

'Oh . . . Well, I huvna seen him the day. Have you seen Dreep the day?' she called to Mr Bryce.

'No, I huvna, now that you mention it. Come to that, I didna see him yesterday either.'

'It's no' like him, no' to put in an appearance two days in a row,' Mrs Bryce said. She sounded worried.

'He's all right,' Dot said. 'I had Hooligan home with me yesterday. He wouldna have come if Dreep was in bother.'

'Right enough,' the man called Arthur agreed. 'They're probably just lying somewhere out o' the sun, the pair o' them.'

Mrs Bryce brought our lemonade over. 'Don't drink it too quickly. You'll get a sore stomach.' She was always saying things like that.

Joe drank his and looked to see how much I had left. I kept it in my hand. 'D' you live here?' I asked him.

'Nuht! I live wi' Da.' He said it as though I was stupid. He could be very annoying.

'I didn't mean *here*, in *this* place, I meant in the town.'

"Course we do. Where else would we stay?'

'Well, where? In a house?'

He sighed and blew his breath out. 'Above our shop, if you must know. You go up the stairs and you're in our house.'

'I was only asking.'

There was a commotion upstairs. Mrs Bryce fairly flew up the steps. You'd never have believed how quickly she moved. 'That's himself up,' she said.

I ran to Dot. She pulled me beside her. 'It's all right, hen. It's all right,' she soothed. She turned to Mr Bryce. 'He came over to Jessie's yesterday. Gave her a bit of a turn.'

Mr Bryce pulled his eyebrows together and leaned over the bar at me. 'He'll be happy once he's met you, Ellie. You don't need to be afraid of him.' He must have seen the terror in my face, even though I tried to hide it. 'There's a lemonade in it for you, if you'll just shake hands wi' him.'

Joe was right beside us. 'No' you,' Mr Bryce said. 'You've met him plenty.' Joseph went back and sat on the sofa, swinging his legs like he didn't care, but I could tell he did.

Mrs Bryce came down the stairs with Hugh. She was holding his hand, and going one step at a time, as though she was afraid he would fall. He could walk fine, though, and was pulling impatiently at her to go faster. He pushed her away at the bottom, and came headfirst towards us. I tried to get behind Dot, but she wouldn't let me. She put up a hand

84

just as Hugh looked like he would fall on top of us, and held him away. He was still smiling, and his mouth was moving as if he was eating something. I didn't want to look.

'Hugh, this is Ellie. D'you remember, from yesterday?'

His head started rolling again. He was trying to nod. 'Aah-gaargh! Uuhrrr-eeeee.'

'Say hello, Ellie.' Dot pulled my arm from my side.

'Hello, H-H-Hugh.' I was shaking and stuttering. It was awful. Just when I thought he was going to shake my hand, he grabbed me right into him and gave me a hug. He was clapping my head, and squeezing the life out of me.

'Let her go, Hugh. Come on, son, let the lassie go now.' Mrs Bryce was pulling him off me. He was trying to speak, and creating an awful lot of spittle. Mrs Bryce laughed. 'Aye, she is. He says you're beautiful, Ellie.'

I forgot to be scared. I couldn't believe she could understand what he'd been saying. I tried to smile at him, but my mouth wouldn't move, and my neck was sore from going rigid. Mrs Bryce took him over to the sofa and gave him a magazine. He sat as good as gold, with the magazine right up at his face, and didn't even try to get up.

Dot lifted her eyebrows. It was as much as to say 'I told you so'. I didn't go back to the sofa. Joe had finished my lemonade, but I didn't mind. I said 'No thanks' when Mr Bryce offered to pour me another.

'We'll go and look for Hooligan,' I said to Dot.

'Right-oh. Don't wander too far. You know where to find me,' she said.

I tried not to make it obvious that I was tiptoeing out. I beckoned to Joe. He got up, and came after me. The street was cooler. I took deep breaths. Dad showed me how to do it once; I think it was the first time the doctor came for Mam.

'That's the worst over,' Joe said, as though he knew how I was feeling. I felt better then. We stopped in front of the grocer's. It was the only shop I hadn't been in.

The sign said 'Alexander's'. It was wooden, and stretched across both windows. The paint was flaking, and the door and the window-frames looked just as decrepit. Tins were stacked in neat pyramids in one window though, and there was a display of Surf and Omo in the other, with tubes of SR toothpaste between them. None of the labels was faded, nor the sign on the door, which had a black cat with 'Craven A' above it, and 'Closed' below.

'Is that Mrs Alexander's shop too?' I asked Joe.

'Nuht. It used to be. Well, it was her and her husband's. She took over the paper-shop when he died. The Corbetts were moving to Locheirnan.'

'Who're the Corbetts?'

'They used to have the paper-shop. Before it was a post office.'

'So who's got the grocer's?'

He sighed, and started walking again. He kept

making me feel he couldn't be bothered with me.

'The Fishbeins,' he answered.

'What kind of name's that?'

'Everyone says they're Jews. They had to get out of Germany during the war. Dad says Mr Fishbein's got relations in Edinburgh, and that's how they ended up here.'

Edinburgh was a long way from Inchbrae. I didn't think that answered the question.

'Anyway, Mrs Alexander let the shop to them, and they've been here for years,' Joe continued. 'Mrs Fishbein still doesn't speak much English, but she's a nice wifie. She sometimes lets me have stuff from the threepenny box, even if I've only got tuppence. He's nice too, but he just gives you what you pay for.'

'Why didn't they just buy a shop in Edinburgh?'

'They couldn't buy one anywhere. They had to leave all their worldly possessions behind.'

'Poor wifie', Dot had said. I felt very sorry for them.

'Do they have kids?'

We were at the end of the street. Joe turned into a lane with some garages, and a bit of wasteground beyond. There was an old pram beside the rubbish. All the wheels were off it, and someone had dumped dirty sacks in it.

'You're no' to mention it, but they had a son who went into one o' thon concentration camps, and was never heard of again.'

It seemed like everyone in Inchbrae was missing

someone. It made you realise that other people must be lonely too. I was just thinking this, and thinking I didn't feel too lonely right then, when Hooligan appeared from behind the rubbish.

He stopped and looked at us, keeping his tail down till I called his name. Then he started wagging it and panting a bit. I couldn't wait to get my hands on him. He let me come right up to him, and I noticed his coat had a sticky patch on it, which I avoided, while I stroked the back of his neck. His fur felt like silk, and it was warm as could be. Joe bent down and rubbed his chest, and Hooligan began to back off.

'He doesn't like you to pet him too much,' Joe said.

'I know,' I answered. I was sure I could change that. Something moved in the pram. I stiffened, and Hooligan let out arrow growl. I looked at him. He was growling at me.

The sacks sat up. It was a man. I nearly screamed. I looked at Joe, but he wasn't a bit scared. The man threw an arm over the side and Hooligan pushed up against it. I knew then that it was Dreep, the wino.

His face was almost covered by his moustache and beard. He was brown and grey and filthy from top to toe. His legs were somewhere under him, but you couldn't see them, and his coat – or whatever it was – had a big hood on it. He must have been sweltered with the heat and all those clothes on him.

'How y'doing the day, Dreep?' Joe asked.

'Fucking beautiful.'

I gasped.

'We're taking Hooligan for his supper,' Joe said.

'On you go.'

We started walking away. Joe snapped his fingers for Hooligan to follow. I didn't want to look back to see if he was coming, but then I heard him padding along behind us. We turned back on to the High Street.

'He must be near sober,' Joe remarked. 'He never swears when he's drunk.' He started whistling 'Tom Dooley' and Hooligan passed us up and laid down at the door of the Jacobite.

'He said the "F" word.'

'So?' Joe said, and carried on whistling.

'I only ever heard Walter Cummings say it.'

'Who's he?' Joe asked, not really interested. 'Po-or boy, you go-o-na die . . .'

'He's a wicked, evil boy. He hardly ever gets to do lessons, he's in the corner so much. Once, when he was put in the corner, he called Mr Ballantyne an effing basket, and Mr Ballantyne threw the duster at him. It looked like a good aim. We all thought it would get him on the back of the head, but it missed him – just.'

'We've got a teacher who throws dusters. It's sore.'

I looked at Joseph, wondering what he'd done to deserve that. He was running his hand along the wall, and I knew he wasn't going to tell me.

89

I shrugged. 'Anyway, at playtime, Gordie Mitchell – who's nearly as brave as Walter – said that Walter shouldn't be calling anyone a basket because he was one himself. D'you know what I mean . . . basket?'

"Course! It's baby talk anyway. We say bastard here. We just say it, right.' Joseph looked at me, throwing back his shoulders. I knew he didn't say it. His face was red.

He watched me watching him. Then he moved on. 'So?'

'So what?'

'So what happened?' he asked, closing his eyes and making me feel stupid again, which I wasn't.

I waited. He slowed, and turned back. 'Don't tell me then. I couldn't care less.'

Somehow, it was important for him to care.

'Walter kicked him between the legs, and Gordie was off school for nearly a week. His mother had to take him to the hospital for tests, and she came to the school about it. Walter got the strap in the Headie's office, but it hasn't stopped him saying the "F" word – or kicking people.'

I had never talked to a boy about the 'F' word, or things between your legs, or *anything* before. But I'd never been made to feel stupid, either. In our class, it was the boys who were stupid, even the clever ones. They were always pushing each other, and having pretend fights – and sometimes real ones, like Gordie and Walter. And the Jannie was always having to mend the door of the boys' toilets, because they couldn't go through it one at a time like civilised people. Janet and I were in the cloakrooms once, and actually saw *four* of them trying to beat each other out of the way to get in first. Janet said she couldn't imagine ever having a boyfriend, and I had to agree.

Joseph seemed just the type to be involved in the same kind of nonsense, and didn't seem a bit impressed with what I'd just told him. If he was, he certainly wasn't going to let on, but then maybe he hadn't spoken to girls much either. I think we were both relieved to see Dot coming out of the Jacobite. She walked out to the middle of the street and looked up at the windows above Joe's father's shop.

'No signs o' life?' she asked, of no-one in particular.

'I'm supposed to be at your house,' Joe retorted. 'That's where they'll come for me.'

'We better get going then,' Dot answered. Hooligan was already on his way.

None of us talked much on the way back. I was feeling quite tired and hungry, too, now. Joe told Dot we'd found Dreep. She was glad he was all right, but he was old enough to look after himself, she said.

We weren't very far along when we saw a tractor coming towards us. The driver was turned away from us, and was waving on the car behind. It pulled out around him and then stopped beside us. It was Rita. That made the farmer have to pull out to pass *her*. He gave her a 'V' sign and she gave him one back. Dot laughed and waved at the farmer.

'Grand day, Dot,' he called. His bad humour hadn't lasted a minute.

Rita opened the passenger door from the inside. 'Where the hell were yis?'

'You never said when you'd be back for him,' Dot said.

'Get in the car,' she shouted at Joe.

'I will not,' he said. It was just like earlier.

'For the love o' God, will you just once do what you're told!'

'Where's Da?' Joe asked. He had a very surly expression on his face.

'He's at the house. If you get in now, we'll have time to go to Locheirnan for fish suppers.'

He still didn't move. Rita got out her side, and slammed the door. She came right up to Joe. He moved back, but just about half a step. 'Are you coming – or are you not?' She seemed more exasperated than ever.

Joe got in the car, and then he slammed *his* door. It was a lovely car. Dad said you should never abuse property; not your own, and especially not someone else's.

'Well?' Dot said. She was staring at Rita, as though she expected to be told something. I knew it was to do with Rita wondering whether or not to marry Mr Conroy.

'I'm none the wiser, so don't be asking me,' Rita flung back. There was dust for miles when she drove off.

Hooligan was waiting at the back door. After he ate, he went to lie down in the shade of Dot's shed. The sun had made the wood warm, and there was a gorgeous smell off the creosote. I breathed it in all the way down to my stomach.

Hooligan let me sit beside him, and after a while I laid my head against his back. His tongue had been hanging out the side of his mouth, but he held his breath for a moment when he felt me lean on him. I put my arm round him, but he wasn't too sure about that, so I took it off again and just stroked his neck. He stretched his legs out, and quivered. I could hear his heart beating. I really loved him.

I told him about Mam and Dad, and about Johnny Starling, and how much I wanted a grandad. I'm sure he understood.

Dot said I fell asleep right there, and she'd carried me inside and put me to bed. She said I never even opened my eyes, but I had once. We both knew it.

CHAPTER 8

Dot must have lit the fire, because the water was roasting the next morning. I had a good wash in the sink, and we had Mrs Bryce's steak pie and tatties for breakfast.

The whole morning had a more cheerful feel to it. Billie Holiday was singing 'Them There Eyes', which was a very catchy tune and not sad like the others. I told Dot I liked it, and she left the arm off the record player so it kept playing for me. The sun was burning off the haze, and Dot had all her windows open, and both doors. I was sure Mam would be feeling better by now. The sun just naturally made people happier. I asked Dot if she agreed.

'Without a doubt, Ellie. Although I've known people who could be just as happy when it rains.'

'Mam doesn't like the rain. She says it's depressing.'

'I've never found it to be so,' Dot said. There was a blue gingham curtain round the sink. Dot lifted it aside, and pulled out her whisky bottle, which was next to the Parozone. She poured some whisky into her coffee. I had never seen that done before, but I didn't remark on it. I was already getting coffee; I didn't think I was ready to try whisky.

'D'you think my mam will be up by now? Y'see, Dad'll be back to work today, and there'll be nobody there for her.'

'Och, I'm sure she'll manage fine. If your dad's got any sense, he'll take a couple of days off ... spend some time with her.'

'Oh no,' I said, 'he couldn't possibly. He's got a very important job, and he doesn't get his holidays till August.'

'No job's that important, but God forbid he'd have to change his routine. I never knew a bairn that would get more upset at being out of his routine than him.'

I couldn't imagine Dad as a little boy. He was just so ... grown-up.

'Was he a very good bairn?' I asked. I was sure she would say he was, and I felt guilty even asking.

'He was good, aye. But awful wrapped up in himself. I used to think it was a form o' protection.' Dot blew some smoke at the ceiling. 'It became an arrogance with him. He's no' the better for it.'

'What was he protecting?'

She smiled. 'Himself, and I canna blame him. He didna have an ordinary childhood. I tried to be father and mother both, but there's no' a living soul that can manage to do that.'

I wanted to ask about this, maybe get some clues about what happened to Mr Starling. I was chewing on my pinkie nail and wondering how I could get round to it without mentioning the letter, when the nail came off. It got stuck in my throat, almost in my ear, and I couldn't work it back out.

'What's wrong wi' you?' Dot asked. She was peering at me and frowning.

The nail came out of my ear, and I swallowed it. 'It's all right now,' I answered.

'I don't suppose your father talks about me much?'

I didn't know what to say.

'Well, there's my answer,' Dot said. She said it softly. 'You'll no' have heard the story then?'

Suddenly, I didn't know if I wanted to hear it. My heart was going fast again. 'You don't have to tell me anything you don't want to,' I said.

'Bloody right!' She looked angry for a minute. I hoped I hadn't spoiled the day already.

'Och, don't look so worried, Ellie. There's no' much to tell. I got in trouble with a man when I was young. He wasn't free to marry me, and he wouldn't have married me even if he had been. I knew that when I laid with him.'

There was a bit of sweat on my forehead. I shuffled back a bit on the chair so the sun wouldn't make me any hotter. Dot got up and walked to the living-room window. 'Stay away from lilac trees, Ellie. They've a powerful scent to them.'

I would never go near a lilac tree again. Apart from the fact that I was afraid of bees, I now knew that lilac trees had something to do with Mr Starling and S-E-X.

Dot came back to the table. 'Well, the long and the short of it is, I couldn't stay around here. I'd been brought up in this house with my Auntie Mary, and she wouldn't have me round her wi' a big belly and no man to support me. No' that I'd beg a man for support, you understand?'

Indeed I did. She hadn't even posted the letter.

'So off I went to Glasgow. I had rooms with my cousins there, and I went to work after your da was born. He had as good a time of it as I could give him, but I couldn't give him much. He used to tell folks his father was dead, so they wouldn't call him a bastard, but I refused to call myself "Mrs" when I wasn't. I think he hated me for that.'

I couldn't imagine Dad hating his own mother. I couldn't imagine him hating anyone.

Dot carried on as though it wasn't important. 'He did well at the school, though . . . won a couple of bursaries. They used to torment him more for being "lang-heided" – that means scholarly, y'know – than they did for being born on the wrong side o' the blanket.' Dot laughed. I still hadn't got used to her sense of humour. I thought it was an awful story. Poor Dad.

'He went into the Civil Service after the war, and then he met your mother. He's still ashamed of me though . . . to this day.'

Poor Dot. 'He's not ashamed of you!'

'Aye, hen, he is, but that's his loss. He's got no idea of the magic that's around him. Never will have.'

I didn't know who to feel sorry for any more.

'When did you come back here?' I asked. It seemed a safe question. I was hoping she'd mention Newcastle.

'Just after your mam and dad got engaged. Auntie Mary was fair done, and needed someone to look after her. She was a miserable old bitch right to the end. I can't tell you how happy I was when she drew her last.'

I wasn't a Catholic, but I'd seen them crossing themselves and I did it mentally. This was exactly the kind of thing that gave people the creeps with Dot.

'So, here I am,' Dot said, sighing. 'The house is mine now. She didn't have anyone else to leave it to, and I can suit myself when I come and go.'

'D'you not miss having a husband?'

'*Miss* it? Indeed I don't. I can do whatever the hell I feel like, and no bugger to tell me different. It's a great life, Ellie. A great life.'

Although they seemed very different, I could see how Dad was like Dot in a way – not letting anyone interrupt him, and always so sure that what he said was right – which of course it was, most of the time. It's just he had a more boring way of saying things, like a teacher or something. Mam had said to me once that she hated being lectured. I wasn't sure if I was supposed to agree with her, but I knew what she meant.

'Did Dad ever get to know his father at all?' I don't know how the words got out, because I was holding my breath when I asked.

Dot frowned. 'He did not,' she answered, 'and that's not something I have to explain to you.'

' 'Course not. It's none of my business.'

She roared, and nearly gave me a heart attack. 'Hah! You're no' as green as you're cabbage,' she laughed, which made no sense at all.

'Matter of fact, Ellie, it was all for the best whether he thinks it or no'. It's just a pity we don't see eye to eye. He's a good enough sort – in his own way.'

'Why don't you see eye to eye? I miss having a granny.' It was the first time I'd said it, and I embarrassed myself. I looked down, away from her.

'We did once, after a fashion.' Her voice was as quiet as I'd ever heard it. She lit another cigarette and puffed on it for a while.

'They used to come to see me, your mam and dad. I like Sylvia, always did. She had a rough time of it after her mother left; I think that's what drew Adam to her. He was working in Kilmoran after the war, in the government buildings there, and she was in the Clarks' shoe shop on the High Street.'

I knew it. Mam was still taking me there for my shoes. I hated wearing those big clodhoppers when Janet and *everyone* already had flatties and some even with Baby Lou heels. Mam never said she worked there though.

'Anyway,' Dot continued, 'he always felt a bit cheated himself, on account of his upbringing, and before I knew it they were married, quietly – the way they wanted it. In those days they came down often to see me. They were so happy with one another, it did your heart good to see them.

'Then your Dad got promoted and you came along, and all of a sudden there was no room for me. Well, no lost sleep there. Still, I thought they were all right until . . . that last time.'

'When I was here?'

'Aye, hen. D'you remember it at all?'

I shook my head. 'Not really.'

'Just as well,' Dot said, stubbing out her cigarette and lighting another. I don't know how she managed to talk and smoke so fast at the same time.

'Thing is, your dad left the three of us here, and decided to go into Locheirnan – he wanted to look round the new gents' outfitters there for a new suit; he likes to look smart – and I could tell there was something going on between the two of them. Your mam wasn't the lassie I'd remembered. She seemed . . . different.

'Well, I committed the cardinal sin – I got her drunk.' Dot laughed, but it was a quiet, sad laugh, like grown-ups sometimes did instead of talking. She kept on, though, and I was listening really hard by now.

'Seems your mam wanted one of two things – to go back to work, or have another baby; she wasn't sure. You were in school, and her days were long. I told her to make up her mind which she wanted, and just to do it. Your dad didn't want either one, apparently. "One child is quite sufficient," he'd told her, and he definitely didn't want her back in a shoe shop. He's a bloody snob, of course. Always was.

'By the time he got back from Locheirnan, I'd filled us both full of Dutch courage, and there was an awful commotion. So he bundled you both up and took you home. It's the last I've seen of any of you – until now.'

I looked at Dot. Her eyes were squinty and damp. I wasn't sure if it was from the cigarettes or not.

Mam hadn't gone back to work, and I was still an only child.

She got up. 'Are you ready?'

'What for?'

'We'll go in and take a look at Lil's guest. He's arriving today.'

There was nothing else to do. We got the bikes out of the shed and started off.

Dreep was sitting in the close just before the paper-shop. You could see his tackety boots sticking out. They had no laces. He was wearing the same clothes, but his hood was off. His hair was very thick, and whiter than his beard and moustache. It stood out all over his head like Oor Wullie's. There was no sign of Hooligan.

'Another fine day, Dreep,' Dot said, coming off her bike.

'We are blessed indeed,' he answered. There was a lemonade bottle beside him on the pavement. It was inside a brown bag.

'D' you have a droppie in your bottle the day?' Dot asked.

'I do,' he answered, 'and I extend my gratitude to you for your concern. It's a wondrous thing in these soul-wearying times for another human . . .'

'Aye, aye . . .' Dot said, and walked on into the Jacobite. I followed, leaving Dreep still murmuring to himself.

Hugh was walking up and down in the lobby. He didn't try to speak to us. Back and fore he went, over to the window, back to the sofa, over to the window. Mr Bryce looked up from polishing the bar.

We said hello and walked across. I kept watching Hugh. He was looking down as he walked, and taking short quick steps. His fists were curled, but both his index fingers pointed straight down as though he was marking his passage across the floor.

'Is he here yet, Eck?'

Mr Bryce knew immediately who Dot was enquiring about.

'Herself's fit to be tied, Dot.' He leaned a bit closer. 'He's a darkie.'

'A darkie?'

'Aye. Thon must be a made-up name, Gerald Smith. You'd never guess from that.'

'I'm sure it's his real name, Eck. He's English, isn't he?'

'Are you no' hearing me? He's a bloody darkie . . . here in Inchbrae!'

Outside, a passing car tooted its horn. 'That'll be the BBC then,' Dot announced.

'Oh, you're the smart one, right enough,' Mr Bryce said. He glared at Dot. Then Mrs Bryce appeared at the hatch. 'Is that yourself, Dot?'

She appeared with an armful of towels. Mr Bryce held the bartop open for her. She still had to squeeze through. Hugh looked up, but he didn't break his stride.

'Did Eck tell you?' She looked very upset. Dot nodded. 'Oh Dot . . . my good sheets!' She sounded like she might cry.

Dot shook her head. 'His colour's no' going to come off on your sheets, Lil. For God's sake . . . !' She was cross again.

'You huvna seen him, Dot. He's well-spoken, I'll give him that. He doesna have thon awful Geordie accent . . . but my God he's black.'

Geordie accent. Of course! Mr Bryce had said the darkie came from Newcastle. I couldn't believe my luck. I'd thought I would never be able to find my grandad, and here was the answer to my prayers, staring me in the face. Why would a darkie *ever* come to Inchbrae – just when I was here myself – if it wasn't a sign from God? I'd been meant to read the letter, after all. I'd been meant to find my grandad. The darkie must know Mr Starling, surely. Newcastle couldn't be that big of a place. Even if he didn't know him, he would know how to find him. I was positive. I knew I was smiling with the excitement of it all.

'He's black as the Earl o' Hell's waistcoat, so he is,' Mr Bryce added, frowning at me. He couldn't understand what I was smiling at.

'Will y'listen to the pair o' yis?' Dot said. 'The man's just a man, black or no' – and a paying guest at that.'

'That's no' the point,' Mrs Bryce said, flinging herself down on the sofa. 'He never *said* he was black!'

'Come on,' Dot said, pulling my arm. 'Let's get out of here.'

'Don't go getting on your high horse, Dot,' Mr Bryce warned. 'It's no' your bed he's sleeping in . . .'

We were almost at the door. '. . . and he put Hugh all wrong as well,' Mrs Bryce added.

Dot turned. 'God pity the pair o' yis in yir ignorance.'

'Aye, go on then.' Mr Bryce was nearly shouting now. 'Jews next door, darkies up the stairs . . . We'll be having the bloody English next.'

'He *is* bloody English!' Dot shouted back, and hurled me through the door. I nearly fell, but she pulled me up by the arm before my face hit the ground.

'Did y'ever hear the like?' Dot asked. We were in Rita's. We were the only ones in the shop, but there was a lady looking in the window.

Rita pushed Dot aside. She walked to the door and smiled at the woman. 'That's a lovely wee costume you're looking at. Perfect with your colouring, too.'

The woman smiled back. She put her head to one side, and looked again at the outfit. 'Mm-mm. It *is* rather smart.'

'Isn't it though?' Rita agreed. 'Not every woman could wear that particular blue, *and* there's two guineas off it at the moment – only till Friday, I'm afraid.'

Dot looked at me. 'It's navy blue,' she said. 'Tell me the woman who can't wear navy blue.' She seemed to be getting into a worse temper by the minute.

'Well, I'd like Neville to take a look at it. He's got such good colour sense. Maybe I'll come back on Thursday.' The woman smiled again at Rita, and walked on down the street.

Rita flounced back into the shop. It seemed like everyone was in a bad mood. 'See what *Nev*-ille thinks,' she said, very sarcastically. 'Damn cissified boy that she has. It wouldn't surprise me if *Nev*-ille started wearing dresses himself one o' these days.'

'I can't believe my ears,' Dot said. 'The boy's an artist. Of course he has good colour sense . . . good enough to see it's navy blue.'

Rita wheeled on Dot. 'It's FRENCH navy, and what would you know?' She gave Dot the once-over, and looked away in disgust.

'I know you've been in a hellish mood for weeks now. That's what I know.'

Rita sighed. She walked back to the door, and

leaned against it. She was looking across at the butcher's and shaking her head slowly from side to side. Her arms were folded across her chest and she pulled her shoulders up as though she was cold.

'Are you home the night?' she asked.

'Where am I usually?'

'You wouldn't mind me coming over?'

'Do I ever?'

Rita turned. 'Dot . . .' Her voice was pleading. She looked very beautiful with the sun shining on her hair. I was sure Mr Conroy was hopelessly in love with her.

'I'll bring Lil if she can get away,' Rita said.

'Huh,' Dot answered. 'She'll probably be too busy boiling her sheets!'

Rita grinned. 'Imagine though, a darkie. I bet her face was a picture when she saw him.'

They both laughed. I was glad they were laughing.

The lady who'd been looking in the window came back. 'Mrs Gilchrist?'

'Yes,' Rita answered, leaving us standing there. 'Have you changed your mind?'

'Well, perhaps I could try it . . . while I'm in town.'

'Certainly, Mrs Robertson. As a matter of fact, why don't you take it home on appro? I'm sure Neville's going to agree that's it's just perfect when he sees it on you, and there's the smartest wee hat to go with it. It has your name all over it.'

The lady was beaming as Rita walked over to the dummy.

'See you later,' Dot said, and we stepped back into the street. As we passed the window, Rita was removing the jacket from the dummy, and swaying from side to side. 'See you later, alligator . . .' She was mouthing the words at me.

I mouthed back, 'In a while, crocodile.'

She winked.

CHAPTER 9

I looked across the road just as Joseph came out of the grocer's. He was sucking an ice lolly.

'Can I buy one Dot?' I asked. 'I've got some money with me.'

'I'll buy us both one, hen. It's years since I had an ice lolly.' We crossed the street.

'Where y'going?' Joseph asked.

'Nowhere. We're getting ice lollies.'

He came back into the grocer's with us. The shop was bigger than it looked from the outside. There were some sacks of flour by the door, and a smell of coffee like you got in Lipton's. Beside the flour, a wrought-iron stand was laden with ironmongery things, and some pans of different sizes hung from hooks above that.

The tinned goods were stacked behind the counter, and there was a row of glass jars with sweeties in them. All the other sweeties were in boxes under the glass. A second counter stood next to the big one, with a row of open biscuit tins attached to the front, and wooden trays with bread and rolls on top of it. A man was standing behind the smaller counter, scooping sugar into blue paper bags and weighing them.

'Good day,' he said. He had thin grey hair, and a small moustache. He had a sad look to his face, but then he smiled and I thought maybe I just imagined that, knowing he was a Jew who had lost all his worldly possessions.

Dot nodded and walked to the back. She opened the big lid on the freezer. 'What kind, Ellie?'

'Chocolate, please.'

'I'll have banana,' she said, and took them both over to the man. 'How's business, Mr Fishbein?'

He pushed down the big buttons on the till and it flew open. 'No' bad, Miss Fairbairn. Ist not for complaining.'

You could tell right away he was foreign, but Scottish-sounding at the same time. His wife came through from the back shop, wiping her hands on her overall.

Dot nodded at her. 'You're well?' she asked.

'Goot, goot,' Mrs Fishbein answered. I took the wrapper off my lolly, and Mrs Fishbein held out her hand and took it from me. Very gently she touched my face.

'A child to be proud of,' she said. Her eyes were really sad, and I wasn't imagining it.

Joseph had finished his lolly. I looked at Dot. 'You'll no' be allowed another one before your dinner,' she told him.

He didn't answer. He just stood there.

'Well, I'll no' tell if you don't,' Dot said, going

back for another chocolate lolly. We went outside and left Dot talking to Mr and Mrs Fishbein.

'Are you doing anything?' he asked me.

'I don't think so. We just came in to see . . . Well, I don't know if we're doing anything or not.'

'R.S.'

'Randolph Scott.' I didn't even have to think about it.

'A.G.,' I challenged back.

'Is it a man or a woman?'

'That's not fair.'

'I bet it's a woman. Ann . . .'

'It's not Ann anything.'

'Ava Gardner.'

'Right. Your turn,' I said.

'Did y'hear about the darkie?'

'Aye. Dot's mad with Mr and Mrs Bryce. She says they're ignorant. Have you seen him?' I asked.

'Nuht. He's got a car. He went off somewhere to take photos.'

'D'you know when he's coming back?' I asked. I had to meet Mr Smith, had to find a way to talk to him.

Joe shook his head. 'Hope I'm here though. I want to see a real darkie. Wait till Malc hears what he missed.'

'And what is it Malc's missing?' Dot asked, appearing behind us.

'Seeing a real darkie,' Joe answered. I looked at Dot. She was shaking her head again. 'He's no' something to be stared at,' she said.

'I thought that's what we came for.' I don't know why I said it. I just felt that Joseph didn't need another telling-off, and Dot *had* said we were coming 'for a look'.

'Well, that's not what I meant at all,' Dot said. She sounded a bit surprised. 'It's just that we don't get many people here on business, and I . . .' She smiled at me, then she laughed. 'I'm glad to hear you speaking up at last,' she said, ruffling my hair, which was quite sore the way she did it. I didn't mind.

Mrs Bryce came out of the Jacobite, holding Hugh's hand. He was still looking down, and as they came closer I could see he was trembling slightly. Mrs Bryce sort of tossed her head as though she was going to ignore us, but Dot stood right in front of her, blocking her way.

'C'mon, Lil,' she said. 'There's no point in us falling out over a stranger.'

'It's no' me that lost the head,' Mrs Bryce answered. 'Did I ask you to start shouting and bawling? I did not.'

'Maybe not, but you canna be that prejudiced, Lil. God, d'you no' remember thon time Dodo's pal came up to see you? You made him as welcome as anything, and there was no word about him being black.'

'That was different, Dot. He was in the war with Dodo. He was a Yank. And besides, it was just a visit. He didn't *stay* with us.'

'But didn't Dodo write a poem about prejudice?

And weren't you the proud one when it got published?'

'Aye.' Lil smiled. 'My brother the poet.' She drew a deep sigh. 'Well, he *is* very polite.' She let go of Hugh's hand, but he grabbed it back again. 'I'm just away in next door for a loaf. Will you wait and have a bittie dinner with us?' Mrs Bryce asked.

Dot glanced at me. I knew from her expression I wasn't to mention having the steak pie for breakfast. 'Aye,' she said. 'We'll wait.'

Joe sat down on the kerb, and I sat beside him. Dreep had disappeared. Mrs Bryce and Dot and Hugh came back with the loaf and went back inside the bar, but before we had a chance to start talking again, Dot reappeared with Hugh. 'He wants to stay out here with youse.' She helped him down to the kerb. His legs sprawled a bit, but he pulled them close to his chest, and sat rocking.

'Don't let him go on the road,' Dot warned, and left us.

'Did the darkie give you a fright, Hugh?' Joe asked. I felt like kicking him. Hugh didn't say anything. I could hear a sound coming from him, like the hum of a plane, but his mouth wasn't moving.

'Be quiet,' I hissed at Joe.

'Will not,' he said. I think he just naturally said 'no' and 'will not'. I remembered one day when Dad had remarked that Mam was in a contrary mood. I thought that contrary was a good word to describe Joseph.

I looked at Hugh. He had very small ears for

such a big head. He turned towards me, but his head was so low on his chest that he had to squint up at me. I smiled at him, and he smiled back. It was a funny kind of smile. I didn't like thinking it, but it was almost sneaky. I got the feeling that maybe he knew more than he let on.

'Are you going in for your dinner?' I asked Joe.

'In a minute. Da closes at one.'

'Does he cook for you?' I thought it would be strange for a man not to have a wife. I couldn't imagine how the dusting and the washing and everything else would get done.

'None o' yir business,' Joseph said. He was bent on being unpleasant, even after getting the ice lolly.

'D.D.'

'Doris Day,' he sneered.

'Wrong.' D.D. was a good one, because there were quite a few film stars with those initials, and you could always say it was someone else.

'Dan Dailey.'

'Wrong again, and you're no' getting another guess.'

'Who cares?' He rose, and headed for his father's shop. I felt a bit panicky, being left alone with Hugh, but I wouldn't show it. Joe turned when he got to the door.

'Bet it *was* Dan Dailey!'

'As a matter of fact, it was Dan Duryea,' I answered. It was true. Hardly anyone ever guessed him.

'I was half right,' Joe called back. He put his

thumb to his nose, and stuck out his tongue, waggling his fingers at me. I did it back. So did Hugh. Joseph laughed and pointed. 'Look, he's doing it!'

I laughed too. Hugh kept doing it. 'See you after dinner,' Joseph said.

'Right-oh.'

'Errr-ohh.'

There was a horrible smell of cabbage in Mrs Bryce's kitchen, but you could tell that it usually smelled nice in there. We had boiled ham and tatties with the cabbage, and half a tomato each. There was butter in the cabbage, and it tasted better than it smelled. The bread had a lovely black crust. Mam once said it was a relief to her that I liked crusts, as most children refused them. I always liked her to see me enjoying them after that.

Mr Bryce ate his dinner at the bar. The man called Arthur had come in with a friend, and they were playing dominoes again. You could hear the occasional swearword even back there in the kitchen, and Dot said a well-mannered darkie was much to be preferred. Lil said Dot had been put on this earth to try her, but they didn't fall out again.

I tried not to watch Hugh eating, because he wouldn't keep his mouth closed and it looked a bit disgusting. Mrs Bryce cut up all his food for him, but he fed himself. He had a lot of tomato sauce on his plate, and he pushed all his food round and round in it. He made an awful mess, but he ate the lot, and Mrs Bryce wiped his mouth and gave him a kiss when he was finished.

I thought it would make Mrs Bryce happy if I invited Hugh to play with me and Joseph. I felt it was the least I could do, but Mrs Bryce shook her head.

'He has a wee nap after his dinner, hen. He gets fair tired in the afternoons,' she explained. I was relieved.

Hugh was nodding wildly, and trying to say 'yes'. I was beginning to get the gist of some of his words, but it nearly gave you a sore head concentrating on them. He didn't look a bit tired to me, but Mrs Bryce made him wave cheerio and took him upstairs. Dot said I could call for Joseph and we'd take a walk down to the river, and come back for our bikes later.

The man called Arthur asked me if I was enjoying my holidays as I went past, and I said that I was. He said I was a good sight bonnier than my granny, but there was a lot of Fairbairn in me. It didn't sound like a compliment, and I wasn't sure whether to thank him or not. His companion said it would suit him better to leave me alone, and pay more notice to his hand. Arthur said he was 'chapping', whatever that meant, and I left them to it.

Mr Conroy was slicing some meat when I walked in.

'It's yourself,' he said, smiling at me. 'Didn't you just put the sunshine back in my day?' If I

115

was Rita, I would've married him straight off. I heard a toilet flushing somewhere, and then Joe appeared.

'D'you want to come for a walk with us?' I asked him.

'Who's "us"?'

'Me and Dot. We're going to the river.'

Mr Conroy stopped the slicing machine. 'Is it Dot now?'

'I . . . I . . . I haven't got used to "Granny",' I said, knowing it must have sounded disrespectful.

'Well, she's still Miss Fairbairn to you, Joseph. See and remember that.'

Joe slid his eyes downwards. 'And it's *Mrs* Gilchrist to you,' he murmured.

Mr Conroy fixed him with a look. 'What's that you're saying?'

Joe shook his head. 'Nothing.'

'That's right,' Mr Conroy said. 'Off you go then.'

Dot was leaning against the wall when we came outside. She was smoking a cigarette, and looking down the street. Dreep was approaching. He held his arms out wide from his sides, and walked very straight. He wasn't carrying anything, but his paper bag with the lemonade bottle was weighing down one of his pockets. He'd acquired a black eyepatch. Hooligan was behind him.

'What happened t'yir eye, Dreep?' Dot asked.

He stopped level with her, and bowed. 'I have decided to view the world from a different perspective, Miss Fairbairn . . . to narrow my vision; for the

116

whole of life is too much to behold. I hope to learn something from it.'

'God's sake,' Dot said. 'You canna see where you're going now!'

'Your estimation of my ambulatory progress may be correct. Nonetheless, I trust you will indulge me in this temporary affectation.' With that, he turned around and began marching back in the direction from which he'd come.

'Aaah, Christ, he's getting worse,' Dot said. Her voice was sad. She ground out her cigarette on the pavement, and ushered us in front of her. Hooligan stood for a moment, not knowing who to follow, but I beckoned for him to come with us and, with a last look after Dreep, he did so.

'Is Dreep his real name?' I asked Joe. He was kicking a rusty tin towards Hooligan, but Hooligan wasn't interested. Joe picked it up, and threw it down the close beside the bus stop as we passed. He seemed to enjoy throwing things. It was like spitting. It was something boys, and men, enjoyed. It seemed to me that they were always trying to get rid of something, though I hadn't worked out what.

'Nah,' he answered. 'No-one knows his real name. Did you look at his nose?'

I hadn't.

'He's always got a dreep at the end of it, summer and winter. Even when he wipes it on his sleeve, it comes right back. Sometimes he licks it.'

'Gyudders!'

Joe grinned at me. He really looked nice when he smiled. 'I know,' he agreed.

We went through the fields again. The bull was gone. There were some sheep on the other side of the road which hadn't been there the day before. I wondered who moved the animals about, and why. Joseph didn't know, but he pretended he did and said the country was a mystery to 'townies'.

Hooligan wandered off as usual, but he didn't make for the sheep. Dot said it was worth keeping an eye on him, just the same. There was a car parked off the road, close to where we were heading. Joe said it was probably some 'townies' out for the day, and they'd ruin it for us, but Dot disagreed. She said it was an English number plate; probably some holiday-makers enjoying the view, and we were to be nice to them and not give them a bad impression.

When we got to the river, we saw a man lying on his belly on the shingle. There was a tripod beside him, with a camera on it, and he had another camera in his hands. He didn't even notice us.

'You'll no get a bonnier photo, son,' Dot said. He jumped, dusting himself off as he rose. I had never seen a darkie before. Joseph and I stared. We couldn't help it.

'Dot Fairbairn,' Dot said, walking forwards to shake his hand. 'You'll be Mr Smith.'

He smiled, and shook her hand warmly. He had the most beautiful teeth I'd ever seen. 'You've heard of me then?' he asked.

'Lil 'n' Eckie are friends,' Dot answered. 'And we don't get that many visitors.'

'Not like me,' the man answered, still smiling. 'I'm afraid I gave them something of a surprise.'

Dot roared. 'That you did!' She wiped her eyes and pulled out another cigarette. 'D'you smoke, son?'

He nodded, and thanked her. 'Call me Gerry,' he said. 'It's a pleasure to meet you—' He raised his eyebrows, and Dot nodded. 'It's a pleasure to meet you, Dot.'

He looked across at Joe and me. Joseph had moved closer to me without realising it. I think he was a bit scared. I was too.

'Your children?' he asked, looking back at Dot.

She roared again, and started coughing on her cigarette. I wished she would either stop smoking or stop laughing; she was a bit of a worry.

'You havena much of an eye, if it's a photographer y'are,' she answered. 'Where would an old wifie like me have bairns that age?'

He drew on his cigarette. 'Youth is like beauty, Dot. It's in the eye of the beholder.'

'Away wi' you,' Dot said, but I could tell she was pleased. 'Are you getting some good photos?'

He nodded. 'It's another world. I've done my share of travelling, but this . . .' He shook his head, gazing off at the hills again. 'What are they called?'

Dot shrugged. 'I just call them "The Old Ones",' she answered. 'They've all got Gaelic names, which I couldna rightly pronounce.'

'You don't speak Gaelic?' Mr Smith asked. Hooligan had come back. He was watching the stranger, no more at ease than us.

'*Slàinte*! That's all the Gaelic I need to know,' Dot laughed.

'Which means?'

'Good health!' Dot took a hipflask from her trouser pocket, and held it out. I hadn't seen it before. It was silver, and very pretty.

Mr Smith nodded again, and took the flask. 'You don't mind?'

'I'm Billie Holiday's biggest fan,' Dot answered.

Mr Smith lowered the flask. 'I prefer Connie Francis,' he said. There was a stillness to him, and things went very quiet. All you could hear was the slap-slap of the waves, and the wind soughing in the trees.

'I'm sorry, son,' Dot said at last. Her voice was quiet now too. I wasn't sure what was going on, but I knew she'd offended Mr Smith in some way. I thought it would help Dot if I took Mr Smith's mind off it.

'How d'you do?' I said. I held out my hand. 'I'm Ellie.' I felt very brave.

'My grand-daughter,' Dot said. There was pride in her voice. I knew I was beaming. I was warm with the feel of it.

'Joseph Conroy,' Joe said, pushing in front of me. Hooligan growled a bit at all the sudden movement.

'It's a pleasure to meet you both,' Mr Smith said.

'Ellie ... Joe ...' He shook our hands, and his palms were pink like ours. It looked really strange. Then he raised the hipflask to his mouth. He had very big lips. They were purple.

'Slange-a, Dot.' It didn't sound quite right, but it was close.

I wanted to wait and talk with Mr Smith, but I could see Dot was settling in for quite a blether, and Joe had already lost interest now that he'd finally seen the darkie. We set off along the bay, with Hooligan between us.

I looked back once or twice. Dot and Mr Smith were sitting on the shore, smoking and talking and drinking together. They looked like they'd known each other for ever. I wondered if Dot might beat me to it, and mention Mr Starling. I didn't think so. She'd said she didn't miss having a husband. She seemed quite definite about that.

I caught up with Joseph. I was still feeling brave, which was a new experience for me.

'What happened to your mother?' I asked.

CHAPTER 10

Joseph turned and glared at me. He stamped off, climbing up into the dunes, pulling up tufts of grass as he went. I kept after him. I wanted to know.

'Where's your mother?' I asked again.

He stopped. Lifting his leg, he looked down at his sandal.

'Cack,' he said, and started rubbing it on a grassy clump. I waited while he cleaned it off. He sat down with his back to me. Hooligan was sniffing about the grass where Joseph had stood. Joe picked up a twig and threw it.

Hooligan peed on the grass, watching where the twig landed. When he was ready, he walked over and chewed it to smithereens. Then he came back.

'Stupid bloody dog,' Joe said.

'He is not!' I retorted. 'I bet I could get him to bring it back!'

'Bet you couldn't.'

I hunted around and found a good thick twig. I tried to pull off some sharp bits which I thought might hurt Hooligan's mouth if he caught it the wrong way, but they just twisted in my hand and wouldn't come free.

'Give it here,' Joe said.

'Give it back to me then.'

He pulled on it once or twice, but he couldn't make it any smoother. 'Fetch!' he shouted, and threw it. Hooligan laid down in front of Joe, with his head between his paws.

'See! Told you he was stupid.'

'You were supposed to give it back,' I said. I thought it might take a few tries for Hooligan to get the idea. I sat down beside Joe, and threw a bit of driftwood. I didn't want to make a big issue of it, so I just said, quite quietly, 'Fetch, Hooligan.' He watched it going past his nose, and looked back at me. Then he stretched out and went to sleep.

'He's just not in the mood,' I said. 'He's not stupid though.'

'He is stupid.'

I sighed. 'Why are you always arguing with people?'

'I am not.'

'See. You're doing it now.'

Joe went quiet. 'She ran off,' he said at last.

I'd heard of people running off and leaving their children, but it was usually men who did such things. I didn't know of any mothers who had run off.

'It's cruel to leave children,' I said.

'She's *not* cruel! She's NOT!'

I bit my lip. It *was* cruel, but I'd upset Joe by saying it. 'I'm sorry,' I said.

He took off his sandals and pushed his feet into the sand, folding his arms across his knees. He leaned his head on them and stuck out his chin, as though he was clenching his teeth very hard.

'Her name's Faith. Da says that's a laugh.'

'What else does your da say?' I wondered if Rita's name had come up at all. I was sure that it had, her being so close to marrying Mr Conroy. I didn't think Joe was going to answer; it was a long time before he said anything.

'He used to say she'd run off wi' the milkman, and he'd make a joke of it. Once, he was getting drunk in the house, and I asked him, for real like, what happened. He said it wasna the milkman, it was his mate – his "compadre", he said, like in the cowboy pictures. Then he started greeting. I said she'd be coming back, and for him no' to be crying over it.'

Joe got up, and walked on a bit. He picked up the twig I'd found and started twisting it again. I followed him. We went through a fence and into a field that was just grass and clover. Hooligan had squeezed through behind us. Joseph threw the twig away without even looking where it went, but Hooligan caught it and came back with it in his mouth.

'I *told* you!' I was delighted. 'He just wasn't in the mood earlier. He's even smarter than I thought!'

Joseph didn't answer me. I knew he was still thinking about his mother.

'Did your da stop crying?' I asked. I had the feeling that he wanted to finish his story, now that he'd started.

'Aye, he did. He belted me one and told me to get to my bed, out of his sight. That's how I know it's my fault she left. It must've been something to do with me.'

'Oh no, Joseph. You would remember surely – if it was.' He was a bit difficult, but I couldn't imagine him doing something bad enough to make his mother run off. Even Walter Cumming's mother hadn't run off, and he was much, much worse than Joseph.

He shrugged. 'I dunno,' he said. He sounded very forlorn. He threw the stick again, and again Hooligan caught it and brought it back. Again and again Joe threw it, harder and harder. Then he hurled himself down on the grass, with his face in the clover. 'One day she'll stop wi' her running and come back to us. I *know* she will!'

I watched Hooligan. His heart was bursting in his chest. He laid down with his head across Joseph's back, and looked up at me. He was panting, but his eyes were sad. He knew Joseph's mother wasn't coming back. We all did.

We were nearly back at the shore before we remembered about Joe's sandals. They were half-covered with sand, and we were lucky they were still there.

I'd lost my gym shoes once. I hadn't strapped my saddle-bag properly, and they'd fallen out. I never did find them, and I didn't get any pocket money for two weeks, but Mam took me to see *The King and I* to make up for it. We didn't tell Dad.

Dot was on her own when we got back to where she was sitting, and my heart sank. She said Mr Smith had gone down the road a bit to get photos of the old cairns, but she'd invited him to stop by her house on the way back if he had time. I cheered up.

Hooligan headed off towards Dot's house. He had obviously decided that it was a waste of time coming back to Inchbrae, just to have to turn around again. He was really very clever.

Dot took us back to town, and I said cheerio to Joe. He'd gone quiet on me, and I still wasn't sure if he knew about Rita or not.

Dot told Mrs Bryce that we'd met Mr Smith, and what a nice man he was. Mrs Bryce said she was browned off with the whole thing, and she wasn't going to say any more about it. Dot said it was good she was browned off; it might give her an idea how Mr Smith felt. Mrs Bryce lifted her brush to Dot, and we left. Dot laughed on and off all the way back.

I mentioned to Dot that I'd found Mr Smith to be very nice too – even though I'd been a bit afraid of him at first.

'Ellie, when you came here, you were as much a stranger to me as Mr Smith, d'you know that?' Dot asked

'But I'm your grand-daughter, and I'm not . . . black.' I nearly said 'a darkie', but I knew it would have been the wrong thing to say.

'A stranger just the same,' she said, 'and if we canna take a stranger to our hearts, we're a poor class of people indeed.' She seemed quite firm about this.

'Have you taken me to your heart, then?' I asked.

She smiled at me for a long time. 'I have that,' she answered. It made me happy.

Mrs Bryce had given Dot a flask of lentil soup and a wee parcel with a piece of beef in it. We had it for our supper, and Hooligan got a big hambone that Mr Conroy had saved for him. Dot said Mr Conroy was very good at saving scraps and bones for Hooligan, but he wouldn't feed the dog personally, as he didn't want Hooligan hanging about his door.

I'd seen Hooligan lift his leg on the wall of the butcher's shop, and could understand Mr Conroy's point of view. I made up my mind to try to discourage Hooligan from this behaviour. Dot laughed when I told her. She said dogs were like men – they didn't care where they peed.

Dot seemed very thoughtful after supper. She asked me if I'd listened to the words of 'Strange Fruit', which was one of the Billie Holiday songs that she played a lot. I said that I hadn't. Dot put it on, and I had to sit quietly and listen to it.

'Does it make any sense t'you, hen?'

'It sounds very sad.'

'Aye,' she said. 'It's always Lady Day's finale. It's about black people.'

I must have looked confused. 'Is Billie Holiday black then?'

'She is, aye, and proud of it. The strange fruit she's singing about is all the black people who were hanged from the trees in the South . . . in America.'

'What for?'

Dot shook her head. 'Just for being black, mostly. It all comes from the days of the slave trade, but a lot of them are slaves to this day. They're not allowed to mix with white folks; still living in the hope of being free.'

'I thought that's what the Civil War was for,' I said. 'To set them free.'

'Aye. Nearly a hundred years since, and they still canna call themselves free. Brother fought brother in that war, Ellie. It makes you wonder if we ever learn anything. God knows, if you were up in that Sputnik thing looking down, you couldna see the first one o' us. And yet we canna be at peace wi' one another for two minutes.'

'D'you think God can see every one of us?' I asked. It was a question which often bothered me, and I knew God was even farther away than the Sputnik. I'd never asked anyone before, but I felt that Dot would give me an honest answer.

She looked at me for a minute. 'If you believe that He does, then He does.'

I was disappointed. It wasn't really an answer. We were taught at Sunday School to have 'Faith

Above All'. That made me think of Joseph's mother.

'What time's Rita coming?' I was wishing she'd hurry up, so she'd leave before Mr Smith arrived. If not, it might be complicated trying to talk to him on my own.

Dot glanced at the clock. 'She'll be over in a wee whilie, hen. Would you mind playing outside when she gets here?'

I had never been asked if I *minded* leaving grown-up company before. I thought it was most polite of Dot to ask.

'No, course not.'

'You're a good bairn, Ellie, no bother at all,' Dot said. I was just feeling pleased with myself when she added, 'Those parents o' yours need a good kick in the arse.'

'They do not!' I exclaimed. It was nearly a shout. 'Mam's SICK!'

'Sick o' yir father, I wouldn't wonder.'

Her words frightened me. What if it was true? What if Mam got to feeling like Joseph's mother, and ran off and left us? She couldn't. Not Mam. I felt the tears in my eyes, and started towards the door. Maybe Hooligan was still about.

Dot called me back. 'Ellie, hen, it's just my foolish way of talking. I didn't mean to put you wrong.'

I stood there. The tears came out of my eyes and rolled down my cheeks. Dot reached over and lifted me on to her knee. Nobody had done that to me for a very long time. Even though I was crying, it felt nice. Her shirt was rough and hairy against me, and there was a bit of a sweaty smell off her, but it wasn't a bad smell, just warm.

'Wheesht, bairn,' she said, rubbing my back. 'Your mam'll be fine, and no doubt they're *both* missing you. How could they no?' She took a big man's hankie from her pocket, and wiped my nose and my eyes too.

'Could we phone?' I asked.

She nodded. 'If it'll make you feel better, we'll phone tomorrow.'

It did make me feel better. It seemed like I'd been away for such a long time.

Dot took me to the back door and whistled for Hooligan, but he was standing right there. We hadn't noticed him behind the purple flower. He looked at us as though we were daft, and we both laughed. I was feeling much better. Dot went back inside, and I took Hooligan for a walk down the lane. I was careful not to go all the way to the road, in case he decided to carry on and leave me.

I told him that I wanted to find my grandad before I left, but that Mam was probably wanting me home now, and maybe I wouldn't have the time. I thought he was nodding his head to show he understood, but when I bent down beside him, he was just chewing on something or other he'd found on the road. Still, he stayed beside me all the way to the road. It was the first time he hadn't wandered off by himself, and I knew then that he was beginning to love me back.

* * *

I heard a car just as were turning to go back up the lane, and waited to see if it might be Mr Smith. Sure enough, he slowed to a stop beside us, and Hooligan didn't even growl. Omens didn't have to be bad all the time like Mam said; sometimes there were good omens too.

Mr Smith rolled down his window. 'Ellie, how nice to see you again.' I wished my smile was as beautiful as Mr Smith's.

'Are you coming up to the house?'

'I'm sorry,' he answered. 'It was most gracious of your grandmother to invite me, but I'm rather hungry – it's been a long day – and I wouldn't want Mrs Bryce holding up dinner for me. Would you give Dot my regards and apologise for my absence?'

I sighed, and he seemed surprised at my disappointment.

'Ellie . . . ?'

'I was hoping to talk to you . . . in confidence.'

From the corner of my eye, I noticed Hooligan lifting his leg against Mr Smith's tyre, but I didn't scold him. He didn't know any better.

Mr Smith looked puzzled, but he was still smiling. 'What did you want to talk to me about?'

'Well, there's somebody in Newcastle I would like to find . . . well, I think he's in Newcastle, but he might not be any more . . . but I don't want anyone to know I'm looking for him . . . not till I find him . . . if you could help me find him, that is . . .'

131

Mr Smith lifted his eyebrows. They were like crow's wings. 'Newcastle's a very large city, Ellie. Who is it you're looking for?'

'Mr Starling, Mr Johnny Starling ... do you know him? He's my grandad ... I think.'

Mr Smith rubbed his nose. Then he took a cigarette from his shirt pocket, and lit it. He opened the door, and stepped out of the car. I looked up, but he put his hand on my shoulder and knelt in front of me. His face was even blacker close up, but he looked very kind. There were two long lines from his nose to his mouth which I hadn't seen before, and I thought they made him look a bit sad. I was always thinking people looked sad.

'Don't you know? If he's your grandad?' he asked.

I shook my head. 'You see, I just got to know Dot ... well, I always knew her but not like I know her now, and I found a letter ... she's a Miss ... she probably told you ... she tells everyone and it doesn't seem to matter ... but I found a letter she wrote ... before my dad was born ... and it was to Mr Johnny Starling ... and I think he's my grandad.' I was out of breath.

Hooligan was circling around us. He didn't seem comfortable with us so close to each other, but Mr Smith ignored him.

'And why don't you ask your grandmother about this?' Mr Smith said. He leaned even closer 'And what were you doing reading someone else's letters?'

'I found it . . . by accident. I tried . . . a bit . . . to ask Dot, but she says she's glad she's not married, so she couldn't have tried to find him . . . before. She never posted the letter.'

Mr Smith rubbed his nose again. 'Ellie, you have to trust grown-ups to decide what's best. I'm sure, knowing Dot, she did what was best.'

'But maybe *not*,' I pleaded. 'Maybe she was scared to try harder. People get scared. They do!'

He nodded. 'Yes, they do,' he agreed. 'Do you have this address, for Mr Starling who may or may not be your grandad?' It sounded as though he was making fun of me, but when I looked right at him, I could see that he wasn't – he was just being nice.

'I memorised it. It's c/o Mrs Parkin, 20 Seaton Road, Newcastle.'

He brought out a pen and a small leather note-book with an elastic band round it. Carefully, he wrote it down.

'I've never heard of Seaton Road, Ellie, and it would seem that that wasn't even a permanent address for Mr Starling.'

'But you'll try to find him? You will, won't you?'

He stroked his hair. It looked very soft and wasn't all covered in Brylcreem like the darkies you saw at the pictures. 'I promise I'll look it up for you when I get home. If you give me Dot's address too, I'll write to you personally as soon as I've checked on it. OK?'

'But . . . But that might be too late. You see, I might even be home myself by then, and I don't know when I'll get back here. I might *never* get back, Mr Smith.' I bit my lip. 'Do you think you could please do something sooner? Please?' I knew I was being rude, pestering him like that, but I couldn't help it.

Mr Smith sighed. 'Well, I'm going on over to the west coast tomorrow, but I'll be back on Wednesday – sometime in the evening. In the meantime, I'll make some phone calls and see what I can find out. How's that?'

'Oh thank you, Mr Smith.' I nearly hugged him with relief, but it would have been forward.

Mr Smith rose, and opened his car door. He turned back to me. 'Ellie, don't build your hopes up. It's very unlikely I'll have anything to tell you. You do realise that?'

I was beaming at him. 'I know ... but it's possible, isn't it? It's possible.'

CHAPTER 11

It wasn't long after that when Rita arrived. She had probably passed Mr Smith on the road, although she wouldn't have noticed him. Rita drove too fast to notice anyone. Hooligan headed for Inchbrae. He seemed to know that Rita was more of a hazard than Mr Smith, and I was glad of that.

The Murchisons had a dog once who ran after cars. Not many cars came down our street, but one day one of them hit the Murchisons' dog, and he had to be put down. Dad said it was a wonder it hadn't happened sooner, but I still felt sorry for the dog. It had just been a game to him.

Rita was on her own, and I went inside with her. When I told Dot that Mr Smith was sorry he couldn't stop she didn't say anything, but I was afraid she somehow knew what I'd asked him. I turned to Rita to hide my face from her.

'I'll just play outside so you can talk to Dot in private,' I said. She looked a bit surprised, then she said she hoped I'd be spending a lot of time with Joe – he could stand a lesson or two in manners.

I cycled up and down the lane a couple of times,

then I thought I'd got a puncture in my back wheel. I couldn't see anything on the tyre, it just looked a bit flat, so I walked it back to the house. Dot's bike was under the kitchen window, and I didn't think she'd mind me borrowing her pump. It was quite hard to fix it on to the Cameron boys' bike, but I could hear Dot and Rita talking, and I didn't want to interrupt them.

I finally screwed it on to the valve, and had just begun pumping the tyre when I heard Dot and Rita coming into the kitchen. Dot was telling Rita to sit at the kitchen table, and I could hear her pouring them both a dram. I wasn't sure whether to stand up and let them see me, but I thought they would surely hear the sooch of the pump, and probably weren't bothered at me being there.

'So what did you do?' Dot was asking.

'God, I was near off my head, Dot. I'm damn near scalded with all the hot baths . . . and I'll never drink another gin as long as I live.'

'Why didn't you tell us?'

'I don't know. At first, I thought I was just late, and then Pat kept saying . . . that if it was meant to be, well, we'd make the best of it.'

'That's a man for you. It's just no' the same worry to them.'

'Well, you know me, Dot. I've never wanted children. Lil can say all she likes about it no' being natural, but it's just not in me, and there's no sense in pretending it is.'

'So you're better then?'

'Aye. I got some quinine from that drunken old chemist in Locheirnan. I had to bring him a sunray skirt for his fancy bit, but it was worth it.' I heard Rita sighing. 'I'll never really be sure if I was or I wasn't, but I started the next day, so that's that.'

I was on my knees on the ground. I didn't understand everything Rita had been talking about, but I thought it was awful that she never wanted children. I hoped Rita wouldn't marry Mr Conroy after all.

'Well, you better marry the bugger before you get caught again,' Dot said. I nearly stood up then, and told her to mind her own business. She had no right telling Rita to get married, when poor Joseph was still breaking his heart for his real mother – who was never going to come back for him – and now he would end up with a wicked stepmother who didn't even like children.

'It's not that I don't want to marry him, Dot, but that's just what I'm afraid of. I'm thirty-eight now. If I ever *was* going to want a bairn, it would have been a long time ago. And Pat ... well, he canna keep his hands off me, and that's the truth.' She sounded worried about Mr Conroy's hands. Now that I thought about it, I don't think I'd have liked a butcher's hands on me either, however handsome he was.

'You obviously don't want him to. Anyway, it's no' his hands that's the problem,' Dot said. I could tell from her voice she was smiling. 'D'you love him still?'

Rita must have nodded. 'Well then, marry him, Rita. It can get hellish lonely on yir own, y'know.'

I was getting angrier by the minute. Now Dot was telling lies. She'd told me she was *glad* she didn't have a husband. Maybe nobody had ever *wanted* to marry her, and it served her right.

'Then there's that boy of his to contend with,' Rita said, sounding even more worried. I held my breath.

'He's no a *bad* bairn, Rita. He's bound to be missing thon hoor of a mother, and I'm sure he's wondering what's going on between you and Pat. Poor thing doesna know if he's coming or going half the time,' Dot said.

I was glad then I hadn't stood up. At least Dot was taking up for Joseph.

'Has Pat spoken to him?' she asked.

'He's tried. *I've* tried. Joe just closes up and won't even listen. He doesn't *want* to believe that I care for him . . . in my own way,' Rita added.

I let my breath out. My face must have been as purple as the flower. Rita *cared* for Joseph. I had a sore head, between holding my breath and all the confusion of it; and besides, there was a funny smell off the purple flower that I hadn't noticed before.

'Well, give him a chance,' Dot said. 'He'll come around in time. You'll just have to wheedle him along in the meantime.'

'I'm no bloody wheedling anyone,' Rita answered. 'He's going into the Academy after the summer. He's old enough to accept things as they are.'

'Tread softly, Rita. He's been abandoned once. How d'you think he's going to feel getting shipped off to the hostel, while you and his dad play hoosies?'

'God, Dot, I never thought about it like that.'

There was a silence. I held my breath again.

'But I'm no' giving up my own house,' Rita continued. 'I set myself up wi' the money Colin left me, and if Pat Conroy wants me for his wife, he's going to have to move in with me. Joseph too.' She sighed again. 'I could make up a right bonny room for him – if he'd let me – but he'll never accept me as his mother, Dot. Mind, I wouldn't be a threat to her memory – no matter what she was.'

'Well, at least Colin's no' a threat, God rest him.'

'Jeez, Dot, I wouldn't even remember what he looked like, if I didn't have our wedding photo to remind me. Come to think of it, I don't even know where it is . . .'

'Poor bugger,' Dot said. 'One furlough, and bang!'

'Best man I ever had,' said Rita. 'Wasn't around long enough to make a pest of himself, and left me a nice wee nest-egg when he went.' They both laughed. 'We'd never have lasted anyway,' Rita added, and she wasn't laughing now. 'It was the war . . .'

'I know, hen. Time seemed in short supply to everyone then,' Dot said. 'Bring your dram through wi' you. I'll put on a record.'

I waited until I heard the trumpet solo of 'Lady Sings the Blues' before I tried to rise. My legs were cramped, and tiny stones were stuck into my knees and all down my shins. Eventually I got up and put Dot's pump back on her bike. My tyre was flat as a pancake. It was punctured, after all.

Dot called me in when Rita left. She said it had been a long day, and as I'd been so good, I could have some peaches and cream before I went to bed. But when she went into her press there weren't any peaches left. She said she didn't remember us eating that many. I had an apple instead, and a piece with butter and sugar, which was fine, but I'd have preferred the peaches.

I asked Dot if Rita had decided to marry Mr Conroy, and she gave me a funny look. I pushed my legs behind the spar of the chair. You could still see the marks all over them, where the stones had got stuck.

'Does it matter to you?' Dot asked.

'I was just thinking about Joseph.'

'Well, I can assure you Joseph's no' thinking about you,' Dot said. 'Eat your piece.'

I'd nearly given the game away. I made a bit of a show of eating my crusts to make up for it.

'I enjoyed Mrs Bryce's soup,' I said. 'Do you think Mr Smith'll be getting it for his supper?' I knew Dot would be happy to talk about Mr Smith again.

She gave me another funny look, then she laughed.

'Rita says he was buying everyone a dram when she went in the night. He'll be needing a good bowl o' soup by the time they're through with him.'

'They won't mind him buying drams,' I agreed. The people in Inchbrae didn't seem to mind who bought the whisky. They all enjoyed drinking it. It worried me. What if Mr Smith got drunk and forgot to make his phone calls – or worse, what if he told anyone our secret?

'You're right to look worried, Ellie,' Dot said. 'This morning he wasna long out o' the jungle. Before the night's over, he'll be a gentleman and a scholar.' Her voice was a bit sad, the way she said it.

Perhaps there was a chance we'd catch him tomorrow before he left for the west coast. It would put my mind at rest to know if he had stayed sober or not.

'Do you think we'll see him, when we go in to phone Mam?' I asked.

Dot shook her head. 'We're no going that early, Ellie. I'm sure he'll be well on his way by the time we get in. The poor man's going to have the sheets wheeched from under him before the light's hit the earth,' Dot said. She laughed again. She wasn't sad any more.

I tried to laugh with her, but it sounded a bit loud, so I changed it to a smile. I couldn't wait to go to bed and think about everything. Also, I couldn't wait to talk to Mam.

* * *

We decided to phone from Mrs Alexander's, as Rita had two customers in her shop, which Dot said was because Tuesday was market day and the farmers' wives were happy to get a few hours to themselves. She said they didn't buy that much, but Rita had a good sale, and wasn't just marking things down because they were rubbish like the stuff they sold in Locheirnan. I didn't think Dot shopped at Rita's by the look of her clothes, but it was a fact that every woman knows a bargain when she sees it. Even Dad agreed on that point.

Mrs Bryce was sweeping her doorway, and shouted to Dot that the bar was hotching wi' folk. Dot said she was glad; it was good revenue, and didn't Hugh enjoy all the attention.

I was going to bring all of my money with me, in case we had to buy bus tickets, but Dot said half-a-crown would be plenty, and we'd have time to get the rest if it was needed. She'd slammed the back door when we left, and I thought that I'd maybe made her angry. She said I could go on her bar, or we could walk, seeing as my bike was punctured. I said the bar was fine, and would she apologise to the Cameron boys, if I had to leave before I got a chance to mend the puncture.

'Don't worry about it, Ellie,' she said. She was really staring at me, and her eyes had a wild look to them. I didn't know what it was that had made her so angry. When we got to the road, she lifted me on to the bar, and then she said a strange thing to me.

'If you had to leave this very day, Ellie, there's

142

no-one would be more pleased than me.'

'Don't you like me being here?'

'I never knew how much I missed you, till I had you,' she said. This made no sense at all, but I knew she wasn't angry with me. I knew it must have been something else.

Even the paper-shop was busy. There were two ladies laughing over some rude postcards, and a man at the counter was buying a miniature Bagatelle. He said it was for his nephew, but one of the ladies said, 'Since when did y'have a nephew, Hamish? Isn't it yirself that likes a shottie o' a bairn's game?'

Hamish told them to clack their tongues somewhere else, and the two ladies laughed at him when he went out. 'Big bloody bairns, every one o' them,' the older one said.

Mrs Alexander smiled. 'And where would we be without wir bairns?' she asked. She looked very fresh and powdery.

She bent down, and lifted a comic from below the counter. '*Girl's Crystal*, just in,' she said. 'One of your favourites, if I haven't missed my guess.'

I held out my half-crown and nodded. 'I'll save it for the bus,' I told her. She looked astounded. 'Och, surely you're no' leaving us already, Ellie. I've barely had a glimpse at you.'

'I might have to go home by the end of the week, Mrs Alexander. My mam'll be needing me. Eh, Dot?' I turned in time to catch Dot giving Mrs Alexander one of her looks, but just too late

143

to be sure what kind of look it was.

'Can I use your front room, Jessie? Ellie wants to phone her mother.'

Mrs Alexander nodded. Then she looked back at Dot and shook her head. The excitement was leaving me. The two ladies had been listening to us, and they left without buying anything.

My heart was pounding again. It was as if I was in the hospital or something. Everyone seemed to know something about me, something that was making them feel sorry for me! I stared at Dot. 'What's wrong with me?' I asked.

'Nothing at all, Ellie. We're jist no' ready to let you go,' Mrs Alexander said. She was smiling at me, and looking her normal self. 'Can you blame us?'

I wasn't sure. Mrs Alexander took my half-crown and rang up her till. She counted the change back into my hand, and (I never even saw her getting it) put a white chocolate mouse with it.

'Go ahead, Dot,' she said.

I started to follow Dot, but Mrs Alexander stopped me. 'Wait, dearie. She'll call you as soon as she gets through. We wouldn't want you trapped in the post office again, would we?'

'Och, I've met Hugh, Mrs Alexander. I'm not scared of him now.' As soon as I said it, I knew it was true. It was like saying you were going to be a film star.

'I'm going to Hollywood,' I told her.

Mrs Alexander pushed her glasses up her nose.

'I wouldn't doubt it,' she said. She was a really nice lady, but I got the feeling that she did doubt it; I think it was the thing with the glasses.

'Honest to God, I am,' I assured her. 'I'm going to be a film star.'

She stood back, and crossed her hands in front of her stomach. 'Will you remember your friends, when you're a film star?' she asked.

'I will,' I answered. I was waiting for Dot to call me to the phone. 'I'll leave you my autograph before I go, if you like.'

'That'll be lovely,' she said.

Dot came back. 'Did you not get through yet?' I asked.

'I got through, Ellie. Your mam's feeling better, but she's no quite right just yet. Maybe by next week . . .'

I was furious. She hadn't even *tried*. She hadn't even let me speak to Mam when that was the whole point of us coming here.

'You didn't call me!'

'Your mam was . . . tired. She asked me to tell you that she's missing you . . .'

'You didn't let me speak to her. If she heard my voice, she'd *know* . . . she'd know she couldn't just leave me here!'

'Ellie, it's only been a couple of days. You've got to . . .'

'I don't have to do ANYTHING!' I threw my change on the floor. The white mouse skittered all the way to the counter, as though it was alive. It

145

was going to get stood on by someone who didn't care. People *didn't care*.

I ran outside, and straight into Dreep. I didn't even see him.

'Fuck off!' he said.

'Fuck off yourself!'

I'd said it. The first time in my life I'd ever said the 'F' word.

It wasn't that good a word, not *that* good.

CHAPTER 12

I looked up and down the street. There was nowhere to go. I was sobbing. I could hear Dot behind me, and Dreep was staring down at me. He had eyes like currants. I hated all of them. Rita's car was parked outside her shop. I ran to it, and climbed inside. I would sit there, with the doors closed, and not talk to anyone, ever again.

Dreep came marching after me. Just as I got inside the car, he threw out his hand to stop me closing the door. It was too late. I looked up and saw his fingertips jammed in the door. His nails were black with dirt. I remember noticing that – and some yellow paint on one of his knuckles.

He started screaming blue murder. Rita came running outside and pulled the door open. 'Aaarghhh!' Dreep screamed. 'Ooyah, ooyah. Aaarghh!' Then Rita started howling at Dreep, and Hooligan came racing from nowhere. Dreep was running in circles, and Hooligan was throwing himself in the air and barking his head off.

People started pouring out of the Jacobite and Dot was racing around behind Dreep, trying to catch a hold of him. I covered my ears; it was the most awful commotion I'd ever heard. Then Joseph was pulling me out of the car.

'What did you do? What did you do?' He kept asking it, over and over. I was shaking my head. I felt like my ears were going to burst, and I was crying so hard I was seeing two of everyone.

Mr Bryce had Hugh pinned to the wall outside the bar, and was bawling at Dot, and Hugh was stotting his head off the window, and roaring as loud as Dreep. 'For Chris'sakes, get a hold of him!' Mr Bryce was shouting. I didn't think Dot could hear him.

'Dreep . . . Dreep, for God's sake, open yir hand,' she kept saying. 'Open yir hand, Dreep!' She'd caught his sleeve and was hanging on for dear life.

Dreep stopped birling. The whole place went quiet, even Hooligan. Dreep lifted his hand to his face and inspected it. He spread his fingers open, and then gave them a bit of a shake. 'It's no' as bad as I thought,' he said. He started walking away.

He gave me a murderous look as he went by. 'Y'wee bitch that y'are!' he said.

Dot took out a cigarette and lit it. Everyone went back inside the Jacobite, and Rita reappeared with some keys. She locked the car doors and glared at Dot. 'What a carry-on,' she said, and marched back into the shop. In seconds, the only people left on the street were me and Dot and Joseph.

Mrs Bryce took a little round box of tablets from

her overall pocket and gave one to Hugh. He calmed down quite quickly, and sat beside us at the table, looking at his magazine. Mrs Bryce made us all drink hot tea. Joe said he would have preferred lemonade, but she said hot tea was the thing for shock.

'It wasn't me that got the shock,' Joe muttered, but he still didn't get any lemonade.

Dot told me that if I said I was sorry one more time she'd take the lug off me, and she and Mr Bryce had two large drams to help them get over it all. The man called Arthur got a large one too, as he said he had a bad heart, and he wouldn't want his death on anyone's conscience. Nobody was listening to him, and I think he got the drink by mistake.

It occurred to me then that God had seen all of this, and that I would have to stay the whole two weeks in Inchbrae to make up for my bad behaviour, and maybe never find Mr Starling, ever. It would be my punishment, and was probably better than the burning fire.

I tried to remember how it was to feel brave, but I couldn't. More than anything, I hoped that Hooligan didn't hate me now. I'd never meant to hurt Dreep.

Joe was very nice to me, and assured me that Hooligan had seen Dreep in worse shape than this. He even said that Hooligan was clever enough to know it had been an accident. Mrs Bryce bent to give him a cuddle when he said that, but he threw himself sideways, and she nearly landed in my lap.

Dot said we should go back and apologise to Mrs Alexander; that she was the one who had been hurt most by my behaviour. I dreaded going in, but she was as nice as ever. She had gathered all my change up, and she gave me and Joe two white mice each, and refused to let us pay for them. I kissed her on the cheek, and she kissed me back. I wanted to cry again, with her being so kind to me, but she said there had been altogether too many tears for one day, so I didn't.

I asked Dot if we should try to find Dreep too – to apologise. She laughed, and all the tiredness left her. 'I couldna stand to look at that graveyard o' a mooth twice in one day,' she said.

Joseph and I waited to see what we should do next, but Dot said she was going home for a bit of sustenance, and she hoped it would be daylight before she came to. 'It *is* daylight; it's just the back of two,' Joe remarked, looking at his watch, which didn't have a minute hand. He said it was 'contemporary'. I thought it was useless, but I'd said enough already, so I pretended to admire it.

Dot asked Mr Conroy if I could stay and play about the place with Joseph. He said it made no difference, and he thought Rita wouldn't mind driving me home later. He said they had no plans for the evening, so there was no reason for her to hang around.

This seemed to delight Joe, and he actually offered to take me to a place he knew, where the gypsies were camping. Mr Conroy said we were to stay away from them. He'd been cursed enough in his time, and Joseph would be to blame if there were any more troubles heaped on their heads.

'It's always *me* to blame,' Joe grumbled, but he was still in a good mood. I didn't care what we did. I felt like Dot; I just wanted the day to be over with.

'M.M.'

'Marilyn Monroe,' I answered. I knew he'd given me an easy one to cheer me up. It was nice of him.

We left town at the Locheirnan end, and carried on until we came to some fields. We had to cross through two of them, which were planted with tatties, but we kept to the side so as not to damage them. The camp was in a sort of clearing, surrounded by trees, and there was a wee burn at the far end. Joe said the stream came from the River Eirnan. He said we had to be quiet if we were going to watch the gypsies, because they didn't like intruders.

We hunkered down behind some bushes. There wasn't much sign of life, and I was beginning to think they'd moved on when I noticed some smoke coming out of one of their tents. They weren't real tents, just layers of oilcloth and bits of blankets heaped on top of each other, and the chimney was an old pipe sticking through the roof of the tent. There were two carts beside the burn, and a couple of ponies grazed quietly beside them. The ponies weren't what you'd call well cared for, but they seemed happy enough.

'They'll be leaving soon,' Joe whispered. 'They've been round the doors already, and they usually go on past Locheirnan to work the fields on their way to Blairgowrie. They're never here more'n a day or two.'

'Where are they all?' I asked. Joe nipped my arm.

A woman pulled aside the door of one of the tents, and peered out. She sniffed the air, a bit like a dog would do, and then trailed out a big foot-locker, which was very old and dented. She sat down on it, leaning on her knees, which were wide apart, and lit a pipe. I'd never seen a woman smoke a pipe before. Her hair was long and matted, and she was wearing a black skirt and a flowered blouse. Over the blouse was a black cardigan with big holes in the sleeves, and a bright blue scarf was knotted at her throat.

The sun broke through the clearing, and shone right over her, and I wondered how her hair could gleam the way it did, and be so dirty-looking. I pointed this out to Joe. He whispered that the ones who came round the doors were quite clean. They probably washed themselves in the burn, he said.

'Maybe they've left her behind, 'cos she won't bother to wash herself,' he suggested.

Just then, we heard a child crying. It was coming from inside the tent. The woman mumbled a few words, but you couldn't make out what they were. She rose and disappeared back inside the tent.

'They have their own language,' Joe informd me. 'Rita says it's called "the cant".' He sniggered. 'Da

152

says it's called that 'cos tinks *can't* talk right.' He looked at me to be sure I'd got the joke.

The woman came back out, carrying a baby on her hip. She sat down on the locker and began crooning to it, laying it on its belly across her knees. It was a bonny bairn, with big squeezy cheeks and bright red curls. It was swaddled in a tattered plaid, and was quite a few months old. I didn't have enough experience of babies to say just how old, but I'd have guessed about six months. I saw Joe staring at it, and it seemed to me that the baby was staring back at us.

My legs were beginning to hurt, and I shifted a bit to lean back on my heels. There was a rustling noise where I'd disturbed the leaves, and Joe nipped my arm again. The woman's head shot up, and I got a good view of her face. She looked too old to be the baby's mother; maybe she was its gran, and had been left to look after it. She stared across at where we were hiding, and we both held our breath: then she smiled to herself – a very sly smile.

The baby girned, and she sat it up. The plaid fell away for a moment, and we could see it was a boy. The woman pulled open her blouse, and the boy wrapped his fist round her bosom, and began to suck.

I didn't want to watch them any more then, and I looked away. My face was burning, and my stomach had started to rumble. Joseph must have felt just as embarrassed. 'Let's go,' he whispered.

We were well clear before he said anything else. 'Filthy bloody tinks!'

His good mood seemed to have vanished, and I didn't feel like talking either. We wandered back through the tattie fields. Joe went down one of the drills, and swiped at some of the plants. After a while, he spoke again. 'When y'going home?' he asked.

'I'm not sure,' I answered. It was the very last thing I wanted to talk about.

'Yir ma's still sick?'

'It's none of your business,' I snapped. He looked startled.

'I was just bloody asking!' he retorted. 'I won't ask anything else, then.'

'Fine.'

'Right then.'

'Right.'

He had tried to be kind to me today. He had taken me to see the gypsies. He didn't have to do that. 'She's a bit better, I think. I might be going home this weekend.'

'Who cares?'

We were back on the roadside. 'I wouldn't mind being a tink,' Joe said. 'You could just go where you pleased, and never have to mind anyone.'

'I wouldn't like it,' I said. 'Living in tents and things . . .'

'Let's build a tent!' Joe brightened at his own suggestion. I don't think he'd even heard me.

'What with?' I asked.

'We'll find stuff. We can look around the dump. There's always stuff lying about down there.'

'It'll be all dirty.' I didn't want to build a tent, especially not with stuff from the dump.

'Well, we'll ask around. We're bound to get something.'

'Where would we build it?'

'Down by the river. There's plenty of sticks there. I know how to build a fire, and we could cook fish, and boil tea and things.'

'What fish? I hate fish.'

'You're a pain in the arse,' Joe complained. 'We don't *have* to eat fish. We can cook sausages, or . . . There's plenty of things we can cook.'

'Why would we want to?'

'Arghh!' He looked like he might punch me. 'I should have known better than to waste a good idea on a *girl*!' He started to run. He was round the corner and out of sight before I could react. I ran after him.

He was sitting on a milestone waiting for me, and pretending he wasn't. I was out of breath, and near to tears again. 'I don't even *know* this road,' I told him.

'It only goes one way. You can't get lost,' he answered, shaking his head at my stupidity.

'Why were you waiting for me then?' I was fed up, and angry – especially with Joseph Conroy.

'Was not!'

'Yes you were!' My hands were on my hips, and I know my face was red.

Joe grinned. 'C'mon, *ba*-by. I'll take you back, don't worry.'

I was still fuming as we walked on. 'I said the "F" word today,' I told him. I knew it was wrong to brag about it, but it was far more impressive, I thought, than building a stupid tent.

He stopped and looked at me. 'Who to?' he asked.

'To Dreep,' I answered, 'but he said it first.'

Joe was starting at me. He believed me, and there was admiration in his eyes.

'I often say it,' he retorted. I wasn't entirely sure that he did, but it seemed important to him that I believed him.

'D'you like saying it?' I asked.

'Aye, it's grand.' He started walking again. 'Do *you* like saying it?'

'Oh aye,' I answered. I didn't though, and I was already sorry I'd mentioned it. Now Joe would be expecting me to say it again, and he'd probably start saying it too, which would be worse somehow.

'Hugh says it,' Joe volunteered.

I was aghast. 'How d'you know?'

'Malc taught him. He doesn't say it much, though.'

'Has Mrs Bryce heard him saying it?'

'Nuht,' Joe smiled. 'He's no' that daft, is Hugh.'

'I'm not scared of him any more.'

'He's OK. You just have to know him. He gets bored.'

'Aye,' I agreed. I was sure that he did.

'We could take him to our tent!' I gritted my teeth. He hadn't forgotten about the tent, and now Hugh was to be our guest. Joe spent the rest of the way back planning this new adventure.

I hoped I'd be home before the tent got built.

CHAPTER 13

Rita was pushing in her awning with a long pole as we came up the High Street.

'There yis are!' she said. 'I thought I was going to have to send out a search party.' She didn't sound too cross with us.

'You wouldna be sending any search parties for me!' Joe said. There was a challenge in his voice, and Rita turned to look at him.

'Aye, Joseph, I would,' she said. You could tell she was trying to be patient with him. 'And it's yourself that knows it.'

'Doubt it,' he sneered, and pushed past her.

Rita was shaking her head after him. 'I could wring his neck,' she confided. I knew how she felt. She was looking particularly beautiful, especially compared to the tinkie wifie we'd seen, and she seemed to have forgotten about the problems I'd caused earlier.

'Are you ready for home?' she asked, smiling.

I nodded.

'I'll lock up and say cheerio to Pat, then.' Her smile became more mischievous. 'D'you want to wait in the car?'

I shrugged.

She opened the passenger door. 'In you go,' she said. 'God, you're a relief to that awful boy.' She finished with the awning and went back inside. As she reappeared to lock the door, she called to me. 'I'll no be a minute, Ellie,' and with that she ran across the road to Mr Conroy's shop.

I looked at myself in the wing-mirror. My face was turning brown, but the freckles on my nose had got bigger, which was depressing. I'd scrubbed them with Vim once, and Mam had made me promise never to do it again; she'd said I'd ruin my complexion, and anyway freckles were a sign of beauty. Mam had a lovely complexion. I knew that there wasn't anything beautiful about freckles, and I wondered where that expression had started.

Janet said she thought it was only if you had a fair skin that you got freckles, and maybe folk had thought fair meant beautiful – as it sometimes did – instead of pale, which is what it more often meant. Janet had been Dux of our school. She was very clever.

Joseph had huge freckles. It hadn't come up, but I knew that he must hate them. Still, we were both lucky not to have carroty hair. His was more auburn, I suppose from his mother, because Mr Conroy's hair was jet black. I was still looking in the mirror and thinking all of this, when I saw Mrs Alexander hurry out of her shop and go into the Jacobite. That was when I remembered about my

Girl's Crystal, and that I'd left it at Mrs Bryce's table.

I opened the car door and started to cross the road just as Rita came out of Mr Conroy's. 'Where are you off to now?' she asked.

'I left my comic at Mrs Bryce's,' I answered.

We both went in. Mrs Bryce looked like she'd seen a ghost, and Mrs Alexander had her hand on Mrs Bryce's arm, as though she was trying to comfort her.

'What's going on?' Rita asked. Mrs Alexander turned to look at her, but didn't answer.

Rita moved forward. 'Lil? What is it?'

Mrs Bryce ran her hand across her mouth. 'There's been a phone call . . .' she said.

'From who?' Rita asked. 'What is it, Lil? Is it bad news?'

'No . . . No, I don't think it is.'

'Well what?' She grabbed at Mrs Bryce's sleeve. I shivered. Was it Mam? Had Mam phoned? Or maybe Dad? Maybe Mam had got sicker after Dot phoned. Please God, let Mam be all right.

Mrs Alexander spoke. 'I had an enquiry, Rita, about accommodation . . .'

I relaxed.

'*You* had? Who from? Who'd be phoning the post office for accommodation?' Rita asked.

'Well, that's just it,' Mrs Alexander answered. 'This gentleman wasn't sure if there was somewhere locally for him to spend a few days. He was calling from England. The operator booked the call through to me.'

'From *who*? For God's sake, it's worse than pulling teeth.'

Mrs Bryce walked over to the sofa and sat down. 'It's Johnny, Rita. It's Johnny that called.'

Rita threw her hands up, and turned on Mrs Alexander. 'Johnny *who*?' she demanded.

'Starling,' Mrs Alexander answered. 'Johnny Starling.'

My heart leapt. Mr Smith had found my grandad. He'd really done it!

Rita whirled. 'Oh, Lil, are you sure? Are you sure it's him?'

'The call was from Newcastle,' Mrs Bryce answered. She still sounded a bit dazed. 'He told Jessie he wanted to come up for a visit. He's calling her back tomorrow.'

'Didn't you know, Jessie . . . that it was him?' Rita asked.

'Aye, fine I knew,' Mrs Alexander answered. 'But I didn't want to go giving him any information before I made sure it was all right with Lil. I said I'd look into it for him.'

'Didn't he recognise *you*?' Rita asked.

'No, dear, he didn't. There wasn't a post office here when he left.' Mrs Alexander pushed her glasses back up her nose.

'God, Lil, are you going to put him up? When's he coming? I never thought I'd get to meet him. Did he say how long he's staying?' Rita was going nineteen to the dozen.

'I'll have to talk to my man,' Mrs Bryce

interrupted. 'I'm no sure Eckie'll be happy with the idea.'

'I don't imagine he will,' Rita continued. 'But why doesn't Starling stay at Locheirnan? There's three hotels there now. He wouldn't need to be bothering...'

'He would come here just the same,' Mrs Bryce said. She stood up, and wiped her hands on her overall. There was no reason for this. She just did it.

'Will you let me know?' Mrs Alexander asked, touching her arm very gently.

'Aye, Jessie,' Mrs Bryce answered. 'I'll speak to Eckie the night, after he closes the bar. No sense in taking his mind off his work sooner than I have to.'

Mrs Alexander left. Rita was leaning against the bar. 'Wouldn't you want to see him, Lil? After what you told me, I'm damn sure he'd be getting a piece o' *my* mind!'

'It was a lifetime ago,' Mrs Bryce answered. She shook her head, as though clearing her thoughts. 'Someone's going to have to tell Dot,' she added.

'I'm taking the bairn home,' Rita said. 'I'll tell her, if you like. She knew him pretty well herself, didn't she?'

Mrs Bryce turned to look at me. I hadn't moved. I couldn't. My heart was hammering, and I began to worry again. There were tears in Mrs Bryce's eyes. I hadn't meant to upset anyone.

'Can I get my comic? I left it in the kitchen.' I couldn't think of anything else to say.

'Aye, Dot knew him,' Mrs Bryce murmured, as though she hadn't heard me. 'I wonder what she'll think about it?'

What was Dot going to think about *me*? And how had Mr Smith found Mr Starling so quickly? And why wasn't he here to explain it all? And how was *I* going to explain it all? I would have to admit to reading the letter . . . and the rest of it. Please God, please God, let me go home.

Rita drove quite fast, and very straight. There were a lot of potholes in the road, and she drove right over them instead of trying to avoid them as Dad always did.

I would try reason with Dot. I would let her know that I had a right to know my grandad. Everybody did. Dot believed in people having rights. She would understand.

I was feeling sick with the worry of it, and Rita driving over the potholes and my teeth clattering in my head. I wondered how much Rita knew. She had heard about him, I knew that from the things she'd said to Mrs Bryce.

'How long have you been staying in Inchbrae?' I asked.

'God, it must be years,' she answered. 'My sister used to live here, and I spent a lot of time with her. Then her man got shifted to Aberdeen. They'd just finished building the house, and the shop came vacant at the same time. I thought I could do worse than buy them both . . . cool my heels for a while.'

She laughed, but it was more of a snort. 'Good old Rita. Never known to make the right choice, when the wrong one's there for the taking.'

Crunch! I bit my lip, and sucked it. 'D'you not like being here then?' I asked – when I was sure it wasn't going to bleed.

'I like it fine, Ellie,' she said. 'I just don't like feeling . . . trapped, y'know?' She turned to me as she said it. I looked ahead before I nodded. I was glad there wasn't anything coming.

'Did you know Dot and Mrs Bryce – from when your sister was here?' I asked.

'Not that well, no. I can't say we were friends, not like we are now. Why?'

'It's just . . . well, I hope you don't mind me saying it, but you're a lot younger than them, and I was wondering if you knew the same people.'

'Mind? It's thrilled I am. Imagine a wee lass like you commenting on that!' She looked in her mirror, and rubbed her lips together as though she'd just put on lipstick. She hadn't, that I knew of, but she always looked as though she had.

'I'd've thought we'd all look like old fogeys to you and Joseph.' She paused. 'Does Joseph talk about me?'

She was watching the road again. I wasn't interested in talking about Joseph, not at all. I was also hoping that she had noticed the big lorry getting ready to turn in front of us. She did, at the last minute, and I hit my forehead on the dashboard.

'Sorry, hen,' she said. 'Bloody men, think they

own the road!' I caught a glimpse of the lorry driver's face as we passed. He was as white as a sheet.

'Not really,' I answered. 'He doesn't talk about you.' I wasn't telling lies. He'd mentioned Rita, but he hadn't *talked* about her. He didn't have to; it was clear how he felt. I was trying to get back to the subject of Mr Starling, but she kept on.

'He doesn't? Well, that's good then, I suppose.' We were nearly at our turn-off. 'Has he said if he likes me?'

'No, he hasn't,' I replied, wishing I had more time. All I'd wanted this morning was for the time to go quickly, and now, now it was going too fast to keep up with.

Rita grimaced. 'Has he said anything about me and his da then?'

'No. Rita. . .'

'His ma?'

'Aye.' It was no good. We were home already. Rita swerved on to the lane in front of Dot's house, and I bounced against the window.

'What does he say about her?'

'Maybe you should ask him yourself,' I said. I didn't care about Rita and Joseph at that moment, but I knew what I'd said had sounded cheeky, and I didn't mean that either. I could do nothing right – nothing.

'Begging your pardon!' Rita said, jamming on her brakes. I'd made her cross.

The house was wide open as usual, and Dot was

165

nowhere to be seen. 'Where the hell has she got to now?' Rita bawled. 'She *knew* I was bringing you home. Could she no' just stay put for a minute?'

We got back in the car. 'We'll try the river,' Rita said. 'If she's no' there, you're coming to mine, and she can bloody well look for us!'

I didn't say anything. I knew Dot would be there.

She was sitting looking at her hills, and smoking. Hooligan was at her feet, and when he saw me his tail thumped on the stones once, twice, three times. At least he'd forgiven me. It made me sore inside with the gladness of it.

He watched me as I walked towards them. Rita was in front, but he ignored her, and smiled as I came closer. I rubbed his ear and he let me kiss his nose. Dot smiled at both of us. 'Did the day improve for you?' she asked.

'Im-*prove*?' Rita said. 'I'm all over the country looking for you. How long've you been here?'

'Hundreds and hundreds of years,' Dot answered. She had a way of riling Rita; I still wasn't sure if she meant to do it.

'Yir well named,' Rita went on. 'Dotty as they come. Daft as a ha'penny watch, so y'are!'

'No' as daft as Joe's watch,' she replied. 'I suppose you bought it for him?'

'What if I did?'

Dot shook her head. So did Hooligan. He knew everything that went on.

'Well, thanks for bringing my bairn back.' The tears stung my eyes, and I buried my head in

Hooligan's neck. She had no idea that I had betrayed her confidence.

'Any time, Miss Fairbairn. We're here to serve!' Rita snapped. 'I'm away home,' she said then. 'Have you got something for the bairn's supper?'

It seemed an endless cause for talk, that Dot was poorly prepared in the line of foodstuffs. I'm sure I would have been insulted with all the prying if it was me, but it never seemed to bother her any.

'I'm not hungry,' I said.

'We'll no' starve, none o' the three of us,' Dot assured Rita. That meant that Hooligan hadn't eaten yet, and would be coming home with us. It made me feel better – a bit.

Rita shook her head. 'There's four chops in the car. I'll no' eat more than one myself, and they're good gigot chops – it's a shame to waste them. I'll go and get them,' she offered.

'Maybe Pat thinks you need fattening up . . .' Dot mused.

Rita wagged her finger. 'If you mention . . .'

'Me? Where would I say a word?'

They both laughed then. Hooligan stood up at the thought of a chop, and gave himself a shake. He must have been in the river at some point, because drops of water that you couldn't see on his coat flew in every direction. Rita screamed and jumped backwards, but Dot just laughed some more. She looked at me, no doubt wondering why I wasn't laughing too, but she didn't say anything.

Rita ran back to the car, and Dot took out her

hipflask and lit another cigarette. The flask was back in her pocket by the time Rita returned. It wasn't that she was trying to hide it; it just didn't take her long to take a drink.

'I nearly forgot – ' Rita said, trying to hand Dot the parcel of chops without Hooligan getting to it first. (He was very determined, and it took more than one try.) 'Lil asked me to let you know. Johnny Starling's coming back.'

Dot dropped the chops. She'd been holding them quite loosely, and Hooligan decided to take advantage of this sudden opportunity. There was quite a tussle before Dot got the parcel back, and the brown paper was torn in a couple of places, but he hadn't quite got to the meat.

'I hope you've something else in the house,' Rita remarked. 'I wouldn't put that in my mouth now.'

'Nothing wrong with it,' Dot answered, blowing some sand off one of the chops. Then she wiped them with her hand. 'We'll put them under the tap,' she promised me. 'They'll be fine.'

She leaned back against a divot of wild grass. 'What was that you were saying, Rita?'

'If you're finished blowing on that chops, I'll tell you,' Rita answered. 'Jessie got a phone call from Newcastle. It seems it's this Johnny Starling looking for a bed. Lil said she'd have to talk to Eckie about it. He's phoning back tomorrow . . . says he's coming back for a look at the place.'

'Does he now?' Dot murmured, her eyes burning holes in the water. There was a plopping noise, and then a ripple appeared, spreading all the way to the edge of the shore. 'Well, I always thought he'd be back . . . some day.'

Rita swatted at something. 'I'm no' hanging about, Dot. The midgies are eating me alive. I'll see you in the morning.'

'Aye.'

'Thanks for the lift, Mrs Gilchrist,' I called after her. I didn't want her to leave me alone with Dot.

'Och, call me Rita, Ellie. And Dot, don't be keeping those chops out here in the heat. They've had enough abuse as it is.'

Dot rose, and Hooligan bounded ahead. There were long slavers coming from his mouth, and I knew he was drooling at the thought of the meat. I was afraid he'd be half-dead with anticipation by the time Dot had them cooked.

Dot played her records non-stop when we got home, and didn't say much of anything. I tried, once or twice, to confess what I'd done, but I couldn't. Then, just before we sat down to eat, Dot said she hoped I'd be home before things got sticky. She seemed quite melancholy.

The chops were very tough, but Hooligan loved them. He had his own, and Dot's too, and most of mine. Then he set off back to Inchbrae in search of Dreep, but he did lick my face before he went. His breath was nice, and his tongue was wet and dry at the same time. I told him I'd see him tomorrow, and that I loved him with all my heart. He seemed pleased. Anyway, I believed that he was. Dot had told me that if you believed it, then it was true. I'd believed that I'd find Mr Starling, and it seemed that I had.

Dot finished her whisky from under the sink, and got another bottle from the press. When I went to bed, Billie Holiday was singing 'Some Other Spring'. Dot wasn't sitting in her chair. She was standing at the window, looking out at the lilac trees.

CHAPTER 14

We did some housework on Wednesday morning, but it wasn't like the housework me and Mam did; it was more of a tidy-up. Dot washed some clothes, and I helped her hang them out. It was another fine day. Dot didn't have a pole for her washing line. She said she did have one once, but she couldn't remember what had happened to it. Mam had three washing lines, but Dot had only one, so she put the towels and two of my dresses over the hedge to dry.

'I think my clothes would dry better on the line,' I suggested, because I was a bit worried that earwigs would crawl inside my pockets.

'They'll be fine where they are,' Dot answered. 'Unless you want your socks and knickers on the hedge . . . ?' I shook my head, trying not to shiver. Dot mentioned that it was half-day closing in Inchbrae, and Rita would probably call in to spend the afternoon with us.

'Will she be bringing Joe over?' I asked.

Dot shook her head. 'No, Pat likes to spend what time he can with him, and they usually go to the pictures in Locheirnan on Wednesday afternoons.'

'Doesn't Rita go with them?'

'Och, she's no' one for the pictures, hen. It would mean sitting too long in one place. She's a restless woman, is Rita.'

'Could we go to the pictures sometime?'

Dot screwed her face up. 'Well, I'm no' too fond of sitting inside when the weather's good,' she answered. She saw my disappointment, and added, 'Still, I suppose if you're going to be a film star, you'd be needing to study other folks at the acting. Maybe . . . if we get a droppie rain before the end of the week.'

I hoped we would be at the pictures when Mr Starling arrived. Maybe, if he couldn't find us, he'd just give up and go home again. But then I'd never get to know him. I didn't know what I wanted any more.

After our housework Dot and I made some sandwiches and took them outside to eat. We laid a blanket out on the grass and I read my comic for a while, but then I felt a bit sleepy and laid down on the blanket to watch the clouds. There weren't many. The sky was so blue it hurt my eyes.

It was nearly three o'clock when Rita drove up.

'What's new the day?' Dot asked, as Rita came round the corner of the house.

'Not much,' she answered. She was wearing tight black trousers, and an off-the-shoulder white blouse with a big ruffle and black polka-dots. I couldn't take my eyes off her. She straightened out Dot's blanket before she sat down.

'Is this clean?' she asked.

'Clean enough,' Dot answered. 'Are you for a dram?'

'Och, it's a bit hot. I'll have a shandy, I think.'

'Is Mr Smith back yet?' I asked.

Rita shrugged. 'No . . . come to think of it, I didn't see his car.'

Dot rose, and Rita leaned back. She pushed her blouse further off her shoulders, and turned her face to the sun. Her bosoms stuck out. She had big ones. Mam's were quite small. Rita caught me looking, and I blushed.

'You'll have them too one day, Ellie. Be sure you wear a well-fitting brassière. Good foundation garments are the best investment a woman can make.' I resolved to remember her advice; I couldn't wait to have bosoms.

'Don't be filling the bairn's head wi' nonsense,' Dot said, appearing from the back door.

'It's not nonsense. It's a fact, and you'd do well to pay heed yourself.'

Dot snorted. 'What kept you, anyway? I thought you'd be here hours ago.'

'I took Pat and Joseph into Locheirnan. We went to the tea-rooms and had a bite to eat before the pictures. That Joe ate *three* cream cookies. Pat ruins him.' She shook her head. 'Anyway, they're taking the bus back, so I'm all yours.' She looked at her watch. 'I hadn't realised it was this late.'

'What's on?' I asked.

'I didn't notice. Oh yes, it's *Inn of the Sixth Happiness*.'

'Oh . . .' I hadn't seen it yet, though I knew the story. We'd been reading about Gladys Aylward at school, and I'd been looking forward to it for ages.

'We'll maybe catch it before it leaves,' Dot said. 'Ellie's going to be a film star herself,' she told Rita.

Although I was quite sure about it, and had told Joe and Mrs Alexander, I somehow felt that Rita wouldn't take me seriously. 'Well, it's what I'd *like* to be . . . if I could . . .' I stammered. I was blushing again.

''Course you could,' Rita said. She didn't sound too interested, but she hadn't dismissed the idea, and that was the important thing.

'Did you see Lil?' Dot asked.

'Aye. Oh, she said to tell you she hadn't heard any more from that Starling bloke. Jessie said it would probably be later in the day before he phoned again.'

'What did Eckie have to say about it?'

'He says it won't put him up nor down. It'll be up to Lil . . . if she wants him around or not.'

'*And* . . . ?'

'And what?' Rita asked.

'And . . . what did she decide?'

'She's still swithering, but she didn't seem to be so anxious about it today. I think Eckie settled her down a bit.'

There was a long silence. I kept my arm across

my face, pretending the sun was in my eyes, which it was, but not that much.

Rita carried on sun-bathing, and Dot wandered back into the house to change her records. Then she came back and sat down, and got back up again. She went over to the hedge, and began turning the washing over.

'What about yourself?' she asked Rita.

Rita sat forward and hugged her knees. 'What about me?'

'Are you going to go for the shop?'

Rita shook her head. 'I'm a fool for myself, Dot, but I called the solicitors in Locheirnan this morning . . . let them know I wouldn't be putting in an offer.' She didn't sound very happy with her decision.

'Have you told Pat?'

Rita shot Dot a warning look. I knew it had to do with me being there. Grown-ups often looked at each other like that – as though you weren't supposed to notice it.

'It's all right, Rita,' Dot said. 'The bairn's been better brought up than to repeat what she hears. Haven't you, Ellie?'

'What?' I asked. I pretended not to have been listening, as I wanted to hear what Rita had to say. Dot gave me a look, and I knew I hadn't fooled her.

Rita was staring at me. 'I'm well brought up,' I assured her. Well enough brought up to know it was a bad thing to read other people's letters.

'I've told Pat. We're going to wait a while, before we say anything,' she answered.

So Joseph hadn't been told yet.

'I'll have that dram now,' Rita said. I knew she just wanted to go into the kitchen with Dot so she could talk to her some more. They were inside for a long time, but Rita didn't look any happier when she came out. In fact, they both seemed out of sorts.

It was hard keeping up with grown-ups' moods. I wasn't very good at knowing when Dad was going to be in a bad mood. Even when I could hear the start of it in his voice, I had to watch his face very carefully to know *exactly* when it would happen. Once, I'd started crying before Dad went into a bad mood, and he'd sent me to bed. I would never cry after that. It was important to be there – to watch them, so you were ready for it. I wondered how angry he was going to be when he found out what I'd done. Very angry, I imagined. Very, very angry.

Dot and Rita weren't talking much, and I asked if I could go down to the river. Dot said I could, but Rita thought it was too dangerous on my own. Dot gave in, which wasn't like her, then she thought better of it. 'We'll all go,' she announced. 'I need to stretch my legs.'

'I'm not going to the river,' Rita stated. No wonder she didn't get on with Joseph; she argued as much as he did.

'Nobody's forcing you,' Dot replied. 'You can stay here till we get back.'

'I'm no staying here by myself. I'd be as well at home.'

'Go home then,' Dot said.

'I think I will,' Rita agreed. She didn't seem to mind. 'I'll have a bath and wash my hair.' She looked at me. 'You won't have had a bath yet, Ellie?'

I shook my head.

'Well, Dot comes over on a Friday for hers. You can come with her if you like.'

I thanked her. I was quite sure her house would be lovely inside. Mam always said you could spot good taste a mile off. Mam's good taste was a bit different to Rita's, but they both had it. You could tell.

We didn't make it to the river. We were almost there when we found Mrs Fishbein, sitting on a stile. She didn't even see us. Her hands were across her face, and we were almost beside her before we realised that she was crying.

Dot touched her shoulder. 'Greta ... Greta, what's wrong?'

She turned, and I've never seen anyone look so sad. I had to swallow hard.

'Ach, Miss Fairbairn. Ist today ... his birthday being ...'

Dot stared at her, and then took both Mrs Fishbein's hands in her own. 'Your boy? Is it your boy's birthday?'

Mrs Fishbein nodded, and sobbed some more. Her nose was running a lot, and her face was very blotchy, so I knew she'd been crying for a long time. Dot reached in her trouser pocket for her hankie, but Mrs Fishbein pulled one from her own pocket first. There was a straw message-bag at her feet, and she put the hankie inside it and brought out another. Her whole body was shaking with crying. It was very frightening.

'Mein Abel. Only seventeen, Miss Fairbairn. A boy, he vas.' She spread her arms before her. 'From mein arms they pulled him. Und still he smiled. His smile, I neffer forget . . .' She broke down again. I thought she might choke, she was crying so hard.

I wondered if I should run for the doctor, but I didn't think there was a doctor in Inchbrae. I looked at Dot. She seemed to have forgotten I was there, and I could feel the panic inside me. They were ignoring me, and I didn't know what to do. All the fear I'd been feeling choked up inside me, and I wanted to run, and keep running.

Dot was standing with her arm around Mrs Fishbein. Mrs Fishbein buried her head in Dot's stomach, and Dot kept stroking her back. 'How old would he be today?' Dot asked. Her voice was calm and gentle. I wanted her to keep talking . . . to put the panic away.

'Thirty years und four,' Mrs Fishbein answered. She looked up at Dot. 'You see . . . ? The same . . .' she whispered.

'Aye,' Dot answered. 'As many years as he lived.' She let Mrs Fishbein cry a bit more, stroking her all the while. 'Do you know for sure what happened to him?' she asked.

Mrs Fishbein shook her head once, violently. 'Knowing ve can neffer do!'

Dot eased Mrs Fishbein to her feet. 'He'll aye be seventeen to you, Greta, and nothing can ever hurt him again. That much you do know,' she said.

Mrs Fishbein nodded. Dot took the hankie from her and wiped Mrs Fishbein's tears away, then she made her blow her nose, and she wiped that too.

'Will we walk with you, Greta?' she asked.

Mrs Fishbein nodded again. Dot signalled to me to carry the message-bag. I picked it up, and realised it was empty. For some reason that made me feel sadder than ever, knowing Mrs Fishbein had come all this way with an empty message-bag.

We started back to town. I held Mrs Fishbein's hand, and Dot took her arm. A couple of times we had to break up to let the traffic pass, but it was always Dot who fell behind. Mrs Fishbein never once let go of my hand. She talked a little from time to time, but I had a hard job understanding her. Dot would nod and ask a question or two, but mostly we just walked.

I found myself thinking about Dot, and my father. She seemed to understand Mrs Fishbein's terrible heartache and all, but she had her own son who was still alive, and she never even bothered to come and see him. And why didn't Dad visit *her*? He couldn't be that angry just because she liked her whisky. Maybe he was angry because she hadn't let him have a father of his own. Maybe once Mr Starling arrived, Dad would meet him and they'd love each other, and Dot would love them both, and everyone would thank me for bringing them all together.

Maybe not.

Then I felt ashamed of being so selfish with Mrs Fishbein breaking her poor heart, but it was true to say that I was frightened too. I hoped God knew what I meant. Everything got so complicated when you started thinking.

We had just reached the High Street when we saw Dreep. He was coming towards us, on the other side of the road, and he was wearing a fur coat.

Dot stopped. 'For the love o' God,' she said, 'will you look at that?'

Mrs Fishbein raised her head, and looked across at Dreep. As he came level with us, Dot called out to him. 'Are you no' rushing the season a wee bit, Dreep?' He waved back at us – a very cheerful wave. I was included in the wave and immediately felt better. Dot and Mrs Fishbein turned slightly to look after him.

'Where did he find a beaver lamb coat in Inchbrae?' Dot wondered.

'Jessie,' Mrs Fishbein said. 'Vun she has. Beaver lamb, ja.'

'It's no' Jessie's,' Dot said, shaking her head. Dreep had disappeared round the corner. 'Thon coat belonged to a tall woman. Did you see how well the sleeves fit him?'

'Ja, ja,' Mrs Fishbein answered. She was no longer crying.

Dot started laughing. 'He must have been all the way to Locheirnan. Some poor dame got conned out of her fur coat the day. It's a wonder he never got lifted!' She laughed and laughed, and Mrs Fishbein began laughing too.

We walked on. Mrs Fishbein took the shop keys from her pocket. 'Is your man home?' Dot asked.

Mrs Fishbein turned back to us. 'Ja,' she answered. 'Now ve vill pray together. Thank you. Ist very kind you haff been. I vill tell mein Abel . . .' Her eyes were full of crying again.

Dot touched her arm. 'Just tell him "Happy Birthday" – from Dot.'

'And Ellie,' I added.

Mrs Fishbein smiled and nodded. Then she went inside, and closed the door quietly behind her.

I started into the Jacobite. With a bit of luck Mr Smith might arrive while we were still here. I could feel Dot hesitate. 'Are we no' going in?' I asked.

She took a deep breath. 'I suppose,' she said. 'God knows what I'm going to hear next.'

CHAPTER 15

Hugh was sitting on the sofa. He had a word-puzzle in his hands, and was moving the squares back and forth. I knew that he couldn't read, and would never solve the puzzle, but he seemed to be enjoying it. Mrs Bryce was coming backwards down the stairs, polishing the banister as she went.

'The bar's no' open yet,' she called over her shoulder.

'It's me,' Dot answered. Mrs Bryce stopped polishing and nodded at Dot. They headed for one of the tables. Dot had lit a cigarette before we came in, and Mrs Bryce took a clean ashtray from the counter, which had 'Glenfiddich' in big writing all along the side. I thought of Dad drinking his whisky at Christmas. Maybe this year Mr Starling could stay with us for Christmas.

I went over and sat by Hugh. He looked at me and handed me the puzzle. The letters were all over the place, but he did have one line correct. 'Look, Hugh,' I pointed. 'You spelled "farm".'

He pulled it back and squinted at it very closely, but I could tell he still didn't know what he'd done.

He watched me moving the squares around. I almost had it, and stopped to work out what to do next, but I must have done something wrong, because Hugh started his awful roaring, and kept jabbing at the puzzle with his thumb.

I brought it over to Mrs Bryce. 'What does he want?' I pleaded. He was beginning to make me all nervous again.

'Oh, Ellie, he has to have the empty square in the middle when you stop. He doesn't like you to fill it in.'

'But it won't work like that.'

'Humour him, pet.' She looked worried, but I didn't think it was because of Hugh, as she must have been used to his roaring by now. Anyway, I put the empty square back in the middle, which spoiled the whole thing. Hugh smiled at me, and we sat back down. I didn't want to play with it if I couldn't do it right, so I handed it back to him, and he clapped my head a couple of times. Dot was telling Mrs Bryce about us finding Mrs Fishbein in such a terrible state.

'Poor Greta,' Mrs Bryce said. 'You just canna imagine the wickedness that went on; tearing bairns from their mothers' arms. What an awful thing.' She was looking over at Hugh as she spoke. You could tell she loved him very much, even though he was . . . whatever he was.

'I'll look in on them when Eckie gets back,' Mrs Bryce added. 'There's a nice pan of broth just made. I'll bring them some over.'

'I don't think she'll be feeling up to it, Lil,' Dot said. 'They might just want to be alone. If you could have seen her ... She was broken-hearted, poor soul.'

'Aye well, a good plate of soup works wonders.' This went on for a minute or two. They weren't really arguing, but they weren't talking properly either. It was as though they didn't know what to be saying to each other, and I was getting a bit impatient, waiting for them to talk about Mr Starling, and wondering when Mr Smith would be back.

Suddenly the door burst open, and I caught my breath, but it was only Mr Bryce.

'You'll never guess what I just saw, Lil,' he said, pulling off his bicycle clips. I didn't know where he'd been, but his face was redder than ever and his hair was sticking up as though he'd been in the wind. He smoothed his hand over it, and flattened the sticking-up bits.

'What, Eck?' Mrs Bryce asked. She'd risen from the table as though she was expecting bad news.

'That idiot Dreep's wandering about the place in a fur coat! In this weather!'

Dot laughed. 'Oh aye, I forgot to tell you, Lil. We saw him ourselves, just a minute ago.'

'My God, he'll be ripe,' Mrs Bryce said. She looked relieved though. She was smiling too.

'He's never anything else,' Mr Bryce remarked. 'Maybe it's a good thing. Maybe the fur'll keep the smell in.' They all had a laugh about it, and Mr

Bryce poured himself and Dot a dram.

'Has Jessie been over?' he asked. Mrs Bryce shook her head and Dot lit another cigarette. She didn't usually smoke them this close together.

'Och well, maybe he'll no bother calling back. What would he be wanting to come here for anyway – after all this time?' Mr Bryce put his arm round Mrs Bryce and gave her a squeeze. She slapped at him, but made sure she missed.

'Best thing he ever did was get out o' the place,' Mr Bryce added. 'Did us all a favour, eh, Lil?'

She touched his cheek. 'That he did,' she answered. I looked at Dot. She was smiling at them both, but it wasn't in her eyes; there was something else there.

The door opened again, and in came Dreep. Hugh dropped his puzzle. 'Rrrugghh!' he roared, curling both his hands into claws and slashing at the air.

'Be quiet, Hugh,' Mr Bryce said. Hugh fell silent, but he kept clawing the air, and I wanted to laugh at him.

'What're you after now, Dreep? I've told you before – you're getting no drink here.' Mr Bryce looked quite ferocious.

'My dear fellow, it is not the want of liquid refreshment which brings me across your venerable threshold. Indeed no. Rather, I have decided to share with you my good fortune.

'For today I was yet again made aware of the goodwill that exists on this earthly plane, and I am here to pass on "the Word". That love in its glorious infinity is available to all men . . .'

'You've got five to get out,' Mr Bryce warned him.

Dreep bowed low. 'Then leave I must. Felicitations to you all.'

Mrs Bryce waved her duster in the air where he'd been standing, holding her other hand over her nose and mouth. I could smell Dreep myself, even from the sofa. Hugh was rocking from side to side, laughing madly. It sounded much like his other roaring, but I was getting to know him better now, and laughed with him.

Things settled down. A few men came into the bar, and Dot and Mrs Bryce went back into the kitchen. Hugh and I followed. Mrs Bryce was fussing around, and wouldn't sit, and Dot seemed to be irritable again. Then we heard Mr Bryce talking to Mrs Alexander. Mrs Bryce stood stock still, and Dot looked down at her glass and began moving it in circles.

'Go on through, Jessie. They're all in the kitchen,' we heard Mr Bryce say.

Mrs Alexander came in. She was wearing a hat with a long feather on it, which really suited her. I was about to admire it, but Mrs Bryce spoke first.

'Did he phone, Jessie?'

'Aye, Lil. A few minutes ago. I was just on my way out.'

'Well, and what's the good word?' Dot asked. She looked up from the table, and her eyes were glittering. I stared at her.

'He's coming up next week. He says he can get the train to Inverness and be here on Tuesday if it's all right with you.'

Mrs Bryce was hugging herself. She looked at Mrs Alexander for a minute, then shivered as though she had felt a draught. 'Did he say how long for?'

'I gave him your number. He said he'll call you himself tomorrow.'

Dot had lifted her glass, but now she slammed it back on the table. It was all but empty, thank goodness. Hugh and I both jumped.

'For Chris'sakes, Jessie. Could you no' have come and got Lil? All this phoning back and fore . . .'

Mrs Alexander frowned. I thought she looked a bit hurt. 'Well, Dot, I thought . . . I thought it would be best.'

'You did right, Jessie, and I'm much obliged to you, even though some of us round here have forgotten our manners!' Mrs Bryce said, glaring at Dot.

She thanked Mrs Alexander again and walked her to the door. When she came back, she didn't even look at Dot. She started banging soup bowls about, and opened and closed her cutlery drawer three times.

'Don't put any out for us,' Dot said.

'I wasn't going to,' Mrs Bryce retorted. I thought she was though, as she had taken out four bowls, and I knew Mr Bryce wouldn't be eating while he had the bar to tend.

'If there's one thing I can't stand, it's broth,' Dot

187

went on. I couldn't stand it either, especially when there were split peas in it.

Mrs Bryce whirled. She had the ladle in her hand, and for a second, I thought she might take it across Dot's head.

'Since when? Since when did you take a scunner to broth?'

Hugh and I were both getting nervous now. It looked as though there was going to be an awful fight over the broth.

Dot reared up, and then she seemed to collapse back in her chair. 'I'm sorry, Lil. I don't know why I even said that.' She shook her head, and tried to smile. 'It's been a funny day. I think it's the heat that's putting me wrong.'

'It never did before,' Mrs Bryce said. She turned back to the stove, but I could see she had tears in her eyes. I felt sorry for her. I didn't think Dot should have been so rude, even if it *was* hot.

Dot stood up. 'We'll be getting down the road,' she said. 'I'll make a bit macaroni and cheese for me and Ellie.' She paused. ''Course, it won't be as good as your broth, Lil.'

'You're still welcome to it,' Mrs Bryce answered, keeping her back to us.

'No. You were right earlier. The Fishbeins'll probably appreciate it more.'

There was still no sign of Mr Smith. 'I like broth,' I lied. 'Better than macaroni.'

Dot stared at me. 'You'll have macaroni,' she said.

We were at the kitchen door when Mrs Bryce turned around. 'I'll have a better idea of everything when I speak to him myself, Dot.'

Dot sniffed. 'It makes no difference to me if he's back or no'. Do what you want.' She wasn't being rude now, in fact she sounded quite down-in-the-dumps.

'We're still friends, aye?' Mrs Bryce looked like she might cry at any minute.

'Listen to you! It's yourself that's suffering wi' the heat, I'm thinking.' Dot tutted, pretending to smile.

We said cheerio to everyone. I asked Dot to whistle for Hooligan, and she did, twice, but he didn't appear, and neither did Mr Smith. I imagined he would call at the house later to explain everything, but I didn't know how I would get a chance to talk to him in private. I tried to think how Mr Hitchcock would arrange it in a film, but I couldn't always understand his films even when I saw what was happening right in front of me.

I was anxious to get back to the house then, so I was a bit annoyed when we stopped by the river. I tried not to be selfish, though, as I thought it would cheer Dot up if we sat there for a few minutes. It usually did.

There were some sheep on the far bank which hadn't been there that morning. I still didn't know who moved them about. Dot seemed to know most things, so I asked her.

'Who moves them about?'

Dot crunched out her cigarette. 'Dirty bastards. May they rot in hell, every last goose-stepping one o' them!'

I hadn't expected anything like that. I looked around, but there weren't any geese anywhere near us.

'There's no geese, Dot. Just sheep.' I pointed.

She blew out her breath. A lot of smoke came with it, even though she'd finished her cigarette. She must have been holding it in her mouth a long time. It wasn't elegant, like Bette Davis. It was fierce and awful-looking.

'Sorry, hen. I was thinking about Mrs Fishbein . . . and the war.' She shook her head. 'God, how d'you live with something like that?'

I said I didn't know. Dot went quiet again, and I didn't ask any more about the sheep.

'I'll mend your puncture when we get home,' she said. I'd forgotten all about it, and had no idea what had prompted Dot to mention it.

'It's OK. I like walking.'

She turned. We were side by side, except I was on the stones, and she'd found another boulder to sit on.

'You're a nice bairn, Ellie,' she said. She'd said it before, and I thought it was peculiarly satisfying – knowing you were nice. I was pleased to have thought this, as I liked the difference between the meanings of 'peculiar', and knowing how to use them properly. 'Satisfying' was also a good word. It was exactly how it sounded – satisfying.

'You're too nice for your own good,' Dot added, spoiling everything. 'You're going to have to harden up a bit.'

Dad had said that too, the time I cried when he went in a bad mood with Mam, and he'd sent me to bed. They weren't his exact words, but he meant the same thing. 'You'll have to learn to be firm, Ellie – with yourself, most of all.' I hadn't forgotten.

'I've been hardening,' I answered. I wanted Dot to be aware of that fact. It would help her to understand everything when Mr Starling arrived.

She nodded. In the distance, a large bird was circling over Dot's hills, and she pointed. 'D'you see that?'

I nodded.

'It's a hawk, Ellie. Hawks fly alone. Sheep . . . ' She didn't have to point as I knew where they were. 'Sheep herd together. You have to be a hawk in this world if you're to make anything of it. You have to learn to fly alone.'

I'd never been very close to a sheep, but I had the feeling they were much more comfortable to be with than hawks . . . and nicer to touch.

'Och, never mind me,' Dot said at last. 'The war's over, at least for most of us, and we canna all be hawks. Maybe the best thing is just to forgive and forget . . . '

She was quiet for a moment, then she began talking again. 'When your father was wee he got bitten by a dog. I was up half the night with him – between the pain and the nightmares. He's scared

191

of dogs to this day, but it wouldn't be right to blame Hooligan for what some other dog did, would it?'

And now I knew why I was never allowed a puppy. I remembered when I was seven and mam said I could have one for Christmas and I didn't get it, and Mam said Dad thought it was a bad idea, and I could have something else instead. I remembered too that Mam seemed pleased in a funny kind of way, which made me more disappointed than ever. She took me to the pictures twice in one week, but it never made up for not getting a puppy.

'And if you can't blame Hooligan, then you can't blame all the Germans either,' I answered, to let Dot know that I understood her point. Even so, everyone *did* blame the Germans; even at school they did. And the Japanese. Of course the Japanese were very different from us, not like the Germans, who looked quite British.

'And, anyway, how would you know which ones were hawks, and which ones were sheep?' I asked. I couldn't see how one was any better than the other.

Dot threw back her head, and laughed out loud. It was one of her scary laughs. Well, it would have been, but it had become like Hugh's roaring. It wasn't scary any more.

'I think you're ready to mend your own puncture, Ellie.' I knew it was a compliment; I just didn't know what for.

'Were you in the war, Dot?'

'Up to my neck,' she answered. 'When you've

got the time, I'll tell you about it.'

I had the time, right then, but Dot rose and we went home. Hooligan wasn't there. She showed me how to mend the puncture, and then we had our supper. Dot didn't put on her records at all.

It was after eight o' clock, and I was really getting worried by now. Then, at last, I heard his car.

Dot stood up, and went to the window. She smiled, really smiled. 'It's yir darkie, hen,' she said, and opened the back door wide – signalling to Mr Smith to go round.

He had a half-bottle in his hand when he came in, and Dot thanked him for coming by, and for his generosity.

'That's one thing I've learned, Dot,' he said, laughing. 'You can't visit anyone in the Highlands without a wee dram in your pocket. Very civilised, too,' he added.

'I dunno about civilised, son,' Dot answered, 'but it's the way things're done. Yir a quick learner.'

Mr Smith shook my hand again. 'Ellie, how are you?'

'Fine, thank you.' I stared and stared at him, but there wasn't the first clue in his face.

Dot offered Mr Smith a seat, and went through to the kitchen for another glass.

'Thank you,' I whispered. 'Mr Starling phoned twice. He's coming next week.'

'Yes, Dot, very good. Very interesting,' Mr Smith called. Dot had been asking him if he'd had a good trip. He raised a finger to his big lips, and pulled a note from his pocket. I grabbed it just as Dot came back.

They toasted each other, and I could feel the note burning in my hand.

'Now then, Gerry,' Dot said. 'I canna offer you Connie Francis, but I'll no miss the opportunity to educate you about Lady Day. Would you be agreeable?'

Mr Smith laughed. 'Education's a wonderful thing, Dot. I wouldn't be here without it.'

'You've eaten, have you?' Dot asked, remembering her manners. It would be useless if he hadn't. The macaroni was gone, and it hadn't been very good anyway.

'The best soup I ever tasted,' he answered, shaking his head with delight at the memory of it.

'Can I take a look down the road for Hooligan?' I asked.

Dot was just placing the arm on a record. She turned. 'You're welcome to sit by us, Ellie.' It was more of a question than an invitation.

'I . . . I won't be long . . . just down the lane and back.'

She shrugged. I jumped off the chair, and tried not to run from them. As soon as I got round the house, though, I ran past the lilacs and down to the grassy bit just before the road. I opened up the note and began to read.

CHAPTER 16

Dear Ellie

I had some idea that talking with you on my return may prove difficult, so I prepared this letter in advance. I should warn you, however, that I do not intend to leave Inchbrae without informing your grandmother of my actions thus far.

My heart sank. He was probably telling Dot the whole story right now. It was more than I could bear. I read on:

Early on Tuesday morning, I called my office and spoke with my editor. Although I have found life to be full of the most amazing coincidences, I was greatly surprised to learn that he had, in fact, grown up just streets away from Mrs Parkin's lodgings on Seaton Road. He assured me the address was still valid and, although he had little hope of finding Mr Starling there (I did not, of course, divulge my interest in the matter) he agreed to investigate further on my behalf.

I placed another trunk call from Lochcarron

around lunchtime, and was even more surprised to find that Mr Starling is now the owner of the property, and apparently has been so for several years.

My editor (a gentleman of worth, and great kindness) had gone to the trouble of ascertaining Mr Starling's telephone number, and, after serious thought on my own part, I decided to call him. I had little difficulty communicating with Mr Starling, and must tell you that he was both excited and intrigued by my questions. He indicated that he would immediately be in touch, and intends to visit Inchbrae very soon. You may already know this, as he does not seem the type to waste time in achieving what he sets out to do.

Now Ellie, the rest is very much up to yourself and Dot. If I have been mistaken in carrying out my promise to you, then I will no doubt be suitably chastised by your grandmother. I do hope, however, that we will, at least, remain friends, and that Mr Starling is indeed your grandfather.

With best wishes from your co-conspirator,

Gerald Smith.

My heart was beating so fast, it felt as if it might steam-roller itself out of my chest. What would Dot say now? Would she refuse to see Mr Starling? Would I meet him? Would she be very cross with me?

I walked back to the house. The back door was open, as usual, and I could hear Dot and Mr Smith talking. As soon as I walked in they stopped, and Dot looked at me for the longest time.

'Well, miss, and what do you have to say for yourself?'

I looked at Mr Smith. His face had closed down, and there was neither frown nor smile on it. He just sat there, holding his hat in his lap. His trouser leg was raised where he'd crossed his legs, and I could see that he wore suspenders. They were brown, but they looked bright against his black leg. I kept looking at them.

Dot sighed. 'Ellie, life's no' like the pictures. You had no right at all to do what you did. Do you know that?'

'But he's my grandad . . . I just wanted . . .'

'Who says?' Dot barked, making me jump. 'It's for me to know who yir grandad is, and *me* to decide who to tell. First of all –' she pointed her finger almost into my chest – 'you never, *never* read what's no' got your name on it. That much I thought you already knew.'

'I do . . . I did . . .'

'Second, it was unfair of you to lumber Gerald wi' a promise he felt obliged to keep.'

'He off—' I was going to say he'd offered, but he hadn't, not really. I couldn't look at him. Dot's eyes were blazing at me, and I couldn't get away from them. I could feel the tears coming, and swallowed hard.

Dot leaned back, the tiniest bit, and sighed again. 'You have no idea, hen, what you've done here. You canna go pushing things to happen. Maybe . . . maybe people don't want them to happen. D'you understand? It's just . . . It's just no' like the pictures.'

The swallowing wasn't helping. A long snotter came out of my nose, and I tried to sniff it back. I closed my eyes, and the tears trickled out too.

Dot grabbed me, and pulled me on her lap. 'Bairn, bairn . . .' she said, wiping my face with her big hankie. 'Not more tears.'

'Will you see him? When he comes? Will you?' I begged. I was so frightened now that Dot would send him away, and I'd never know him, never truly find out if I had a grandad after all.

She lifted my chin. Her eyes were a cloudy blue, not sparkling clear like they'd been when she was pointing at me. 'I don't know, hen. We'll see. We'll wait and see.'

Mr Smith rose. 'Ladies,' he said, 'I must take my leave. I have yet another long road in front of me tomorrow.'

Dot set me down, and rose with him. She put her arm around his waist and walked with him. 'I don't know if you've done me a favour or not, son,' she said, 'but I thank you anyway . . . for helping Lana Turner here.' She was smiling, and I stopped crying. I ran ahead of them to Mr Smith's car, and opened the door for him.

He put his hat on the passenger seat, and turned to shake Dot's hand. She pushed it away, and gave him a hug instead. She looked very small against him, which was surprising as she usually looked quite tall to me. 'Here's another promise for you to keep,' Dot said, pulling away. 'Promise you'll no' be a stranger. Come back and see me.'

'Us,' I added.

Mr Smith smiled at me and took my hand in both of his. 'I certainly intend to,' he replied. 'Take care, Ellie. I hope everything works out for you.'

I expected to hear more from Dot when we went back inside, but she was very quiet. At last she spoke.

'This letter o' mine . . . where did you find it?'

'In my bedside cabinet.'

'In *my* bedside cabinet,' she reminded me.

I swallowed. 'Do you want me to show you?'

She nodded, and I led her upstairs. When I handed her the letter, she glanced at it, and then tore it in pieces without even reading it. Then she went back downstairs and put the pieces in the bucket.

There were so many questions I wanted to ask. I thought they'd better wait till some other time.

We sat down to breakfast next morning. I stared at the porridge, which looked really horrible. 'What about the war, Dot?' I asked, hoping to delay having to eat it.

'The war?'

'You were going to tell me what you did in the war.'

'Oh aye.' Dot thought for a moment. 'I was

working on the Clyde. I couldn't weld, y'know, but there were plenty o' women who could. There was hardly a job left that wasn't getting done by a woman. It was no bother to us.'

Billie Holiday was singing a song called 'Yesterday', which seemed very appropriate. I was looking forward to Dot's story, even before she began. She had a way of making you do that – looking forward.

'What a strange time it was, Ellie. Half o' Clydebank getting blown to pieces, and those women . . . God, they were hardy. It hardly seems real now, looking back.' She blew on her porridge. It was the first time that she'd made it, and it wasn't like the kind Mam made at all. Dot called it 'brose'. It tasted as bad as it looked.

'We worked almost round the clock,' Dot continued. 'We kept feeding the machines, knowing something valuable was coming out the other end . . . bits o' stuff . . . engines . . . turbines, stuff to win the war.'

'It did,' I remarked. I knew we'd won the war. Everyone knew that.

Dot's eyes went wild on me. 'Ellie, we worked ninety-two hours to earn what the men got for forty-eight. Knocking yir pan in for ninety-two hours! Two pound twelve and six. Would y'credit it?'

I didn't have time to divide it out before she continued. 'We went on strike for equal pay, and we got it. Nineteen forty-three. Women standing shoulder to shoulder, kicking our legs up like the chorus line at the Moulin Rouge. The middle o' the war, and we were fighting for *our* freedom too. We'd had enough.' Her eyes settled down a bit.

'It was a beginning, Ellie – a real beginning – for women. It's up to you to keep that fight going . . . to be sure that women don't work for the pittance that men would have us paid. Know your value! Demand it! The day's going to come when we'll *all* have to stand up and be counted. Mark my words. Mark my words!'

I *was* marking her words, in between wondering if Hooligan would enjoy my brose, and where I could keep it until he arrived. Otherwise, I didn't know what I was going to do with it.

Dot lit a cigarette and leaned back in her chair. 'They were the happiest days of my life,' she said, completely changing her tune. I forgot about my brose.

'What? How could they be?'

'Well, maybe not in a way you could understand, Ellie. But the music was better then. We danced every chance we got. Dancing, working, marching . . . full o' life, we were. And Glasgow belonged to everyone. It was the most desperate, the longest, the very best party. My God, an' it was!' Dot was delighted with herself. The war was making her happy.

It was as good an opportunity as any. 'Where was my dad?'

'Behind a desk, thank God. He stood too close to

a ha'penny rocket when he was fourteen, and ended up wi' a burst ear-drum. He was one o' the lucky ones who couldn't fight . . . or die.' I never knew that about Dad. Maybe that's why he didn't like noise, and why he always spoke so quietly. I asked Dot.

'Naw,' she said. 'You'd think a burst ear-drum would make you want to shout . . . so you could hear yirself better. It's just the way he is.' Dot's mood changed again. I put my hand over my plate. I didn't want her getting upset over the brose and my father all in the same sentence. 'It left its mark, just the same.'

She went through to the living room. The first strains of 'Yesterday' hit my ears again. I waited for the bit where Miss Holiday bopped it up. I liked it when she did that. Dot did too. She was holding an imaginary partner when she came back. I left the table and took her arm. If the brose got cold enough, you couldn't be expected to eat it. We danced, and laughed, and Dot put the record on again, just the bopped-up bit. We danced some more. Then we sat down.

'Was Dad happy in the war?' I asked, panting a bit from the dancing.

'No,' she answered, looking troubled. Then she smiled. 'We were all happier when it ended, though. Then of course, he was offered that job in Kilmoran . . . and he couldn't wait to get away from Glasgow.'

'Why?'

She snorted. 'It was that, or come back to

Inchbrae wi' me. It wisna a hard choice for him.' Dot lit a cigarette, and leaned forward on her elbows. 'He met your mam in the shoe-shop.'

I knew that. Dot rose to put on another record. 'Was Dad's father in the war?' I asked.

Dot screeched the needle over the record. It was a fact that when you did that, you ruined it.

'I have no idea,' she answered. Then she went upstairs, and she had a different turban on when she came down. It was blue chiffon. It was the first time I'd seen it.

'I like that colour. It goes with your eyes,' I said.

'I'll change it,' she said, and went back upstairs. For some reason, I thought about Iona Murchison. She could be very nasty in her own way, but at least you knew where you stood with her. You even knew what to expect from Walter Cummings – which was more than you could say for just about anyone in Inchbrae.

I finished my brose. It didn't taste of anything any more. I could smell the sun. It was everywhere. I felt cold.

Dot didn't change her turban. It was just the same when she came back down, but I didn't say anything. I knew I would just get ignored some more, like at the school prize-giving. There were a lot of pupils who didn't get prizes, most of them in fact, but it seemed as though we were just there so the pupils who did get prizes could enjoy being the centre of attention – along with their parents, who were all very proud.

There had been nobody at the last prize day being proud of me, even though I was only one day short of perfect attendance, and Janet had beaten me by just three points for the English prize, and that was quite something when you had a mother moping about the place every day, and a father who didn't even understand what it was that was making her mope.

It was half-past nine. It had been hours and hours since it was today, and it was only half-past nine. I wished I was in the chorus line at the Moulin Rouge. No I didn't. My father would hate it, and Mam would call me vulgar. I would be famous some other way.

'Did you go to Paris ever?' I asked Dot.

'I didn't. No.'

'Well, I'm going there . . . if I decide not to be a film star, I'll be going to Paris.'

'Why Paris exactly?'

'They might not appreciate me in Hollywood.'

'Oh, I think they will.'

'Well, they might not. And if I can't be a famous film star, I'm going to be a writer.'

'Are you good at the English?'

'Yes I am. As a matter of fact, it's what I'm best at.'

'I see. I understand that writers seem to congregate in Paris.'

'They do.'

'Aye, well, certainly if you're very good at the English, it would be a shame to waste it. I believe the writers in Paris even look like film stars.'

'It's what I've heard.'

'Me too,' Dot said. We began discussing this. She said I might have a tenderance for the writing; it might be a real talent.

'I don't think there's such a word . . . tenderance.'

'Oh aye, there is,' Dot said. 'I just made it up.'

'That's what I mean. It's a made-up word.'

'Well, Ellie, this language they call English really isn't at all,' Dot explained. She was polishing the record that she'd already ruined, but you could tell it wouldn't get the scratch out. 'Y'see,' she told me, 'the language is like a big elastic band. It's made up from French, and Latin, and Norse, and Gaelic. And as long as there's someone speaking it, there's someone making up new words . . . pulling it and pushing it and stretching it.' She put the record back in its cover. 'And so there's always room for a new word . . . like tenderance.'

It was a good word. I would try to use it. Just the same, I felt I should prove that I was good at my grammar.

'You shouldn't start a sentence with "and".'

'Why not?' Dot asked. 'And . . . and . . . and . . . As long as you have "and" there's never an end to anything. It's a great word is "and". And would you just be going to Paris for the writing?' she asked, making her point about 'and'.

I knew the answer. I'd often thought about it. It was Plan B. I knew my compositions were good, and I loved making them up. It was maybe even

205

better than the pictures, because you could be anyone you wanted to be in a story.

'Not just *doing* writing. I'll sit in cafés, in the heat of the afternoon, and talk about writing.'

'That might get tiresome, every day. With the heat . . .'

'No, it won't. I'll be wearing a big hat, and sunglasses. There'll be queues of people waiting at the bookshops for my next book. Some might even be sleeping on the pavements.'

'Anything can happen,' Dot agreed. She lit another cigarette.

'And I'll smoke. I'll drink something called Pernod, and smoke cigarettes.'

Dot shook her head. 'No, hen. If you're going to drink, stick to the whisky. Thon foreign writers will admire you for it. They'll be wanting to come back to your "pension" and be favoured with it – the real whisky. Aye, I believe that your friends would appreciate that.

'The smoking, now . . .' She sucked in her breath. 'Well, I wouldn't advise it, but you'll know if it's not for you. I'm sure you'll give it a try anyway.'

I already had. I thought I was going to die, right there behind the bike-sheds, and Janet had had to push my bike home, as well as her own. She'd tried it too, but she quite liked it. I thought about everything Dot had said, and decided to take her advice. I would also get a good brassière.

'It'll be more to your liking, being a writer . . . in

Paris,' Dot finished. 'Hollywood's getting awful full of trash.'

I agreed. There had been a lot of 'X' films lately. It would be more acceptable to be a writer. It had always been my second ambition, so it wasn't hard to move it up to first. There was only one problem.

'I've told quite a few people now ... that I'm going to be a film star.'

'I wouldn't worry about that,' Dot said. 'A few folk here in Inchbrae ...' She dismissed it with a shrug. 'Besides, they'll be just as proud to know they've had a famous writer in their midst.'

This made sense. I would still be famous. They wouldn't mind at all.

Dot tried to iron my dresses, but she didn't make a very good job of them. There were still a lot of creases left, and she missed some bits altogether. She said it was because she wasn't used to dresses, but the pillow-slips weren't much better. I suggested that maybe the iron would be easier to use if she got the stuck-on black bits off the bottom. She said there was more to life than ironing.

I could hardly believe my eyes when I saw Joseph cycling up Dot's lane.

'What're you here for?' I asked.

He could just as easily have leaned his bike against the wall, but he threw it on the ground instead. 'Did you get any stuff yet?'

I'd forgotten about the tent. 'I don't want to make a tent, Joseph. I told you that already.'

'You said you would!' he accused me.

'I did not!' How could he even think that I had.

'You're useless!' he raged. 'I thought you'd have got *some* stuff by now.'

'Who's wanting a tent?' Dot asked. She'd been in her shed looking for a hammer. She'd noticed that one of the palings behind the hedge was loose when she'd taken in the washing yesterday, and had assured me that it wouldn't be loose for long. Joe looked at the hammer in Dot's hand.

'No-one,' he answered, looking quite fearful.

'I've got an old tarpauleon here, if it's any good to you,' Dot offered. 'It's seen better days though, so don't expect it to keep out the rain.' She looked up. 'If we ever get any.'

I thought about battering her to death with the hammer.

'Great! Ta,' Joe said, nodding with delight.

'Come and get it then,' Dot said, going back inside the shed.

Joe poked me. 'You go,' he whispered.

I sighed, and began to follow Dot. Then I stopped. Why should I? It wasn't me who wanted it. It wasn't me who was scared of Dot.

'If you want it, you get it,' I told him. He glared at me, but I was determined not to give in. He edged towards the shed. Dot must have given up on us. She reappeared with the tarpaulin.

'D'yis want it or not?' she demanded. Joe almost grabbed it from her, but it must have been heavier than it looked, and he dropped it. Dot helped him fold it up again.

'Where's this tent going to be?' she asked.

'At the river,' Joe replied.

Dot straightened. 'Only if you'll look after each other,' she warned. 'I don't want to be fishing yis out o' the water, wi' a mooth full of seaweed.'

Joe looked quite triumphant. He was beaming. 'Tell her she has to come then,' he said, looking at me.

'I'll do no such thing,' Dot said. 'She can go if she wants to go. But if she doesna, you better no' let me catch you bullying her into it.' The hammer was very close to Joe's skull.

'I'll go with him,' I said. 'I don't mind.' At least we hadn't had to get stuff from the dump.

'Right-oh,' Dot said, and turned to Joe again. 'Does yir father know where y'are?'

Joe nodded. 'I said I'd be back for my supper.'

'What about yir dinner? It's no'even twelve o'clock.'

'I've got food for us, for when we get the tent built.' He picked up his bike, and leaned it against the shed. Carefully, he balanced the tarpaulin across the bar of his bike (maybe *that's* what bars were for), and opened his saddle-bag. There were two brown paper bags, but he didn't offer to show Dot what was in them. There were also some sandwiches inside a loaf wrapper.

Dot gave it a quick glance. 'What's in yir pieces?'

'Spam and tomato.' I liked spam. That was OK.

'Off yis go then,' Dot said. 'Be careful, mind.'

'I've got things to tell you,' I called to Joe as we cycled down the lane.

He raced ahead. 'Prob'ly girl's rubbish,' he said.

I had a good mind not to tell him anything then.

CHAPTER 17

We found the perfect spot for the tent right off. It was a natural dip between two of the dunes, and Joe said we would be hidden from intruders, although I didn't agree. I didn't think it would be at all hard to see the tent. I thought about the gypsies, and decided to keep quiet. If we were going to have intruders, I wanted to be able to see them.

It took ages and ages to put up the tent. We had to hunt all over to find the right kind of sticks to hold it up, and then it kept collapsing because we couldn't anchor them properly. Joseph was giving me orders, and I refused to do some of them, so we kept falling out. But in between, we got on pretty well.

We had to eat before we finished putting the tent up. It was hard work, and we were too hungry to wait. Joe had biscuits in one of the bags (including some chocolate digestives which had stuck together), and two bananas and four penny dainties in the other. We decided to keep the sandwiches for when we were finished. We wanted to eat them inside the tent, as a reward.

It didn't take us long to realise that we had nothing to drink. I knew Joseph was very annoyed with himself for having forgotten about that, but he still managed to make it seem like my fault.

'You could've brought *something*!'

'If it wasn't for me, we wouldn't have a tent,' I reminded him.

'It was nothing to do with you. It was yir gran that gave us the tent.' We argued back and forth, but it only made us thirstier. I offered to cycle back to Dot's for lemonade, if Joe would carry on trying to get the tent up.

'Deal!' he agreed.

Dot said I would have to go in the sink when she saw me, but she added that it wouldn't be an adventure if you didn't get dirty. I hadn't thought of it that way – as an adventure – but that's what it was. She was perfectly right, as usual. She gave me a bottle of ginger beer (she'd thought she had some tangerine left, but it was like the peaches; it was gone), and said she'd be cycling into Inchbrae for some messages a bit later on. She seemed unhappy with having to do that, but her press was getting quite empty.

I offered her some of my pocket-money to pay for the messages. I was an extra mouth to feed, after all. She ruffled my hair, and said she didn't need the money; she just didn't feel like going into Inchbrae.

Joseph had his shirt off when I got back. He was wearing his braces over his bare chest, which looked a bit daft, but he was quite a thin boy, so I supposed he needed them to hold his trousers up. I didn't mention it, in case it embarrassed him.

The funny thing was, when we finally got to sit inside the tent, it smelled more like the river than it did when we were outside. The sandwiches were a bit soggy from the tomatoes soaking through, but they still tasted great. I told Joe about Mrs Fishbein while we ate.

'She gave me that four dainties for tuppence today,' Joe said. 'She wasn't crying, though. I've never seen her crying.' He thought about it. 'I'm glad. I would hate that.'

'Did you enjoy the pictures?' I asked.

'It was boring,' he replied. He chewed on his piece.

'I.B.' he shouted, nearly making me jump.

It couldn't have been more obvious. 'Ingrid Bergman,' I answered. 'That was a stupid one.'

'Was not. How did y'know?'

'Rita told me what was on. I know Ingrid Bergman does the Gladys Aylward part.'

'Trust her!' he retorted. He never had anything nice to say about Rita.

'Your dad's handsome.'

'He is not,' Joe said. He sneered the words. He was good at sneering, but I decided to chance telling him.

'I'm not going to Hollywood now. Life's not like the pictures.'

'Never thought you were,' he answered, in

between mouthfuls. At least he was polite enough not to speak with his mouth full.

'I'm going to Paris instead.' Once he understood this, I would tell him about Mr Starling, and how I'd tracked him down. Maybe I would write detective books, like Agatha Christie. She was as famous as Enid Blyton, and probably richer, as grown-ups could afford to pay more for books than children.

'Shite!' I looked up. Joe had dropped a slice of tomato on the ground. He hunted around until he found it, and then he ate it.

'What's to see in Paris?' he asked.

'I'm not going to *see* it. I'm going to live there – as a famous writer.'

It was quite dark in the tent, but I could feel him staring at me. 'You're nuts,' he said, at last. 'That's what comes from staying wi' that creepy wifie.'

He finished his piece. He was about to dismiss the whole idea of me being a famous writer. I knew Dot was on his mind, otherwise he wouldn't have mentioned her, and I knew it would be easy to scare him – here in the dark. I couldn't help it. I leaned right into his face and screamed.

He screamed too and flew backwards, almost bringing the tent down around us. Then he raced outside on his hands and knees. I laughed and laughed. I was still laughing when I crawled out beside him.

He was the most furious I'd ever seen anyone. There were slavers all down his chin where he'd choked on the last bit of his piece, and his knees

214

were scratched and covered in grass stains. It made me laugh even more when I saw the state of him.

'I'll batter you for that,' he threatened, lifting his fist. I had to run all the way to the shore to escape, but by the time he'd caught up with me I could tell he'd decided against hitting me. He started chasing me again, and we ran all over the shore. We ended up both of us laughing, which was good fun. I was glad he wasn't furious with me any more.

He swore he'd get me back, but he didn't mean it.

We covered the tent with branches and sticks before we left. I thought it looked more obvious like that, but Joe was fair pleased with it and said I didn't know what I was talking about. When we reached the road, he offered to walk back to Dot's with me, but I was very used to the road now, and told him I'd manage fine by myself. He pedalled off towards Inchbrae. When he was quite a way away, he turned and waved. I waved back. I'd been watching him. Maybe he'd felt me looking after him.

We must have missed Dot by seconds. She was just putting her bike in the shed when I got to the house. The back door was open, and there were lots of bags on the sink. I would have liked to have had a big basket like Dot's on my bike at home, but I had to admit they were out of fashion.

Dot didn't even bother putting her messages away before she got herself a dram. She seemed very on edge, and wasn't really listening when I told her about my adventure, and how I'd frightened Joseph. I left out the bit about him calling her a 'creepy wifie'. I had to touch her arm a couple of times to get her attention.

'Will I put your messages away?' I asked, when I'd finished my story. She just shook her head.

'Are you no' well?' I was beginning to get worried. She'd had three drams now, which was an awful lot to drink so quickly. Finally, she looked at me. She was going to tell me something bad. I knew it in her face. I didn't want her to speak. I wanted to put my hand over her mouth so she couldn't say it.

'I'm phoning your father tomorrow, Ellie. It'll be better for everyone if you could get home this weekend.'

It wasn't something bad at all. It was the best thing she could have told me – except I wanted to wait now, just until I could meet Mr Starling.

'Dad won't be there, Dot. He'll be at work, but we can phone Mam. She's *bound* to be better by now, and we can explain that I can come home next week after . . .'

'No.' Her voice was very definite. 'I have your father's number at his office. I'll speak to him myself.'

'You can't. You can't phone him at work,' I protested. She would ruin it all. She'd make Dad cross as anything, and I'd never get home early.

She started putting the messages away. 'Don't worry about upsetting your father, Ellie. I'm his mother. I'm entitled to talk to him when the need arises.'

'What need? Why can't you talk to Mam?' I wasn't getting through to her and it was very, very important that she didn't phone my dad's work.

'Please don't phone Dad. Please don't.'

She stepped back from the press, and knelt down so she was looking right at me. It was just like the day I'd arrived, the same smells even. It seemed like such a long time – and like no time at all.

'You want to go home, don't you?' she asked.

I nodded.

'Well then, let's see to it that you do. I promise you everything'll be fine. I promise.' I knew Dot kept her promises, but I wasn't in such a hurry now. What difference would a few days make? She hugged me for a long time, and I thought I felt something wet on my neck, but by the time she let me go, I couldn't feel it any more.

While I was getting washed, Dot heated some tomato soup. We had cheese and toast with it, and then we had peaches and thick cream, not Carnation. It was a super supper. She smiled when I said that, but she didn't eat hardly anything herself.

I think she played all of her records that night. I could hear them, even from bed. Then she seemed to settle on just one. I fell asleep listening to Miss Holiday singing 'Somebody's On My Mind', over and over.

Mrs Alexander was looking through the *School*

Friend with me. I was too het-up to pay much attention, but I didn't want to end up causing more problems for everyone. I knew Mrs Alexander was trying to keep my mind off Dot. We could hear her arguing with my father, and I was really worried by now. Dot had promised she would let me talk to him, but I was so afraid that he would be angry with me, that I didn't think I wanted to any more.

A lady came into the shop with a parcel, and Mrs Alexander had to go into the post office bit. I was sitting on her chair, behind the counter, when I heard a door slamming. Then Dot yanked open the door behind Mrs Alexander, and called me over.

'Your father wants a word with you, Ellie.' She was trying to smile, but she had that fierce scary look on her face.

I just sat there, shaking my head. My feet didn't touch the floor, and I couldn't get down. I didn't want to talk to Dad. I wanted Mam to be there.

'C'mon, Ellie,' Dot urged. 'We canna be tying up Jessie's phone. Your da's waiting.'

Dad was waiting ... I managed to get off the chair, and squeezed past Mrs Alexander. The lady with the parcel watched me. Then she spoke to Dot.

'Your Adam, is it? On the phone?'

'An' if it is?' Dot said. She fixed the lady with one of her looks.

'Oh, n.n.nothing,' the lady stammered. 'How are you keeping anyway, Dot?'

'Fair to hellish,' she answered, and pulled me through by the arm. 'We'll no' be much longer,

Jessie,' she said, and closed the post office door behind us.

We went down the hall to Mrs Alexander's living room. It was quite small, but everything was very clean and tidy. Even being worried, you couldn't help noticing it. The phone looked very big and black on the sideboard. There was a white lace doily beneath it, and Dot had curled one of the corners where she'd laid down the receiver. I straightened it for Mrs Alexander.

It only took a second to do that, but Dot lifted the receiver and pushed it at me as though I'd taken for ever. I swallowed, and it hurt. I thought I was probably getting a cold. That would certainly account for my sore throat, which hadn't been sore until just now. It was very sore.

'Hello?'

'Hello, Eleanor. How are you?'

'Fine, thank you. How are you?' It wasn't like talking to him at all. Even his voice sounded different. He didn't sound angry though. I tried to remember what his real voice sounded like, but I couldn't.

'I'm . . . fine,' Dad answered. 'Are you enjoying being with your grandmother?'

It caught me a bit by surprise. She was just . . . Dot. I looked across at her. She was blowing her smoke out of Mrs Alexander's window, so it wouldn't collect in the room, like it did at home. That was nice of her. 'Aye, I am.'

'Good. You won't mind staying another week?'

My heart sank. I knew he was going to say it, but it made you want to cry when you heard the words.

'Mam's no' any better then?'

There was a silence.

'Are you asking if your mother's feeling better?' He sounded puzzled.

'Aye,' I answered. I was puzzled too.

I could hear the criticism in his voice. 'You're picking up that Inchbrae dialect, Eleanor. And you're talking much more quickly than you used to . . .'

'Oh . . . I . . . How is Mam?'

'Actually, she's much improved. But I think another week could make all the difference. I've managed to move my holidays up. Mr Taylor's retiring soon, so he was kind enough to exchange dates with me. I'll be on holiday from next Friday evening, and I thought it would be nice if you could come home then . . . when your mother's completely . . . feeling better . . . and I could be here with you both.'

It took my breath away. Dad had never, ever changed his holidays. It crossed my mind that maybe Mam wasn't getting better at all. Maybe she was getting worse, and Dad *had* to be at home.

'You're sure . . . about Mam?'

'Absolutely. She misses you, of course, as I do.'

'You miss me?'

'Yes, Eleanor, surely you know that.' There was the faintest hint of annoyance, but nothing like the way he could be *really* annoyed. 'The house seems

220

rather . . . large without you,' he added. I knew he was smiling when he said it. It was far, far better than getting the English prize.

'I'm going to be a writer.'

Silence.

'Dad? Are you there?'

'Yes . . . Yes . . . You're going to be a writer?'

'Aye, Dad. I was going to be a film star, but I'm not now. I'm going to be a writer instead.'

'Good. Well . . . You've always been good at composition.'

'I nearly got the English prize, Dad. There was just three points in it.'

'Were. There *were* only three points in it. Well, perhaps next year. I'm sure you could win a prize, with a little extra effort . . .'

'Absolutely.' I could. I would. Perfect attendance, too. Both of them!

'I need to go, Ellie. I'm afraid the Civil Service waits for no man. We'll look forward to seeing you soon. Goodbye, dear.'

'Bye, Dad. Tell Mam I miss her too. Tell her . . .' The phone clicked off. I put the receiver down.

I turned to tell Dot the good news. Then it hit me.

'He called me Ellie,' I told her. My chest was full of happiness. I had to take a deep breath.

Dot nipped her cigarette, and stuck it behind her ear. Her new turban sizzled, and a large hole appeared. She didn't even notice.

CHAPTER 18

Dot went down to see Rita, and I crossed over to Mr Conroy's. There was fresh sawdust on the floor. I breathed it in. He was serving two customers at once, but he took the time to give me a lovely smile. He had long dimples. Joseph was scrubbing the big wooden table at the end of the counter, but he didn't seem to be putting much effort into it. Joseph didn't have dimples.

'I'm going home,' I told him.

'Good,' he answered. He was surly again. He moved the brush back and forth. It was very half-hearted.

'It's better if you go in circles,' I suggested.

Mr Conroy glanced at us. 'Don't let me have to come over there, Joseph.'

Joe narrowed his eyes at me, but I was too happy to be bothered by it.

'I'm going home next weekend, probably.'

Joe looked up. 'That's when y'were going anyway. Everyone knows that.'

He was determined to annoy me, but I wouldn't let him.

'It wasn't definite. It is now.'

The customers left, and Mr Conroy came over to the table. He stood there examining it, with his hands on his hips. He was wearing a clean white shirt and overall. He was very good at his washing, for a man.

'It would be a grand thing, Joseph, if you could do it right the first time. Then you wouldn't have to be doing it again.'

'It *is* right, an' I'm no' doing it again.'

Mr Conroy grabbed the scrubbing brush from Joseph so quickly that he made us both jump. He waved it in Joe's face.

'The next time . . . the very next time . . . you take that tone with me, I'll be through you like a short cut. D'you understand?' He threw the brush down on the table, just as another customer came in.

'Mrs Girvan, isn't it yourself that's looking as fresh as a windswept meadow? And isn't it a nice bit o' fillet I've got tucked away for you. Only the best – for the best.'

Mrs Girvan giggled. She was not a bonny woman.

'Bastard,' Joe said, but very quietly.

'Are you coming to the tent?' I asked.

Joe brightened. 'Aye. When I'm finished.'

'When will that be?

Mrs Girvan had left. Joe shrugged.

'When can Joseph come out?' I asked Mr Conroy.

'And what would you want to be spending time with an aggravating boy like that for?' he said.

'We're . . . friends,' I answered.

223

'We are not,' Joseph said. He didn't want to be accused of being friends with a girl. I understood that, so I wasn't hurt.

'Well, friends or no', Joseph's needed here today. Friday's a busy day for us, isn't it, Joe?'

Joe moved the brush again. He didn't answer.

'Isn't it, Joe?' Mr Conroy said again.

Joe nodded. 'I'll see you later,' he said. He sounded depressed.

I walked back out into the sunshine. I was so grateful for having a mam and dad who missed me, and soon I'd have a grandad too. I was much better off than Joe.

Hooligan was lying in front of the grocer's, in the sun. He lifted his head when he heard me, and then lowered it again. It seemed like God was being especially good to me today. Maybe He was just catching up on things. Dad often said that he liked to catch up with things on Fridays. I imagined him in his office, even though I'd never been there; catching up on things before his holidays. He would be very busy.

I sat down on the pavement beside Hooligan. Dot was still in Rita's shop, and I could see her stamping about the place. Rita must have put Dot in a bad temper. Rita was a lot like Joseph. I'd noticed that before.

Hooligan lifted his back paw and my heart nearly stopped. The inside of his leg had a deep gash on it, and there was dried blood all over it. The cut had closed over, but his fur was gone, and the skin was purple and bruised. I put my hand under it, and lifted it very carefully. He looked at me and smiled. He was so brave.

I didn't want to go for Dot and leave him on his own. I didn't know what to do. I thought for a moment: Mr Fishbein's small counter was close to the window. I reached up and knocked. Nothing happened. I knocked again.

The shop door opened. Mrs Fishbein came out, then Mr Fishbein appeared behind her.

'Hooligan's hurt.'

Mrs Fishbein was right beside me. She sat down on the pavement and examined his leg. 'Mein Gott. Ist bad, ja.'

Mr Fishbein leaned closer. 'Ach, healing it is. A brave heart he has, eh? Y'canna beat the likes o' him, eh?'

I agreed.

'Bring me the box, Greta,' he said.

Mrs Fishbein ran inside, and came back with a white first aid box with a red cross on the lid. I hoped it wouldn't remind her of the war. In no time Mr Fishbein had Hooligan's wound cleaned and dressed with a new bandage. Then he rose and went back inside, and Mrs Fishbein followed.

Hooligan seemed to know it was safe to stand. He shook himself, and circled a couple of times, testing his leg. He tried to bite at the bandage, but when I explained to him that he needed to keep it on for a while, he gave up.

Mrs Fishbein returned, holding two sugar

225

dummies, a yellow one and a red one.

'Ist you to pick,' she said, holding them out to me. 'Your dog likes any colour, him.' MY dog!

I gave Hooligan the red one. It got sticky when the sugar melted, but he had a great time eating it. His lips were up over his teeth, trying to get the last of it from the roof of his mouth. Then I gave him mine too. He deserved it.

Mrs Fishbein was holding her sides, she was laughing so much at all his expressions. She said that Abel, her murdered son, would have loved a dog like Hooligan. You could understand every word she said. If Joseph had been allowed out, it would have been a perfect day.

Dot said it wouldn't be a good idea for Hooligan to follow us home. He would try to beat us back to the house, he couldn't help it, and it would undo all Mr Fishbein's good work. I didn't want to leave him there, but Dot said he was very used to taking care of himself, and it was a pity there wasn't more around like him. I wished she was in a better mood.

Hooligan limped off back to the dump – or wherever it was that he went – and he seemed to understand that I wasn't forsaking him. He turned at the corner and looked back at me.

I told Dot that Joe wasn't allowed out, and we set off on our bikes. We hadn't gone into the Jacobite at all, and it was very quiet when we passed the door. Dot said it was a lot of nonsense having to go in there every time you came into town. Nobody should feel that committed, she said.

We didn't even stop at the river.

'Will I be going home on the bus?'

'Aye. I think there's one on Saturday mornings. I'll find out.'

'Friday. I'm going home next Friday.'

Dot shook her head. She was hammering away at the palings. She'd already sorted the one that was loose, so I don't know why she felt she had to do them all.

'No. 'Fraid not. Yir da doesn't really start his holidays till Saturday. You'll go back then.'

It was only one more night.

'Do you know what time the bus leaves?'

Dot whirled. 'I told you . . . I'll find out!'

Rita had put Dot all wrong. I sighed.

'Ellie' Dot called. I was almost at the back door. 'Listen, hen, why don't you get yir clean clothes together? We'll be going over to Rita's shortly for our baths. You'll like her house . . . it's no' a bit like mine.'

I'd forgotten about our baths. Dot was smiling, though, so she must have decided to forgive Rita. She was quite a forgiving person.

The walk to Rita's house didn't take long. We had towels and everything, and Dot had her Lifebuoy soap in her sponge-bag, but she said Rita would let me use her Imperial Leather if I asked. I would. I loved the shape of it; it was so different.

Rita's house was very bright inside. She had a lot of contemporary furniture, except for her china cabinet, which was just like the one we had at home. She had Formica chairs in her kitchen, yellow, to match her table. The house was very tidy. Dot was right; it was nothing like hers, which was sort of cosy once you got used to it. Our house wasn't cosy, our house at home. It was clean, though.

Mr Conroy was sitting at the fire. It was an electric fire, with real-looking coal in it. I'd never seen one like that, and thought it must have been very expensive. We had an electric fire at home that we put on the landing in the winter, but it was completely different to Rita's. It wasn't at all pretty, and Dad complained at how much electricity it took to run it. Mam always turned off the top bar before Dad came home, even when it was very cold.

Mr Conroy stood up when we came in. 'Rita,' he called.

She came through from the kitchen, wearing a turquoise dress and bolero. The dress had a huge skirt, and she had black patent shoes and a black patent handbag. I noticed the way Mr Conroy looked at her. I could imagine his butcher's hands on her. It made me shiver.

'Are you cold, Ellie?' Rita asked.

'No. I'm not at all, thank you.'

'Switch the fire on if you like. It's too hot for me, but I wouldn't want you getting a chill.'

Dot walked through to the kitchen. 'It's eighty degrees. Who's going to get a chill?'

'We're going over to Jim and Elsie's for dinner. She found a good recipe for chicken in the *Woman's Realm*. I hope it's better than her last effort – mint lamb. It gave me the boke.'

Mr Conroy crossed his fingers and laughed.

'Where's Joseph?' I asked.

Rita pursed her lips at me. 'Jessie's baby-sitting.'

Joseph must have hated that. Not Mrs Alexander; I knew he liked her, but he was all alone again. I was glad we hadn't gone to the tent, because I would have been talking about finding my grandad and going home, and been all happy, and he would have been more miserable than ever.

'Can he play tomorrow?' I asked Mr Conroy.

'Och, Saturday's worse than . . .'

Rita slapped Mr Conroy with her handbag. He ducked, and laughed again. They were a handsome couple.

'Aye,' she answered. 'I'll see to it, Ellie.'

She leaned into the kitchen doorway. Dot was sitting at the table by herself, smoking. 'Why don't yis stay the night? The bairn shouldn't be trailed home with her hair wet.'

'I'll see,' Dot answered.

Rita took my hand, and led me through to her bathroom. It was like something from MGM. All her pipes were boxed in, and she had matching towels over the bath. There were two bottles of bubble bath, and a saucer with three Imperial Leather soaps. Only one was used.

'Just take what you want,' she said, pointing to the soap and the bubble bath. She reached into her cabinet. 'Don't let her use that soap on your hair,' she added, holding out a blue sachet. 'This has real French perfume in it.' It was called Supersoft, and it was fourpence a sachet. I knew because Janet had used it for the prize-giving. I couldn't wait to try it.

'And be sure to take your bath before Dot. I don't know what state she gets herself into, but it takes a hell of a lot of Vim to get that bath clean after her.'

Dot didn't mind me taking my bath first. She brought me a Pyrex jug from the kitchen to rinse my hair, but I didn't rinse it too much as I wanted the French perfume to stay in it. It felt a bit sticky when it dried.

I hadn't brought my pyjamas with me, but Dot said my clean vest and knickers were good enough. She tucked me into one of the single beds in Rita's spare room. They both had apple-green candlewick bedspreads that smelled new, but Dot said Rita had always had them. It was a beautiful room, like staying in a hotel, which I'd never done, but I knew it would be just like this.

I don't know when Mrs Bryce arrived. I didn't hear a car or anything; just her voice. Dot had left my door open. I hadn't asked her to do that, but she seemed to understand that I might prefer it, being in a strange house. I had been just about to go to the toilet, but when I heard Mrs Bryce mention my father it went away.

'How can you say that about Adam? Your own son!'

CHAPTER 19

'My own son or not, it's true, Lil. He gives my arse the hiccup. That bairn's starved for attention.'

'Starved for attention.' It was me Dot was talking about. How could she say that? Dad had called me Ellie. He said the house was large without me. He said . . .

'And telling me it's my *duty* to look after her! When all this time he wouldn't let me near her . . .'

'That's not true, Dot. You had every opportunity to go down there and see them. Did he keep you away? He did not.'

'And how was I supposed to get there? He's the one wi' the car. Anyway, it's no' me that needs *his* company.'

'Och, Dot. Can y'no' see that he has his pride? He had no idea that thon woman would be such a burden to him . . .'

'Burden, my arse. It's exactly what he wanted – a woman to control, and a bairn too. He never could control me!'

'Could anyone?' Lil sighed. 'They could not.'

Mam wasn't a burden. She wasn't! I kicked off

the covers. I would tell Dot, right now. I looked for my socks. Mam always said not to walk about in your bare feet; you could catch things. *That's* how smart Mam was!

'Is it the change that's on her?' Mrs Bryce asked.

Mam was changing. I decided to wait and find out what it was she was changing into.

'No, it's not. She's no' even forty.'

'Well, look at Annie Macpherson. She was only thirty-nine when it started on her,' Mrs Bryce retorted.

'Far too young! Look where it put her,' Dot exclaimed. 'Ended up in the big hoose, clawing at the walls.'

'That's no' what I heard, Dot. They said it wasna the change; it was thon man of hers, knocking her to the floor near enough every night. That wid put anyone off their heid!'

'Who knows?' Dot said. 'I canna say the change put me up nor down. I don't know what all the fuss is about. Rita says they're even writing about it in magazines now. Mind, that's Rita for you.'

'Am I hearing right?' Mrs Bryce sounded incredulous. 'Who spent months ... *years*, prowling around the place looking for a neck to chew? Was it me? It was not. It was you, Dorothy Fairbairn, and many a poor soul's lucky to be alive to talk on it.'

Dot laughed, far too loud. If I'd been sleeping, she would have wakened me, but she wouldn't have cared.

'Aye, well, maybe it put me wrong for a day or two . . . But that's all, mind! Anyway, what – and who – brought you here the night? Was the bar no' busy?'

'Busy enough,' Mrs Bryce answered. 'Aly Cameron gave me a lift out. He wanted to get home early.' She lowered her voice, and I had to strain to hear. Not for long.

'Talk to me? What did y'have to talk to me about?' Dot's voice was as loud as ever.

I heard the clink of glasses. 'Will y'have one?' she asked. I could hear her moving about. Mrs Bryce was trying to talk, but Dot kept interrupting her. I had to screw my eyes up to make out who was saying what. Somehow that always helped your ears to listen.

'Y'know I never touch the cratur, Dot. Now don't be pouring . . .'

'Yir no' going to die of addiction for one.'

'I said no! D'you listen? Do you *ever* listen . . . ?'

'You used to take a dram . . . when we were . . .'

'Years ago. Maybe once in a . . .'

'For God's sake, drink it!'

Silence. Dot had won.

'I'd forgotten. It's no' that bad . . . A droppie lemonade maybe . . . just to sweeten it,' Mrs Bryce said.

Movement. The scoosh of a bottle opening.

'Aye, that's better.' More silence. 'Anyway, I wanted to talk to you about . . . No Dot, now, the one was fine. Och, what's the use . . . ?'

234

'Well . . . ?' It was Dot. Her voice was rough, and I knew she was smoking.

'About Johnny, Dot. Are you going to tell him?'

'Tell him what?' It was cold, angry, like when the teacher said to you, 'Is that the best you can do, *Miss* Fairbairn?' even when you were doing your best. It was that kind of voice.

'You know what, Dot. You *know*!'

'And what is it you think *you* know, Lilian?'

'I know it was Johnny, Dot. I always knew that.'

'You don't know any such thing. I thought you might be thinking that, but . . .'

'Don't, Dot. What difference does it make now? We've always been friends, haven't we? It never came between us . . .'

Dot coughed. Then she coughed again. They weren't real coughs.

'Dot.' Mrs Bryce's voice was soft now, but quite clear. 'Look, who else could it've been, in a wee place like this . . . ?'

'You were broken-hearted when he ran off . . .'

'I was. But Mam and Dad were here for me then. You had no-one . . . and a bairn on the way. Everyone talking about you . . . yir Aunt Mary telling the world and its neighbour, and folks feeling sorry for you in the one breath, and criticising you in the other.'

'I never cared what any bugger said about me.'

'You cared then, Dot. You just wouldn't admit it. And I was the last one who wanted to hear it from you, that it was . . . his.'

'Jesus, Lil. All these years . . .'

'He was so nice on the phone, Dot. He said he'd never meant to hurt me like that, and how glad he was I had Eckie. We spoke for ages. He got married to that woman he was in digs with. She was a widow, apparently, and a bit older than Johnny. Poor soul died herself from consumption a few years back.

'He was full of questions . . . about you . . . and Ellie. I don't know what Mr Smith had told him, or how Ellie even knew about Johnny. What have you been telling the bairn, Dot?'

'Nothing,' Dot retorted. 'Not a damn thing.'

'Then how?'

The bottle scooshed again, and I knew Dot was pouring Mrs Bryce another dram. I hoped Mrs Bryce was paying attention. I was getting sleepy with paying attention; I wished one of them would finish a sentence.

'Och, don't tell me then,' Mrs Bryce said. She didn't seem to mind. Then she giggled! 'It was a foolish notion, to think Johnny and me wid get married. D'you remember, Dot? Me in a world of my own with 'Roses of Picardy' and reading out Dodo's poems. And you and him, flinging yirsels aboot to "Tiger Rag".

'I think I always knew that he had his eye on you. I just didn't expect him to run off like he did . . .' Mrs Bryce took a deep sigh. 'They were happy days just the same, weren't they? Weren't they, Dot?'

They both laughed then, but not loudly. It was happy and sad at the same time. You often heard grown-ups laughing like that.

'God, not "Tiger Rag"!' It was Rita. She must have just come in, though I hadn't heard the door. 'I'm putting on Elvis, before the two of you ... You're *drunk*!' Rita sounded astonished.

Dot and Mrs Bryce laughed. 'Are we drunk?' Mrs Bryce asked.

'We are!' It was Dot and Mrs Bryce together.

'The likes o' Elvis,' Mrs Bryce said. 'Wiggling himself all over the place like that. His mother must be ashamed.'

'I wouldn't mind him wiggling all over me,' Rita answered.

'God forgive you,' Mrs Bryce said. Then the three of them were laughing, and it sounded really stupid. The last thing I remembered was Elvis singing 'A Fool Such As I'. I was too tired to go to the bathroom.

Dot wasn't well the next morning. I didn't like to say it, but I think she was still drunk. Rita offered to drive us home, but Dot said she'd spew if she had to get in the car with her. We walked, and Dot missed her footing more than once. When we got back to the house, she lay down on the living-room floor. She said she was glad to be home, and she'd be right as rain by supper-time.

We hadn't had any breakfast. Rita had made some toast, but she forgot about it, and her grill-pan nearly went on fire. She started getting ready for work, then changed her mind.

'T'hell,' she said. '*I'm* the boss, and I'm no' opening today.' She went back to bed. I'd asked her if Joseph would be coming over, and she said she couldn't care less.

I thought Dot might feel better if she ate something. I was hungry, so I made us both some beans on toast. I would have liked some chips, but Mam wouldn't let me make them without supervision, and Dot said she couldn't supervise a louse on a bald heid. I didn't know what that meant, except that I wasn't getting chips. When I brought Dot's plate through, she crawled over to the lino, and put her face down against a cold bit. She said to take it away immediately. I'd learned to be forgiving. I ate hers too.

I wondered if I should cycle into town for Joe. I thought it would be best if I inspected the tent first, as Joseph would be very disappointed if all our good work had come to naught. (I loved that expression. I told Janet that all my hard work for the English prize had come to naught, but she said I was getting carried away with myself.)

I was just at the bottom of the lane when Mr Bryce came rushing off the road. Our bicycles nearly collided, but he got control of his more quickly than I did.

'Where is she?'

I knew he meant Dot. He was very angry. I wasn't sure whether to lead him back to the house, but I didn't have to worry about it. He was already ahead of me. He hurled himself into the living room, and stood looking at Dot.

'And how are *you*, Dorothy?'

Dot sat up, almost. 'Rough as a ferret's arse on a frosty morning. How are you yirself, Eck?'

'Yir a coarse one!'

Dot smiled. 'That I am.'

'D' you know what you did to Lil? D'you care?'

'What was that now?' Dot laid back down on the lino.

'She's ill. ILL! Because of you! Because she came all the way out to Rita's in the middle o' a busy Friday night to help you. Yir no' worth helping, so y'are.'

We could barely hear Dot when she spoke. 'Go back to yir wife, Eck. I never asked for anyone's help.'

Mr Bryce squatted beside her. He reached for her arm, and his voice became gentle.

'C'mon Dot, the war's over.' He lifted her back to a sitting position. There had been an awful lot of talk about the war in Inchbrae. Dot was leaning against the wall. She opened her arms wide.

'I wished on the moon, Eck.' It was one of Miss Holiday's songs. Dot began humming it. 'None in all the world to love me . . . ' She hummed some more.

Eck pulled her close and wrapped his big arms round her. And then Dot cried. I walked out into the sunshine, and down the lane, and then I walked back. I didn't know what else to do.

Mr Bryce was just getting on his bicycle. 'She's in her bed,' he said. 'On it, anyway. She'll need to sleep it off. God knows what all they were drinking.'

'Whisky and lemonade,' I informed him.

He stared at me. 'You were up?'

'No,' I answered. 'But I heard Mrs Bryce asking for lemonade.'

Mr Bryce nodded. 'No wonder she's sick. That lemonade'll do it every time.'

I never got sick from lemonade.

'Well, Ellie,' he said, 'Lil's no going to be fit for much, but you're welcome to come back in with me. You can always keep Hugh company.'

I swallowed. 'Thank you.'

'The Conroy boy's probably at a loose end,' Mr Bryce suggested then. I hadn't said anything about not wanting to keep Hugh company. Maybe he just knew. We cycled back in single file, and he looked back a few times, to make sure I was all right. He was turning into a nice person.

Mrs Bryce was in the kitchen. She had her head down on the table, and there was a bucket beside her on the floor. She looked up as we came in, and her face was very, very pale. She did look sick; much sicker than Dot.

Hugh was at the table also, but he didn't seem too worried about his mother. He was trying to spread some jam on a piece of bread – with a fork. He'd made a horrible mess. Mr Bryce took the fork from him, and scolded him for 'taking advantage'.

He wrung out a wet cloth to wipe Hugh's hands, speaking to his wife as he did so.

'Go on up an' lie down, hen. You'll feel better.'

'Dot . . . ?'

'She's no' too great. I carried her up to her bed.'

'You didn't fight with her?'

'Nah! The temper left me when I saw the state of her.'

Mrs Bryce groaned. She was finding it hard to keep her eyes open. 'Ellie,' she whispered. 'I'm sorry, pet.'

I didn't know why she was apologising to me. She hadn't done anything. I looked at Mr Bryce in surprise, but he shook his head, as if to say 'Pay no attention'.

Mrs Bryce pushed herself up from the table. It took two tries, and Mr Bryce put an arm round her. 'The pail . . .' she reminded him. He nodded, and brought it with them. Hugh talked away to me while they were upstairs, but I couldn't make out any of it, except 'sorry' once, when he kicked me under the table by accident.

'Shaah-ree!'

I didn't want to leave as soon as Mr Bryce came down, but he said I'd better let Mr Conroy know that Rita wouldn't be in to her work, and I could see if Joseph was allowed out at the same time. Hugh rose to follow me, but Mr Bryce took his arm and told him he had to stay. I felt sorry for him, a bit, so I said Joe and I would come back in to play with him.

'That's OK, hen. He'll be going down for a nap in a wee whilie.' Hugh was shaking his head 'no'. I didn't think he liked being put down for naps so often.

There was nobody in the butcher's shop when I went in, but Mr Conroy soon appeared from the back. He had a large cleaver in his hand.

'Morning, sunshine.' He smiled. 'I hope it's myself you're here to see. Is it now?'

I smiled back. 'I was wondering if Joseph's allowed out today?'

He put the cleaver down. 'You'll find him across the road,' he said. 'Jessie pays him to cut her grass, but she'll no' let him do it on Sundays. It's the salt o' the earth she is, but she's awful full o' the Bible.'

'Can he play, after he's done the grass?'

'Well now, if it's yourself that's asking, I'm sure we could be persuaded.' He waved the cleaver at the door. 'Don't be encouraging him to rush his work, though.'

'Oh . . .' I had almost forgotten. 'Mrs Gilchrist's not opening her shop today. She's in bed.'

'What's wrong with her?' He looked concerned.

'She was feeling a bit sick.'

'This morning? Was it this morning she was sick?' He was frowning hard at me, and seemed really worried about Rita being sick.

'Aye, but they're all sick.'

'Who?'

'Dot, and Mrs Bryce and Ri—Mrs Gilchrist.'

He took a deep breath, like a sigh of relief. 'What made them sick?'

'We-ell, Mrs Bryce came over, and then Mrs Gilchrist came home, and Dot . . .'

'. . . was feeding them drink,' he finished for me.

I looked down; nodded.

Mr Conroy shook his head. He was still shaking it when I left.

CHAPTER 20

Mrs Alexander said Joe was almost finished, and would we like some lemonade and biscuits. I answered yes for both of us. He had his shirt off again, and was red in the face from pushing the mower. It wasn't a big garden; two squares of grass, and flower borders around them. There were roses planted under the back windows, and you could close your eyes and smell them and the fresh-cut grass at the same time. They were two of my favourite smells. If somebody made a perfume from those smells I'm sure it would be as popular as 'Evening in Paris'.

Joe cleaned off the blades of the mower, and put it back in the shed. Then I helped him to pick up all the loose grass, and we put it in a cardboard box which Mrs Alexander had brought out. She left our lemonade and biscuits on the back step. There were six biscuits. Joe had both the pink wafers and two more, which was only fair as he'd been very busy. Still, I'd have liked one of the pink wafers.

We decided to go to the tent. I'd brought five shillings with me, and by the time Mrs Alexander paid Joe his one and six, we were very well off. He'd got his own pocket-money last night, but he'd spent it all. He said he'd bought sweeties and comics to pass the night by himself. I'd have done the same in his shoes.

Joe went over to tell his father where we were going, and I went into the Jacobite. Hugh must have been put to bed, as Mr Bryce was on his own.

'The road gets busy on a Saturday,' he warned. 'Watch the traffic, and don't go getting in trouble. Will you be back here later?'

'I'll probably just go straight home.'

'Take Joseph to the house with you, then. If Dot's still in her bed, come back here and have your supper with us.' I thanked him and left.

Joe and I went on down to the dump to see if we could find Hooligan, but he wasn't there. Then we went into the grocer's. Mr Fishbein said he hadn't seen Hooligan either, but Dreep had been on the go earlier, and had assured Mr Fishbein that Hooligan was a quick mender. Mr Fishbein said that Dreep was in a most civil mood, which was rather worrying.

Mrs Fishbein served us. She spoke slowly, and didn't get excited. She seemed happier, and let us take plenty of time deciding, agreeing that it was important that the day wasn't spoiled for lack of provisions. She gave us a bag of crisps each for free, and Mr Fishbein spread four rolls with chicken paste, and they were free too. Joe said the heat must have got to him.

We remembered the lemonade this time, but Joe preferred cream soda to tangerine, so we bought that. I liked cream soda.

It didn't take long to get to the tent, and it was just as we'd left it. Joseph said he certainly knew how to put up a tent, and when I reminded him that it had been a joint effort, he said I'd only helped, which wasn't the same thing.

'If you're going to argue all day, I'm not getting inside with you,' I warned him.

'I'd have been able to put it up by myself . . . but it would have taken longer.' It wasn't enough.

'God, all right then,' he sighed. 'It needed both of us. Are y'happy now?'

I was. We crawled inside, and the smell of the river was even stronger today. Joe thought that it was because the tent had lain empty all night. I began telling him about the goings-on at Rita's, but he interrupted me. He wasn't listening at all. It was a bad habit he had.

'I found something out,' he said.

'What?'

'Da's gone and divorced my mam.'

He didn't even sound sad when he said it. It just came out like 'two and two make four'. He was not an easy boy to understand, except most of the time he was.

'How do you know?' I asked.

'Last night, when he got home, he came and sat on my bed. I was reading the *Eagle*, and I threw it on the floor and pretended to be sleeping. I hate the smell off him when he's been with *her*. He's got that gyudders perfume all over him.' Joe was poking a stick into the sandy bits at his feet. He hadn't even thought about eating!

'What happened?'

'He picked my comic up, and said he knew I wasn't sleeping. He said to sit up, he had something to tell me. So I did, and that's what he said, that he'd divorced my mam.'

'But how could he? If she's not even here?'

'He knows where she is. He said she was shacked up with her fancy-man in Huddersfield, wherever *that* is. He's always known where she was. Always . . .' His voice trailed off.

'Oh, Joseph.' I didn't know what to say to him. We were quiet for a while, and I thought about what he'd just said. He must have known by now that Mr Conroy and Rita were madly in love with each other, and he didn't sound too troubled by the news. Maybe he had decided to accept things as they were. I felt I should encourage him to do that.

'Well, I'm glad you're accepting this so well,' I said at last.

Dad had nearly got promoted at his work, and we would have had to go to Edinburgh to live, but he said he'd accepted the fact that it wouldn't be a good idea to move at this point in time, and Mam said she was proud of him for accepting that. Dad didn't seem disappointed at all, but Mam told me it would be something else for her to feel guilty about, and she wished she hadn't said anything at all about not wanting to move.

Besides, she said, he didn't even get the promotion. Somebody else got it. Mam wasn't quite as clever as Dad, but at least she told me things. I didn't even know that we might be going to Edinburgh, not until Dad had accepted that we weren't.

'It's a sign of maturity, Joe . . . accepting things.'

'I'm going to Huddersfield,' he stated, as though I'd never spoken. 'I'm running away.'

I spent hours and hours trying to talk Joseph out of running away. I told him all about Mr Starling, and how we could find his mam some other way, and maybe get her to come here – instead of him running away. He put his hands over his ears so he couldn't hear me, and all of it came to naught. Even when we were cycling up the lane to Dot's house, he asked me if Dot had an atlas so he could find where Huddersfield was.

What scared me most was that, if he ran away before I got to go home, everyone would think I had something to do with it, and I'd probably get stuck in Inchbrae for ever. I was almost in tears with the whole thing, but no matter what argument I put forward, including the one about me not getting home, Joseph just got more and more determined to do it.

When I saw Hooligan lying at the back door, I couldn't help rushing to give him a cuddle. He lifted his lip as if he was going to snarl, but then he let me put my arms round him. His bandage was gone. Joseph looked at his wound, and said it maybe just looked black because it was healing. I hoped he was right, but I could tell it was still very painful, even though Hooligan was too brave to let on.

I kissed his leg, not quite on the scar bit, and Joe said I would have fleas in my mouth, but I didn't. I ran my tongue all over the inside of it to be sure. When I lifted my head, Hooligan sat up and began licking my face. He was a truly perfect dog.

'He could eat the face off you,' Joe said. He was jealous.

'He wouldn't,' I answered, between licks.

'He could though.'

'He *wouldn't*.'

'He might,' Joe said. He always had to have the last word. Mam said Dad was just like that, always having to have the last word; there must be something about their gender that made them do that. We were always told to use 'gender' at school. If the teacher said 'sex' everyone giggled, and it caused 'disruption of the lowest order'. So we had to say 'gender'. But Janet said it was perfectly right to say 'sex', which was different from S-E-X. Personally, I preferred 'gender'.

Joe asked if he had to wait with me, or not. He was impatient to get home, to make plans.

'What plans are you making, boy?'

Joe jumped backwards, out of Dot's view. She'd

been sitting in the kitchen all this time, and we hadn't noticed. She was wearing a man's maroon-coloured dressing-gown, which was far too big for her. I don't know why it annoyed me so much, but it did. She looked better, but her face was still white.

Joe was pressing his foot against the small of my back. I knew he was getting ready to kick me if I said anything.

'I . . . I . . . I was planning . . . to build a kite,' he said. The last few words came out so quick they were all together.

I looked up at him. It was the last thing I would have thought of, but it was quite a good answer. He was gritting his teeth, and giving me huge warning stares with his eyes.

'We-ell,' Dot said. 'You're no' the first man I told to go fly a kite. You'd better get going, while there's some day left in it.'

Joe was on his bike and halfway down the lane before I got to my feet. Hooligan laid down across the space I'd left, and rolled in it. He even wanted the feel of me on him. I was so full of love for him when he did that.

We had corned beef hash for supper, which was mostly hash. Dot cleaned Hooligan's wound again. She agreed that it looked nasty, but when she saw how worried I was, she showed me a scar on his ear (the one which always stuck up) which I hadn't noticed before. Dot said that it had been hanging half-off one time, and Hooligan had just disappeared for a few days until it was better.

'He's a warrior, hen. It'll take more than a scratch to bother that one,' she said, going back into the house and leaving us together.

Hooligan stayed a long time, and I sat with him and told him about Joe. I waited until Dot had turned her records on, so she wouldn't hear me. Hooligan thought I should tell her anyway.

He'd had both his ears up while he listened, cocking his head so he could hear the whole story. When I was finished, he rested his head on my lap. He wasn't smiling. He agreed that it was a bad idea for Joe to run away. When he was ready to leave, I walked with him down the lane, explaining that, if I did tell Dot, I would feel as though I was betraying Joseph, and I knew he understood.

He looked up at me before he set off on the road, and he tried to smile. Neither of us could; but I gave him another hug so he wouldn't be too disappointed with me, and then I went home. It seemed to me that he was limping more than yesterday, and his eyes were very soft.

Rita brought Mrs Bryce out on Sunday afternoon. She said she was taking Mr Conroy and Joe on a picnic, and 'that boy better enjoy himself, or else . . .'

She was referring to Joe, of course, and this was a great relief to me. If he was on a picnic, he couldn't be making plans. Mrs Bryce said she'd be giving Rita some business, as she'd be needing a new outfit for the nuptials. I made a note to look up 'nuptials'. It sounded rude, but Mrs Bryce was never rude, so I knew it would be in the dictionary.

Dot wasn't saying much to anybody. She'd been quiet all day, but very nice to me in every way. She'd apologised for having wasted a precious day. Every day was precious, she explained, especially when you had someone to enjoy it with. We had chips for breakfast, and dinner too.

Mrs Bryce said it was a disgrace when I told her that, but she didn't give Dot a row. I hadn't seen Dot take any drams since we were at Rita's, and Mrs Bryce said that was a blessing, and Dot was better off with chips in the long run.

'May God strike you if you ever touch that poison, Ellie,' she warned. But I knew she was the kind of person who would be most hurt if God ever did strike me, so I didn't take it too seriously.

'Have you seen the papers?' she asked Dot.

'How could I do that? I huvna been over the door.'

'Oh, Dot, they're full o' that Billie Holiday. They arrested her in her hospital bed, the poor soul.'

'It's no' her first trip to the hospital, nor her first brush wi' the law,' Dot answered. 'She'll beat the pair o' them.'

'Not the way they're writing about it, Dot. They're saying there's no bettering in her this time.'

'If that's the case, why the hell would they be arresting her?' Dot asked. 'Bloody papers!'

It was the first I'd heard of this. I asked what it meant, and Mrs Bryce sucked her lips in, as though I'd said something wrong.

'She's a heroin addict, Ellie,' Dot answered. Mrs Bryce made a strangling noise, and I thought she might faint. I was more worried about her than Lady Day. I knew about addicts, but I never heard of anyone liking herring so much. I only liked them when Mam rolled them in oatmeal and fried them, and I certainly couldn't imagine wanting so much of them that you'd end up in the hospital with the police after you.

'Did she steal the herring?'

Dot looked at Mrs Bryce and they both laughed. I didn't know what I'd said that was so funny, and I was embarrassed without knowing why. I knew I was blushing.

'Oh Ellie ... No' herring – heroin! It's a drug, like ... opium.'

I was annoyed at their laughter. 'Well,' I said, getting my own back, 'Sherlock Holmes smokes opium, and he *helps* the police.'

'Aye,' Dot answered. 'But he's no real, and anyway an English gentleman can do no wrong. Haven't you learned *that* yet?'

I remembered about Mr Smith. 'Is it because of the colour bar? Because of the people getting hanged? Is that why she takes the heroin?'

'Partly, maybe,' Dot said. 'But Lady never did have her troubles to seek. I think myself it's more to do with being a woman. It's a man's world yet.'

'My God, Dot, we're no' all heroin addicts. How can you say that to the bairn?' Mrs Bryce had got her voice back.

Dot shrugged. Nobody said anything.

'Will I play outside?' I asked.

They both smiled 'yes' at me. I thought Dot would get a row for sure, but they seemed very at peace with each other when I went in for afternoon tea. Mrs Bryce called it that. So did Mam, when we had it. It was good, except there was more fruit cake, which I was getting tired of.

Rita came back for Mrs Bryce at about five o' clock. Mr Conroy was in the passenger seat, and Joseph was in the back. He squeezed himself right up against the window when he saw Mrs Bryce getting ready to clamber in.

We just said 'hello' and 'cheerio'. I couldn't tell from looking at him if he was still making plans. Rita and Mr Conroy looked very happy, though, and she wasn't bawling at Joe – or anyone. I was sure everything would turn out all right. I was finding that, just when you thought everything had gone wrong, something happened to make it better again.

I mentioned this to Dot after everyone left.

She looked at me for a long time. Then she said, 'Keep a tight hold o' that thought, Ellie. There'll be days you'll be needing it.'

That night Dot and I discussed me being a famous writer again. She said I should think very carefully about it, as you could pay an awful price for fame. I'd heard this before, but it didn't make much sense. People paid *you* when you were famous.

They paid you a lot, and you could take your mam and dad to far-off places, and go to Caribbean islands on yachts – if you got tired of Paris.

Hooligan didn't come by, but I knew he was thinking of me, wherever he was. We had a 'mental communion', which I'd read in a story by someone who'd gone to Africa to follow elephants around; I forgot who. I would write about Hooligan in my journal, and get into the habit of using good vocabulary. I would start a journal as soon as I got home.

Tomorrow would be Monday. I'd soon be meeting Mr Starling, who would also be in my journal, and then I'd be going home, and I'd have so much to tell Janet she'd be jealous. I went to sleep dreaming about it, and being famous.

I'd never have imagined I would need my thought on things getting better so soon, but I needed it on Monday.

CHAPTER 21

Mr Bryce was hammering at the front door before I'd rubbed the sleep from my eyes. He hadn't even come round to the back.

'Christ, Eckie, what is it?'

I could see Rita's car behind Mr Bryce. He must have borrowed it to drive out to Dot's.

'Can y'no' get a phone in the place?' Mr Bryce demanded. He was redder than I'd ever seen him. 'At least I can get hold o' Rita when I need her.'

He was in the living room, and turning in circles like Hooligan did when he didn't know what else to do. Dot grabbed him by the shirt, and I thought she was going to slap him. 'If you don't tell me what's wrong, I'm going to knock the shite out o' you,' she said. She meant it.

Mr Bryce wiped his brow, and then he smoothed his hair, even though it wasn't sticking up. Then he took a deep breath and shook his head. Dot tightened her grip on him, and he peeled her hand away.

'Dodo,' he said. 'It's Dodo.'

Dot leaned her head back, and closed her eyes.

'What're you telling me, Eck?'

Mr Bryce shook his head again.

Dot opened her eyes. 'What happened? Is he dead?'

'Dead as a mackerel.'

'Lil?'

'She's taking it awful hard. She needs you.'

Dot was pulling off her horrible dressing-gown in front of Mr Bryce. 'Get back upstairs, Ellie,' she said. 'Put some clothes on. Anything.'

She pushed past me. Three steps up, she turned back. '*Now*, Ellie!'

We were in the car in no time. I was wearing dirty socks. I hoped no-one would notice. Dot certainly wouldn't. She'd been wearing the same trousers since I arrived.

Mr Bryce was a worse driver than Rita, but he avoided most of the potholes. He didn't seem very aware of the other road users, as we'd been taught to be for our Cycling Proficiency. He kept blowing his horn at people, and almost knocked a pedestrian into the bushes. The pedestrian was quite an old man. He had a sack of something across his shoulders, and he was staggering all over the place trying to hold on to it.

Mr Bryce told Dot that Dodo's wife had found him dead in his bed.

'Eleven o'clock last night, and we just found out an hour ago. She took her time in calling. But she's a rum one, Connie. We always knew that.'

'What happened?'

'Heart,' Mr Bryce said. 'Had to be. He was aye a bit soft for my liking, but he was a nice bloke, Dodo. Wouldn't hurt a fly.'

'Are there any arrangements?'

'Ah-h-h-ah,' Mr Bryce's voice quavered as though he was in pain. Then he began shaking his head. 'I hate bloody funerals!' We jerked to a stop outside the Jacobite. Dot was first through the door.

Hugh must have still been in bed, as Rita and Mrs Bryce were the only ones at the table. Mrs Bryce had on a fluffy pink dressing-gown, and her hair was pushed back with kirby grips. Her face was very shiny. She had a hankie in her hand which she kept twisting, but she wasn't crying, not till Dot spoke.

'I'm awful sorry, Lil. He was a good friend to me, Dodo.'

Mrs Bryce threw her hankie at Dot, and began sobbing. Very angry sobs.

'Why didn't you marry him? *Why* didn't you?'

Dot sat down. She looked stunned. 'What?'

'He would've married you. He offered. But no, not you. You had to do things yir own way, and there's him landed wi' thon sculpture o' a dame who couldn't even call to tell us . . .'

'Sculptor,' Rita said, getting up to boil the kettle.

Mrs Bryce picked up her hankie, which hadn't gone far, and threw it at Rita. It still didn't go far.

Dot reached for Mrs Bryce's hand, and Mrs Bryce let her take it. Rita mouthed to me to get more cups out. I was glad to help. I didn't want to talk about death.

'Lil, she did call you. What was the point of getting you up in the middle o' the night?' Dot said gently.

Mrs Bryce blew her nose and wiped her eyes; then she cried a bit more. Mr Bryce was sitting in the chair beside her. He had his arm around her, and I had to squeeze by to reach the cups. They were both large people. Dot seemed quite small, looking across the table at her, and I'd noticed this before – I couldn't remember when.

'What a pair,' Mrs Bryce said, sniffing loudly. 'Dodo wrapped up in his poetry, and her hacking away at boulders. They were aye in a world o' their own.' Mrs Bryce sounded very disapproving of her brother's world – and his wife's.

Dot sighed. 'They were happy, Lil. We canna all live our lives to please others. Some of us have to do things in our own way.' Dot hadn't said it like she did when she was arguing. It sounded very reasonable, but Mrs Bryce threw another tantrum.

She pulled her hand from Dot's grasp and stamped her feet. Her slippers didn't make much noise. I looked down. They were dark blue tartan with camel pom-poms. Rita was wearing black stilettos. She was always so fashionable, even with death around.

'Lil! Lil, that's enough now!' Mr Bryce said. His voice was quite firm, but you could tell he was a bit afraid of his wife's tantrums.

Rita pointed to the sugar. She held up three fingers. I was to give Mrs Bryce three sugars. I nodded, to show I'd understood.

Dot lit a cigarette and looked at Mr Bryce. 'Have you a dram, Eckie?' She sounded dazed.

'I'll get us a wee something,' he said, and began to rise.

'SIT! Sit where you are, Eckie Bryce, and don't you *dare* go near that bar!'

'Right-oh, Lil.' Mr Bryce sat. 'Maybe later,' he whispered to Dot. We all heard him.

'Try taking deep breaths,' I suggested, putting Mrs Bryce's tea in front of her. 'It sometimes works for me.'

Mrs Bryce stared at me, and then gave me a hug that took all the breath from me, deep ones included.

'You poor bairn. On yir holidays . . .'

'I don't mind,' I said, when I got free. 'I'm sorry about your brother.'

Mrs Bryce sat all the way up, and drank some tea. Then she shivered. 'It's a bit on the sweet side.'

'What about the funeral, Lil?' Dot asked.

Mrs Bryce did take some deep breaths, and was a lot calmer when she spoke. 'It's on Wednesday, one o'clock. I asked if she needed me to come down sooner, and she said I was welcome. They never had anyone close – no family, anyway. I thought . . . maybe I'd be a bit o' help if she needed it.'

It was very typical of Mrs Bryce to be of help. 'The thing is, Dot, Eck would be wanting to come down on Wednesday for the interment, wouldn't you, Eck?' Mr Bryce didn't get a chance to answer. 'So I was wondering . . . if you wouldn't mind Dot . . . if you'd keep yir eye on Hugh for the day? He wouldn't be right – being around mourning, and all.'

Dot was chewing the inside of her cheek. She put her cigarette out, and looked up at Rita. Rita was standing against the sink with her arms folded. When she caught Dot's eye, she lifted her eyebrows. It was her 'nothing to do with me' look.

The phone rang. We all jumped, then Mr Bryce rose to answer it. We could hear him talking, and then he came back through.

'It's Connie, Lil. She'd like to talk to you.'

Mrs Bryce gripped the table, her eyes wild. Mr Bryce helped her up, and led her to the phone, which was in the alcove beside the bar. Mr Bryce waited with her for a moment, then he reappeared in the kitchen with a dram for himself and Dot. They both drank it down in a one-er, and Rita swiped the glasses and put them in the sink before Mrs Bryce came back.

Nobody had heard Hugh getting up. He came into the kitchen headfirst, and smiled at everybody. 'Maahr-nuh.'

We all said 'good morning' back. Mr Bryce sat Hugh at the table, and gave him what was left of his own cup of tea. The spare in Hugh's pyjama trousers was open, and Rita rolled her eyes some more – but I didn't look.

I heard Mrs Bryce put the phone down. As soon as she came in, she went over to Hugh and gave him a hug. 'Yir uncle's gone,' she said. Hugh smiled at her and clapped his hands. Mrs Bryce looked very tired when she sat. She more or less slumped down, but the edge of the table caught her stomach and she had to sit back up again.

'She'll meet me off the train. I'd better get myself sorted out,' she announced. She looked up at Eck.

'I'll give you a hand, Lil,' he said. 'We'll manage fine, and there's no' much doing here on Wednesdays. I can get the morning train from Locheirnan. It's only a couple of hours to Perth nowadays.'

'What about Hugh?' Mrs Bryce asked again. 'Can you keep him, Dot? Just for the day? It'll mean you missing Dodo's funeral.'

'D'you even need to ask?' Dot said.

Mrs Bryce rose. 'Well, I better make a start. The day's half gone already.' It wasn't. Grown-ups had no sense of time, but there was an excuse for Mrs Bryce.

She turned at the kitchen door. 'Dot. Oh my God, Dot. It's tomorrow. Eck, Starling's going to be here . . . tomorrow!'

'Don't worry about that, Lil,' Mr Bryce said. 'I'll make short shrift o' Johnny Starling.'

I looked across at Dot. Her eyes were closed.

Rita went next door to tell Mr Conroy what had happened, and he came in to pay his respects. Mrs Bryce was upstairs getting ready, so Dot said she would pass on the message. Rita got a piece of paper from Mr Bryce and wrote in huge letters, 'CLOSED DUE TO BEREAVEMENT. RE-OPENING TOMORROW.'

She told Dot that it was a handy excuse for her having been closed on Saturday, but Dot said it wouldn't wash. Everyone would know the truth soon enough. She was right. By ten o'clock, the man Arthur and three other people I'd never seen before had looked in to say how sorry they were at the news.

Mr Bryce had taken Hugh upstairs and had got him ready for the drive to Locheirnan station. Now Hugh was sitting on the sofa. He was scrubbed red, and obviously excited at the unexpectedness of a trip in Rita's car. He had an old handbag of Mrs Bryce's on the table in front of him, and Dot asked him what he was doing with it. He told her it was his case, for going to his uncle's.

Dot told me this. I couldn't understand it.

Mr Bryce took the handbag off Hugh and went back upstairs with it. Hugh didn't seem to mind. He was clicking his fingers with impatience to be off.

Two women came in who knew Dot. They were sorry about Dodo. One of them said, 'He was never part of the day-to-day living, poor Dodo.' She was looking over at Hugh when she said it.

'No, he wasna,' Dot agreed. 'He was too clever altogether – to hang about the yokels round here.'

The woman and her friend left.

Mrs Bryce was back in the kitchen. She was very fluttery and weepy, but she was trying to keep things organised, and had a long list of things for Mr Bryce to do in her absence.

'Christ, Lil, it's only a couple o' days,' he said. He was getting a bit flustered himself.

'Don't you take the Lord's name in vain here, Eck,' Mrs Bryce warned him. She went back upstairs.

'She never noticed before,' he complained to Dot. They had another quick dram.

'We'll be off then,' Mrs Bryce said at last. She checked everything one last time, and gave Hugh another kiss. She gave him lots of kisses. Mostly they were absent-minded, as though she didn't notice she was doing it, but Hugh seemed to relish every one.

We all got up and headed for the door, and Hugh and I were first on to the pavement. Dreep was standing against the wall, waiting for someone to come out. He was still wearing his fur coat, although it was a scorching hot day. He had a bunch of wild flowers in his hands which were very colourful; yellow and white and blue, and one reddish-brown thing that was a bit ugly.

Dot and Mr Bryce and Mrs Bryce were behind us. They almost crashed into me and Hugh, and Mr Bryce swore at everyone.

Dreep held out his flowers to Mrs Bryce. 'Condolences, madam.'

Mrs Bryce looked like she didn't quite know what to do with them, but she took them anyway.

264

'Thank you, Dreep. I'm afraid they'll be wilted by the time I get them to the grave.'

Dreep threw back his shoulders. 'My dear lady, they're for you. Flowers are for the living. The dear departed are already wandering in Elysian fields. They have no use for them.'

Mrs Bryce looked confused. 'Aach, can no-one do anything right any more?' she asked. She sounded very forlorn.

Dreep bowed and left. Dot gave Mrs Bryce another hug. 'I wasn't thinking, Lil. What about wreaths?' she asked.

Mrs Bryce was backing into the car. 'There's to be no wreaths,' she answered. She'd started crying again. 'A bunch o' pitiful weeds from an old wino. Aa-ah, Dodo, my poor wee thing.'

It was a sad day. It was also boring. Joe wasn't allowed out. I went next door to ask, but he wasn't in the shop with his father.

'Would you be wanting a bother like that in your hour o' need?' Mr Conroy asked. 'No, he's fine where he is. Maybe tomorrow.' I knew Joseph would be in his room, making plans.

I told Dot. 'Our hour o' need's no' on us yet,' she said. She went back and asked again.

'He's no' forthcoming,' she said, meaning Joe. We waited till Mr Bryce came back with Hugh, then we went home. Dot was too depressed to call Hooligan. She said he'd be wherever he wanted to be, and we should grant him his privacy. Hooligan wasn't as private a dog as she thought. Nobody really knew him, the truth of him. I was afraid he was lying somewhere in pain, and not able to tell anyone about it. But then I thought about what Dot had told me about him disappearing until he was well again, and I tried to stop worrying.

That afternoon the sky darkened. It rained for four hours, and then the sun came out again. Dot mooched about the house. I asked her if she had a spare jotter anywhere so I could start a journal. She didn't, but she found an old Basildon Bond note-pad, and I went through to the kitchen to begin writing. There were only five pages left on the pad, and I spoiled two of them. Then I gave up. I decided to wait until I knew where to start, and read my books instead. I would need to read lots of books if I was going to be a writer. I loved reading. I preferred it to writing, but then I was only beginning my career.

We'd already eaten when Hooligan arrived. He sniffed in Dot's bucket before deciding to eat his dog food, and he didn't eat much of that. His leg was swollen, and he could hardly put any weight on it. Dot couldn't be bothered with either of us, and said I was making too much of it, and hadn't he walked all the way here?

He had, but he didn't look well to me. He kept looking at me as though he was trying to tell me something, but I was always thinking that anyway, and I didn't know whether to be more worried or not.

Dot seemed to want the house to herself, and reminded me that there was an old ball in her shed. I went to look for it. It was a great ball. It was red and yellow marbled, except where it was grey where Hooligan had chewed off some of the rubber. Hooligan recognised it straight away, but when I threw it for him, he didn't even try to catch it.

I started playing 'Plainie, clappie' against Dot's wall, but I was soon bored with that. Hooligan lay down at the back door, watching me. I asked him to stay the night. He didn't say yes or no, but when I went inside he let me kiss him, and he didn't get up, so I definitely felt that he would be there in the morning. I told Dot, but she said you never knew what the next day would bring, and not to get my hopes up.

I kissed Dot too before I went to bed. I thought it might perk her up. She'd been upset all day, even though she tried not to show it. I'd often kissed Mam when she was upset. I would have liked for her to kiss me back, but it was a bit like Mrs Bryce kissing Hugh – except the other way round. Mam always accepted my kisses, but absent-mindedly. That was the invisible part, when you were loving someone and they didn't notice. Dot never made me feel invisible. Even being sad, she kissed me back.

'It's a grand thing, a goodnight kiss,' she said. She was smiling again. 'I don't know what I'm going to do without it.'

I smiled too, but I felt funny when she said that.

267

I think I was ready for going home, but I wasn't sure about leaving Dot. She didn't need me the way Mam needed me, at least the way I *thought* Mam needed me. But she did need me. I liked Dot. I loved her.

CHAPTER 22

As soon as I got up, I ran to open the back door. Dot was at the kitchen table, smoking and drinking coffee. I could smell whisky.

'He's gone, hen. He waited till quite late, though.' She looked at me. 'Later than he ever stayed before.'

'How late?' I asked.

'Well, he was here at ten. I looked in on you, and went down to the river to sit awhile. He was gone when I got back.'

I could feel my temper. It filled my head. I was shaking with it. 'He wouldn't! He wouldn't go and leave me here with no-one to look after me. You *know* he wouldn't!'

'Ach, Ellie. You're in no danger here. God, he waited half the night, and I was back myself when it got dark. I'd no' leave you in the dark, hen.'

I was still shaking. 'He left because of you . . . he saw you leaving, and he . . .'

Dot gripped me by the arms. 'Please, hen . . . Please listen to me. He's a dog. A lone, wandering animal. I've enough to answer for, Ellie. I promise

. . . I'd never, never let anything happen to you. D'you believe that? DO you?'

When I looked into her face, I realised that what I'd found so scary about her eyes (before I knew her so well) was that she never lied. It was the truth in them that frightened you. I felt the shaking leave me.

I nodded. 'Yes,' I said. 'I believe you.'

She hugged me, and at first I thought I'd imagined it. But when I lifted my head from her chest, I heard it again, a scraping noise.

I jerked open the back door. Hooligan was gazing up at me, panting loudly. I lunged at him, but he side-stepped me, and began nosing at his water bowl. 'He's back, Dot,' I shouted. 'He's back.'

Dot leaned against the doorpost. 'So he is,' she said. 'Like a bad penny.' She was smiling. I must have upset her more than I'd thought. It was such a sad smile.

Hooligan waited while Dot filled his bowl. I tugged at her arm; I wanted her to be as happy as we were. 'I'll call you gran, if you like.'

She stopped, turned. 'Dot's fine, Ellie. It suits us both.'

She was quite right. 'I know you're looking after me, Dot,' I assured her. 'I'll tell Dad how well you've looked after me.'

'Well now, am I to be getting a gold star after all?' she asked. Then she laughed, really laughed. It was a great laugh. Nobody in the world laughed like Dot.

'I love you, Dot.'

She had her back to me. She was filling Hooligan's bowl again; he'd been so thirsty he'd already drunk it all. 'I love you too,' she said. Her voice was funny. She had her cigarette in her mouth; that's probably why.

Dot didn't want to leave the house, so Hooligan and I played together all morning. I found out he liked to catch anything you threw, just as long as you didn't mean for him to catch it. He was still limping badly, and wouldn't chase the ball, but he'd catch it if it was anywhere near him. Dot said he had a condescending streak in him. I wasn't sure about 'condescending'. Dot had a dictionary in the alcove on her side of the fireplace, and made me come inside to look it up. I agreed that I would have to be stretching my vocabulary, and looking up words a lot more, if I was going to be a famous writer.

The dictionary was very old. It smelled of kindling that had lain by the fire for a long time. After I found 'condescend' I glanced through the rest of the 'c's'. There was a horrible word that Walter Cummings used beginning with 'c'. He'd told Janet that it was a dictionary word, and he'd been right about 'vagina'. We'd already found that; but we hadn't found the 'c' word yet. Janet said it was just another one of Walter's filthy words, but we kept looking, just in case.

I was helping Dot to peel some potatoes for

271

stovies when we heard the car. Hooligan was lying under the kitchen table. Dot said he'd never done that before. He didn't want to be away from me for a minute.

I thought it sounded like Rita's car, but Dot shook her head. She stopped slicing the onions and just stood there. She was sort of leaning over the sink as though she felt dizzy. There were two knocks on the door before she went to answer it. She was wearing her blue turban, and she pushed all her hair up into it as she walked into the living room. I thought she looked better with some of her hair showing. She had quite nice hair; it was much softer than it looked.

She'd said for me to stay where I was, and I did, but I took the tattie bowl to the table, so I could see through the doorway. I'm not sure who I expected to be there, but it wasn't Bing Crosby.

He was holding a pipe, and he was quite tall, and very thin. He was also wearing a black leather trilby like I'd seen Mr Crosby wearing on a record cover. The first thing that went through my mind was how jealous Janet was going to be when I told her that Bing Crosby had come to my gran's house. She would never believe it.

Of course I soon realised that it couldn't be Mr Crosby. Why on earth would *he* be visiting Dot? And, as soon as I realised that, I knew who the visitor was. It could only be Mr Starling.

'It's been a long time, Dot,' he said. He had a nice wide smile.

'Longer than that,' Dot answered. She didn't invite him in. They just stood looking at each other. Mr Starling put his pipe to his mouth, and let it rest there. It wasn't lit.

'You haven't changed,' he said.

Dot snorted. 'Neither have you, by the sound of it.' She was not at her most welcoming, but I'm sure she was thinking of Mrs Bryce, who'd been left at the altar, and had a dead brother as well.

'You'd better come in,' Dot said. 'And wipe your feet!'

The lane had got a bit muddy from the rain yesterday, but Dot wasn't what you'd call house-proud. I felt embarrassed for Mr Starling.

He wiped his feet anyway. I was feeling a bit nervous, waiting for him to notice me, and took the skin off my thumb with the tattie knife. It was red, but it didn't bleed. Dot marched straight towards me. It was too late to turn back to the sink. I dropped the knife in the tattie bowl, and looked at her. 'We were making stovies,' she said. 'They'll be a while. Are you waiting?'

Mr Starling stood in the doorway. 'Stovies. Well, I . . . I've never said no to stovies.'

'You'd better sit down then,' Dot said. 'This is Ellie, by the way.'

Mr Starling came towards me. Hooligan growled. I was so proud of him. 'It's OK,' I said. 'He's just protective of me.' It was true. I loved telling Mr Starling that.

He bent down and let Hooligan sniff him, and

273

then he shook my hand. 'Pleased to meet you, Ellie, and I can't blame your dog. I'm sure I'd be wanting to protect you too.'

Dot stood watching us. I don't know why she looked so fierce; he seemed like a very nice man. 'Ellie's my grand-daughter, Johnny.'

Mr Starling sat down. 'Ellie?'

'Fairbairn,' she answered.

They looked at each other again. Mr Starling was the first to speak. 'Unusual . . .' he said. 'Mr Fairbairn?'

'There's only one . . . my son Adam.'

Mr Starling nodded. He put his pipe down on the table, and there was another silence. I'd have thought they'd have an awful lot to talk about after all these years, but they'd hardly spoken.

'Lil didn't . . . say . . .'

Dot unfolded her arms. She pulled out her whisky bottle, and reached for the glasses. After she'd poured them both a dram, she sat down opposite Mr Starling.

'Lil wouldn't,' she said. She raised her glass. 'Happy days!' She didn't sound happy, not at all.

Mr Starling raised his glass too, but he didn't drink any. Hooligan was watching me from under the table. He wasn't happy either. I didn't know what had gone wrong. It was like being at home, watching faces, waiting for clues. I didn't like it.

I'd imagined how excited I would be when Mr Starling arrived; how we would all throw our arms around one another and be glad to be together at last. But it wasn't like that at all. It wasn't very exciting – he was just a visitor, a stranger, really. Dot pulled a tabbie from behind her ear and lit it. She nodded at Mr Starling's pipe. 'Go ahead,' she said.

Mr Starling twirled his fingers on the stem. 'It's just habit,' he said. 'I can't give up the feel of it, but I don't smoke. Not any more.'

'What kind o'accent's that?' Dot asked. I gasped at her rudeness. If Mr Starling *was* my grandad he'd probably leave before I'd *ever* get to know him.

'Newcastle,' I answered for him. 'It's a Newcastle accent.'

Mr Starling looked at me. 'You're every bit as special as Mr Smith told me you were.'

I beamed. 'For God's sake!' Dot said in disgust. I looked at her, startled. Mr Starling was being so nice, and she had gone into a bad mood for nothing. Maybe she was jealous because he was giving me more attention than her. Maybe that was it.

'We'll be outside,' I told Dot. She needed time to get used to her old friend. I could understand that. Hooligan rose to accompany me, but he stumbled a bit and nearly knocked the table over. I think his leg had got stiff when he'd lain down, but he seemed anxious to be outside again.

As we started towards the back door, Mr Starling began coughing. He must have swallowed the wrong way. He couldn't stop. Dot just sat there.

Hooligan caught the ball on his first try. I tried to take it from him, but he didn't want me to have it.

He kept it in his mouth, and went back to lie by the purple flower. Then he dropped it.

Mr Starling had stopped coughing.

'How long have you got?' Dot asked.

There was another silence.

'Not long enough,' Mr Starling answered. He sounded sad, as though he had to go back to Newcastle too soon. Then he coughed again. When he spoke, it sounded as though he was smiling once more. 'Straight for the balls, Dot. Like I said, you haven't changed.' It wasn't a very nice thing to say.

Joseph arrived before the stovies were ready. He spent a few minutes looking over Mr Starling's car.

'It's hired,' he announced. 'He's rich.'

'He is not,' I said. I didn't know if he was or not, but it seemed important to say he wasn't. I was angry. I'd been angry, and I didn't really know why. Mr Starling and Dot were getting on much better. I'd heard them both laughing, and there weren't any more silences. Mr Starling was doing nearly all the talking, and he had a lovely soft voice, sort of hoarse like Dot's, but not as certain as she was. Dot always sounded so sure of everything.

Mr Starling had two daughters and three grand-children. He had been married for a long time before his wife died, and all his children had left home. He said he was lonely, which was strange, considering he had all that family. Perhaps Mrs Bryce had been referring to somebody else when she'd said that there was a man out there who was meant for Dot. If it had been Mr Starling, then surely he wouldn't have married anyone else and had children and grandchildren. He sounded so nice, just like you'd want a grandad to sound. And I should be his grandchild, not those others who didn't even care that he was lonely. I kept wishing for Dot to clear everything up, but she was being as awkward as ever, and hadn't even mentioned the lilac trees.

I was still glaring at Joseph. 'Anyway, being rich doesn't make any difference to a person. It's just like . . . being black; and you're an ignorant person if you believe otherwise.'

Joe looked angry then too, but only because I'd hurt him. Men always looked angry when they were hurt. Dot had told me this. She said it was a matter of pride, and men had no more right to pride than women.

'The whole of life's a jigsaw puzzle, Ellie,' she'd said. I think it might have been on the way back from Rita's when she'd said it, but I couldn't remember exactly. 'The men pick out the corners. They enjoy building the frame, you see. But it's always left to us women to fill in the picture.

'And we do it. We fill in all the missing pieces, and then we sit back and let them take the credit; admire their efforts, tell them how wonderful they are . . . when all the time we're the ones doing the hard graft. Let them fill in their own pictures, hen. They need the excercise.'

'Life's a jigsaw puzzle, Joseph,' I said, hoping he

would see the sense of it. He didn't, of course.

'What's your gran got for dinner?' he asked.

There weren't enough stovies to go round. Dot didn't eat, and I wasn't too hungry, so Joe and Mr Starling had most of it – and Hooligan got a taste. I helped Dot to clear up.

'We'll never learn,' she whispered to me. We were putting the plates in the sink, and I wasn't angry any more. I liked it when Dot and me shared things like this.

Mr Starling kept looking at Dot. She must have noticed, but she didn't remark on it. They'd talked about Dodo. Mr Starling said there was a time for all of us, and Dot poured herself another dram. They looked like they'd got used to each other again. It made you relax. It was while I was thinking that I was feeling relaxed that I realised why I'd been angry before. There were too many faces to watch in Inchbrae. You could never relax for long.

I was glad I was going home. I wished Hooligan could come with me. He was so used to everything.

'I found Huddersfield,' Joe said. He wouldn't let it be. I knew he wouldn't. I didn't say anything.

We were in the tent. Hooligan wouldn't come in, but he was lying by the door.

'It's between Leeds and Manchester. I'll hitchhike.'

'I'm going home on Saturday,' I said.

'I'm leaving tomorrow.' As usual, it was as though I'd never spoken.

'I don't think you should go.' I had to try.

'They're going to get married. He hasn't said, but I know they will. I'm going to live with Ma.'

'You don't know her address. She could be anywhere.'

'I'll find her when I get there.' He was certain.

'Don't go, Joseph.' I knew his mother didn't want him. You couldn't really believe that about mothers, but sometimes you had to. He would never believe it.

'I'll stay here tomorrow night. When the heat's off, I'll get a lift to Locheirnan. I can jump a train.'

He sounded like Jimmy Cagney. 'Life's not like the pictures, Joe,' I said.

He went into an awful rage. 'What d'you mean? *You're* the one wi' all the film stars at yir fingertips. I'm going to find her. I WILL! Yir a big baby, Ellie Fairbairn. And *your* mother's nuts! And so's yir granny!'

'They are not!' He was trying to make me cry, but it wasn't working. I was just getting angry again. '*You're* the baby, Joseph Conroy. Going off to look for your mother, who doesn't even . . .' I stopped.

He leaned forward like he was going to punch me. Hooligan put his head through the tent door. I could see Joseph's eyes. They were wet. I was glad. I'd won.

'You better keep yir mouth shut . . . or I'll shut it for you.'

'Will not.' I wasn't afraid of his threats any more.

'Will sot,' Joseph said. Then he thought better of it.

'I'm leaving after supper. I'll pretend I'm going to bed early.' He looked at me, and he wasn't angry now. 'You won't tell . . . ?'

'OK.' I sighed.

Hooligan went back to Inchbrae with Joseph. He was limping very badly now. Maybe I shouldn't have let him play so long. I wanted Dot to look at his leg again, but he wouldn't come with me. It was as though he knew he had to watch over Joe, so I let him go. You couldn't blame Joe for wanting to find his mother, but he was doing it all wrong. He could get lost, or kidnapped, or murdered, or anything.

I had another sore head by the time I got to the house. Mr Starling was gone, and I decided to tell Dot about Joseph's plan. It wasn't betraying him, not really. I wanted him to be safe, and Dot seemed to know how to keep people safe. At least, she understood when they weren't. She accepted things.

'Joseph's planning on running away,' I said. I was sitting on the draining-board while Dot scrubbed behind my ears.

'Where's he running to?' she asked.

I didn't want to say too much. 'Away.'

'It's in them,' she answered.

'In who?' My ears were raw. They had to be clean by now.

'In men . . . aye running.'

'But he's going to do it, Dot. He's going to run away.'

'He'll no' get far.'

'He might.'

'Well then, he'll get as far as he can. Life'll take care o' the rest.' Dot dried me off and helped me into my pyjamas. 'It's out of control,' she said.

'What?'

'Everything, Ellie. We're helpless souls, all of us.' She seemed certain of this.

'I think I should do something?'

'What can you do? Yir no' responsible for anyone, least of all Joseph Conroy. We can't change life, Ellie, not with worry, or bitterness, nor even with love. Life does what it wants with us. You'll have to find a way to come to terms with it. I'm sixty-one years old, and I still don't know what to do with it all.'

Dot didn't know what to do with life! She was crying. She cried like she laughed. It wasn't like Mam; it didn't scare you, it was just crying. We had a good long hug. I don't know why I did it, but I reached for her turban. It took only one tug.

'You have pretty hair,' I said.

'Once upon a time,' she answered. She wiped her eyes, and blew her nose on the towel. I was glad she'd dried me first.

I lay in bed and listened to Lady Day sing 'Summertime'. Dot had said Gershwin and Holiday were unbeatable.

But we were all beatable, even Dot. I tried not to

think about it, but I couldn't help it. I was feeling like Dot; it was all getting out of control.

CHAPTER 23

Mr Starling brought Mr Bryce and Hugh out to the house the next morning, which seemed to annoy Dot. She led Mr Bryce into the kitchen. 'What's he doing here?' she asked, meaning Mr Starling. 'Could you no' have borrowed Rita's car?'

'Y'canna look a gift-horse in the mooth,' Mr Bryce whispered back. 'Besides, I'd still have had to get to the station. Johnny was good enough to offer.'

'So it's "Johnny" now,' Dot said, looking even more rankled.

'He's a decent cratur, Dot,' Mr Bryce answered. 'You could be a bit more amenable, y'know. Poor bugger doesn't know what he's doing here after making the journey an' all. He's waiting for you to come clean, tell him the truth of it.'

'He'll have a long wait,' Dot answered.

'Och, yir an awkward bitch, so y'are. At least we have something in common, him an' me . . . being in the same trade. At least I can *talk* to the man.'

Dot strode back into the living room. 'You'll

no' be back here the day?' she demanded of Mr Starling.

'This evening . . . I'll pick them up this evening. I'll be back then, unless . . .'

Dot just stood there. Mr Starling looked away, and he and Mr Bryce turned to leave. Hugh had sat down quietly by the fireside, looking around. Dot had told me he'd often been to her house before, but he had the gift of always seeing things in a new light. He certainly appeared to be noticing things for the first time.

'He's had his tablet,' Mr Bryce said, glancing at Hugh. 'He'll need a lie down about eleven, and another in the afternoon. Don't let him get over-heated.'

'He'll be fine,' Dot answered. 'Don't worry about him.'

Mr Bryce was wearing a black suit and tie, and a white shirt. His collar was starched and seemed to be bothering him a lot. He kept pulling it away from his neck, but really it was just too tight. I felt sorry for him getting on the train like that. Dot said it was quite a busy train, and for him to take his jacket off when he got to his seat; otherwise his oxters would be soaked by the time he got to the funeral, and Lil would have his guts for garters.

'I could live without this day,' Mr Bryce said, shaking his head.

'So could Dodo,' Dot answered. I thought that was another of Dot's tactless remarks, but Mr Starling grinned, and led Mr Bryce back to the car.

I spent most of the morning going up and down the lane, and hoping it would never get to supper-time. Hugh must have had a built-in alarm clock, because he woke right on the stroke of twelve. I was glad Dot had put him in her bed. I knew it was wrong, but I wouldn't have liked the thought of him being in mine; you got the feeling he slavered on the pillows.

Dot brought Hugh downstairs and we had soup, and custard with lumps in it. I was struggling with my custard when Dot remembered she'd put an orange jelly outside to set. It was still quite watery, but it made the custard better. I was so worried about Joseph running away that I hadn't even noticed the jelly on the kitchen window-sill. We had a fridge at home, so Mam always put the jelly in there. Dot said she'd be getting one soon herself.

'How-an-ever,' she added. 'As I hardly pass a day without a sojourn to the "big city", it's no' a problem to buy fresh.' It was a good point, until you remembered the way she left the potatoes growing in her press.

I got even more worried when Rita arrived. 'That boy's up to something!' Those were her first words.

'What now?' Dot asked, looking at me.

Rita flung her bag on the card table, and sat down.

'Aarr-ohh!'

'Hello, Hugh, how are you?' Rita answered. Hugh was trying to say something else, but she wouldn't wait for him. She hadn't spoken to me at all.

'Would *not* go to the pictures. Would *not* go for a run in the car. Would *not* come out of his bloody room!' she ranted, meaning Joseph.

'Maybe he's no' feeling well,' Dot offered.

Rita rubbed her forehead. She'd taken the sun, and her skin was the colour of Highland Toffee. It was quite exotic.

'So where is he? With Pat?' Dot asked.

'Don't mention Pat,' Rita warned. 'He could've spent the afternoon with me; left that thrawn wee brat in his room – but no! Not our Patrick.'

Hugh was humming in the corner. It was 'The Runaway Train' which Burl Ives sang every Saturday on *Children's Favourites*. It was quite clear, and I wondered if Hugh had the second sight. It was an alarming thought.

'I'm up to here with men,' Rita said, slicing a finger across her throat. 'I should've taken the shop.'

'Well, you didn't,' Dot retorted.

'What's got *your* goat?' Rita asked, frowning again.

Hugh stopped humming and smiled at me. Then he started circling his arms. 'Hoooh-hoooh! Hoooh-hoooh!'

'Chrissakes, Hugh, give it a rest,' Dot said. He stopped, and began rocking back and forth and laughing.

Rita looked at me. 'Ignore him, Ellie. He's just

doing it for attention.' It was the first she'd said to me.

'Why wouldn't he?' Dot whirled on Rita again. 'He's out of his element altogether. Of course he wants attention!'

'Jeez,' Rita said, crossing her legs and straightening her skirt (which was jet black and very elegant). 'Pardon me for living!'

Hugh stopped laughing. Rita and Dot scowled at each other, and there was a moment of dead silence. I felt like being sick. Dot lit a cigarette.

'Is it Starling?' Rita asked.

'What about him?'

'C'mon, Dot. You've been beside yirself since you heard he was coming back . . . and Eckie said he came to see you yesterday. Was it yourself he left Lil for?' Rita was as persistent as Joseph. If you didn't know better you'd think she *was* his mother.

Dot turned away. She was looking out of the window again. 'No,' she answered, 'it wasn't . . . and he didn't.'

There was another silence. Hugh was clattering the poker against the back of the grate, and big flakes of soot were breaking free and falling on to the newspapers. I thought it could get dangerous. The poker was heavy, and if he decided to throw it 'for attention' we could all be dead.

'Dot . . .' I said. She didn't even look at me.

I tried again. 'Rita, Hugh's got the poker . . .'

She held up a hand to silence me. She was watching Dot.

'There's nothing you don't know about me, Dorothy Fairbairn! Now are you going to tell me what's going on here or not?'

Dot turned back to Rita. 'Lil's said nothing?'

'Not to me, she hasn't.' Rita re-crossed her legs. 'Of course, if I'm going to be treated like an outsider after all this time . . .'

Dot smiled. 'Come off it, Rita. You're no' an outsider, and fine you know it.'

'But no' far enough in wi' you both to be confided in. Is that it, Dot?'

Dot suddenly seemed to remember I was there. 'Ellie, why don't you take Hugh for a walk? He's probably needing a bit o' fresh air.' I knew she wanted rid of me. I didn't want to go anywhere, especially not with Hugh.

'Put down the poker, Hugh!' she shouted. She'd just now noticed him.

'Take him out for a while.' She was pleading with me. She looked tired, and worried, and . . . older. She'd appeared quite old when I first arrived, and then – somehow – she'd got younger-looking. Now she looked old again. It was strange.

'Hugh,' I said, touching his arm. He threw the poker on the hearth and ran to the back door before I'd even stood up. We all got a fright. Dot ran to catch hold of him.

'You stay with Ellie, d'you hear me? Stay with her, Hugh.'

Hugh clapped Dot's head, and knocked her turban down on her forehead. She pulled it back up. Rita was looking worried too. 'Don't go near the road,' she called out. 'And for God's sake, Ellie, keep an eye on him. Lil'll do her nut if anything happens!'

I promised to take care of him. He grabbed my hand. His fingers were very long and cold. I thought of Dracula. I shivered, and looked up at him. He was grinning at me, he was so pleased to be getting out. I smiled back. You couldn't help it.

We started down the lane. Hugh wanted to hurry, but I kept him back, and told him to go slow. He began taking Giant Spangs. That made me laugh. Hugh laughed too, and grazed all his bald head against the hedge. It must've been sore, but he never complained. We went nearly to the bottom of the lane, and turned to come back. Hugh let go my hand, and began doing his 'Hoooh-hooohs' again. I felt relieved. Maybe he didn't have the second sight after all. Maybe he just enjoyed being a train. I joined in.

'God, two dafties in the place!' It was Joe. I hadn't heard him come up behind us. He had a big carrier bag under his arm. Hugh turned at the same time, and stuck out his hand. He wanted to shake hands with Joe, but Joseph just looked at it.

'I made it,' he said, ignoring Hugh. 'Da fell asleep reading his paper. It was easy. I kept to the bushes all the way here. No-one's seen me.'

My heart stopped. 'Rita's at the house.'

'So?'

'You can't go now. Not *now*!'

'Why not?'

I didn't know why. 'It's too early.' It sounded silly, even to me. Then I got a brainwave. 'He'll tell.' I nodded frantically in Hugh's direction.

'God, who's going to listen to that?' Joe dismissed the idea. 'Will you come down later?'

I shrugged. 'I might not be able to . . .'

Joe turned around. 'Please yirself!' He was angry with me.

'Don't go, Joe,' I whispered, but he was already at the road.

We walked back in just as Rita said, 'He'll have to be told, Dot.' She looked at me as she said it. Her mascara was smudged beneath her eyes, and I thought she might have been crying; her make-up was always so perfect. They obviously weren't feeling any happier than I was, but at least they were friends again.

Dot chewed on her lip for a moment. 'Ellie, how would you feel about spending the night with Rita?'

I couldn't answer. If I went to Rita's, I wouldn't be able to check on Joseph. And how long would it be before they found out he was missing? Mr Conroy could appear any minute. I was a collaborator, like in the Resistance, except they would all hate me for it.

'I thought you liked me,' Rita said. Her voice was soft. She'd seen the look on my face. I'd hurt her feelings. No matter what I did, I was going to hurt somebody.

'I *do* like you, Rita. Honest!'

'Well then, how about coming back with me? Your gran needs some time with . . .'

'They'll all be here after the station, Ellie,' Dot interrupted. 'We'll no' be very good company.'

'It's OK. I don't mind being here.'

Dot frowned at me. Then she smiled. 'What's worrying you now?' she asked.

'Nothing. There's nothing worrying me.'

Dot shook her head. 'C'mon, Hugh. It's time for your rest.'

Hugh had been the only one in a good mood, but even he seemed dejected now. I went back outside and sat down beside the purple flower.

Hugh leaned out of Dot's bedroom window. 'Err-eeh!' he yelled. I jumped. He hadn't gone to sleep at all.

'Get back in, Hugh,' I called. He was half out the window now, and rocking on his stomach. I couldn't move. Dot came running out, and looked up. 'Omigod! Go in, Hugh!' she shouted. He waved at us with both hands. Dot waved back.

'Coo-ee!' she called again. 'I see you!' She was smiling. I looked on in amazement, and didn't expect the thump she gave me. I reached up to rub my shoulder, and then I realised what she meant.

I ran inside and up the stairs, nearly knocking Rita down in the process. We both came through the bedroom door together. Rita grabbed for Hugh's waistband, but he must have opened his

291

trousers to lie down, and they fell away in her grasp. His underpants came with them. He had the whitest bum I'd ever seen. Hugh reared backwards and pulled his trousers up. Then he turned and slapped Rita across the face. He was furious.

Rita had fallen back on to the bed, and was just sitting there, rubbing her face. She looked stunned. It had all happened so quickly. Then Hugh pushed past me, and made for the stairs. Luckily Dot arrived just in time. She caught him by the arm, and pushed him back down on the bed. Rita stood up immediately.

'The bugger hit me!' she exclaimed, showing Dot her cheek.

'Och, he didn't mean it,' Dot said, as though it was Rita's fault. 'That was dangerous, Hugh,' she told him. 'You could've fallen to yir death.'

Rita stamped off down the stairs, muttering to herself, and Dot tied up Hugh's trousers. Then we all followed Rita. She was in the kitchen, holding a wet cloth to her face.

'I don't think you'll be disfigured,' Dot remarked, making everything worse again. Rita turned, her eyes blazing.

'You don't deserve friends, Dot Fairbairn.'

Dot grinned at her. 'I'm lucky to have them, then,' she said. Rita threw the cloth in the sink, and began to stutter. Then it turned to a laugh. Then they all began laughing; Dot and Rita and Hugh with his awful roaring. I was the only one not laughing.

Dot pulled me to her. 'Did y'get a fright, Ellie?'

I nodded. I could feel my eyes stinging. She stroked my hair. 'You'll be glad to see the back of us all,' she said. It was true. I would.

I couldn't get away to see Joe after that. We were all so busy watching Hugh, and then Rita asked Dot if she had anything in for the supper. 'I'm sure I have,' Dot answered.

Rita got up to look in the press. 'I'll take a run back into town, and get something at Pat's,' she said, not in the least surprised to find the press empty.

'It's OK, Rita,' I said, anxious to dissuade her. I didn't want her to go back and find Joe missing already. 'You don't need to go. We can have left-overs.'

She frowned. 'There aren't any,' she answered. 'I'll no' be long,' she said, her mind made up. 'D'you want to come?'

I shook my head.

Rita arched her eyebrows. 'Are there banners out?'

'What?' I asked, puzzled.

'Are there banners out saying it's "Hate Rita Day"?'

'No, course not,' I answered, trying to smile. 'But we don't need anything to eat. Really.'

'She's got you as daft as herself,' she said. 'It was bound to happen.' She left.

I watched her drive off. Should I try to warn Joseph? Or should I tell Dot everything now –

before Rita returned? Dot would know what to do, I felt sure. But if I did that, then I'd be betraying Joseph.

I felt sick with the worry of it. I knew there was going to be trouble.

CHAPTER 24

Dot had just remarked that Rita was taking a long time to get back when we heard the car. Mr Conroy came in first.

'Have you seen Joseph at all?' he asked Dot. Before she could answer Rita came flying in. She looked much more worried than Mr Conroy.

'He's gone, Dot,' she announced. 'He's taken his good jacket and shirt, and his long trousers. He's run off!'

Joseph wanted to look nice when he met his mother. It didn't surprise me. Dot took a moment to light a cigarette. 'Did he take his bike?' she asked.

Mr Conroy sat down. 'No,' he said. 'I thought he was still in his room. It was only when Rita arrived . . . I went in to see if he wanted to go out somewhere for the evening . . . with me. I . . .' Mr Conroy shook his head, as though he still couldn't believe that Joe had gone.

Rita was tapping her foot. 'I knew this was coming. I knew it! He's probably been planning it all along.'

'Planning what?' Dot asked.

'Running away,' Rita snapped, looking at Dot as though she was daft. 'God, what if anything happens to him? Where could he have gone? We looked all along the road on the way out here, and back in the fields as well. Didn't we, Pat?'

Mr Conroy just kept shaking his head. 'D'you think he might've gone to Locheirnan?' Rita asked, thinking aloud. I'd never heard her so anxious.

I stood by the door, trying not to look at anybody. I concentrated on Dot's clock, but I couldn't tell you what time it was. No matter how hard I stared, my eyes couldn't read it.

'It would be the town he'll be heading for,' Mr Conroy said, nodding now. 'We'd better try looking there. I was thinking maybe he'd headed this way, come t'see yourself, Ellie.' I glanced at him. He smiled at me, but his eyes were cloudy, and my heart lurched. He was far more concerned than I'd thought.

Dot was staring at me too. I could feel her eyes on me, but I wouldn't turn to face her. 'Maybe it's worth a bit more of a search round here,' she suggested. 'You never know.'

'We'd be wasting our time,' Rita said. There were fresh tears in her eyes. 'He's probably off in search of his mother.' Her voice broke.

Hugh was getting very nervous. He was sitting at the card table, across from Dot. She had her hand on his arm, but from the corner of my eye I could see his knees going up and down, faster and faster.

'Then let him find her!' Mr Conroy shouted,

making me jump. 'Her, *and* her fancy-man, *and* their three bairns. Let him see he's the only one she *doesn't* want – MY bairn!'

Rita sobbed. 'Oh, Pat,' she cried, burying her head in his chest.

Dot spoke. Her voice was very calm. 'You're his friend, Ellie. What do you think? Would Joseph be happier, getting all the way down there – just to find that out?'

Of course he wouldn't. Joseph's mother was truly evil. He mustn't find her, not ever. He would hate me for telling, but I had to do it. I was going home soon. He could hate me all he wanted.

Mr Conroy was pacing up and down in front of me. 'He's at the tent,' I whispered.

He stopped. 'Ellie?'

I coughed. 'He's at the tent.'

Rita grabbed my shoulders. 'What tent? Where?'

'At the dunes.'

'Come on,' she said, pulling me by the arm. 'Show us.'

I tried to pull back. I didn't want to be there when they found Joseph. 'I'll tell you ... I'll tell you where to go,' I protested.

Rita kept dragging me with her. Mr Conroy was out of the house. 'Would yis hurry!' he yelled back at us. I turned to Dot. She knew I didn't want to go. She saw me crying, but she urged me on with a wave of her hand. I hated her for that. We were almost at the car when I heard Hugh roaring.

'Maa-ah! Maa-ah!'

He sounded like a demented sheep. Why did everyone want their mothers all of a sudden?

Mr Conroy was out of the car almost before it stopped. I pointed in the direction of the tent, and Rita rushed forward, stumbling in the sand. Her skirt was covered with it, but she carried on. We were both crying.

'Joe! Jo-seph! Jo-seph!' Mr Conroy called.

Joe came out of the tent. He didn't look at his father or Rita – only at me. Then he charged.

Mr Conroy grabbed for him, and missed. I tried to duck behind Rita. She caught Joe by the arm, and spun him away from me. He swung back his leg, and kicked her full force on the shins.

She screamed, and collapsed on the ground, but she still had him in her grasp. Mr Conroy clambered back towards us, and lifted Joe clear of Rita. Joe was still yelling and lashing out with his feet.

'Cut it out!' Mr Conroy gasped. 'Stop it, Joseph. Stop it, are y'hearing me now!'

Joseph stopped. Mr Conroy set him down. Rita and I were still crying. Her stockings were ripped, and her leg was already turning purple.

Joe charged again. This time Rita was his target. She put her arms out to stave him off, and Mr Conroy made another grab at him, losing his own balance. Joseph fell between them, his head in Rita's lap. He struggled to get up, but she held him there, her arms tight around him.

'You're safe. You're safe,' she sobbed. 'Oh, God, you're safe.'

I forgot to cry. Rita had been injured twice in one day. Her clothes were ruined. She didn't want children. She was glad Joseph was safe!

Joe was crying too. His face was beetroot with rage and tears. 'I hate you, Rita. I hate ALL of yis!' I was definitely included in that statement. Mr Conroy dropped down in the sand beside them, his head in his hands. He didn't seem to know what to do. Dot was right. Men were mostly useless.

Rita lifted Joe's face. 'It doesn't matter. It doesn't matter if you hate me. Just please, please promise not to do this again. We were worried sick . . .'

'YOU weren't worried,' Joe sobbed. 'You *want* rid of me!'

Rita held him tighter. 'I do not,' she whispered. 'I only want you to be at peace, Joe.' She stopped crying, and her voice became quite strong again. 'I'm going to marry your father, and you're going to be my son – whether you like it or not,' This enraged Joe even further.

'NOT!' he spat. He actually did – spit. It landed in the sand beside me. I stepped back.

'Either way, it's going to happen. It'll be new for us both, Joe. Maybe we could try helping each other out for a change . . .'

Joe stared up at her.

'I love you,' Rita murmured. 'I didn't realise it till you knocked me half-sick with worry.' She lifted his chin. 'I love you, Joe. Honest to God, I do.'

Joe laid his head on her shoulder, and cried as though his heart would break. Rita looked at Mr Conroy, and he leaned over and put his arms around them both. I was too embarrassed to watch them. I moved away.

I would have liked to put my head on someone's shoulder, and cry like that. It occurred to me that in all the world there was only one shoulder I could cry on. Dot's.

Mr Starling's car was parked at the house when we got back. Joseph refused to come in, and nobody forced him. He'd stared out of the window all the way back, and wouldn't talk to me, but somehow I knew he'd forgiven me in his own way. I think he realised that I'd betrayed him out of concern for his wellbeing.

Whenever Dad checked me for anything, he always said it was from 'concern for my wellbeing'. I'd never really understood what he meant. I think I did now. It didn't matter if Joseph didn't want to talk to me. I didn't feel like talking to anyone either.

The house was full of people. Mrs Bryce seemed more like her old self, and hugged Rita right away. 'Thank God the boy's found,' she said. 'They're nothing but worry.' Then she stood back and took another look at Rita. 'Lord save us! What a mess yir in!'

Rita just smiled. Mr Bryce and Mr Starling were discussing football. Mr Bryce had taken his jacket and tie off, and seemed altogether more comfortable than when he'd left. Hugh was hugging everyone he could, and Mr Conroy had to scoot down and move back against the wall to get out of his embrace.

Dot was in the kitchen. 'I'm proud of you,' she said, squinting at me through her cigarette smoke. 'I know it was hard.'

Before I could tell her just how hard it had been, Rita appeared at Dot's side. 'We'll get going, Dot,' she said. 'Lil's full o' the interment, and it's really the last thing I want to listen to.'

Dot nodded.

'Will I take her?' Rita asked, meaning me.

'No, hen. See to yir own bairn,' she answered, squeezing Rita's arm. She sighed. 'It doesn't look like we'll get any privacy the night anyway. They're here for the duration.'

'What about your supper?' Rita asked.

Dot nodded at a large message-bag on the table. 'Lil packed some food for the train. There's enough here to feed the Royal Scots.'

Rita giggled. 'If you're sure.' She leaned into Dot. 'You *will* tell him?'

Dot avoided her gaze. 'Who knows? If it comes up . . .'

If what came up? I was exhausted. What more could there be?

Rita put her arm around me. 'Thank you, Ellie,' she said. Even with all that had happened, her smile was as beautiful as ever. It made me want to be a film star again. Rita and Mr Conroy said cheerio, and Mrs Bryce began fussing around in the kitchen. Dot gave up and left her to it.

Mrs Bryce was cutting the sandwiches into quarters. 'They look more when you do them that way,' she said, stepping back to admire them. 'And did Hugh behave?'

'He did, aye,' I answered. I wasn't going to clipe twice in one day.

'He's a darling,' Mrs Bryce said, handing me the sandwiches. 'Bring them through for me, like a good girl.'

After everybody had eaten, I went outside to look for Hooligan. I felt sure he must know Joseph was safe by now, and would come looking for his supper, but he didn't. I went back inside and sat down on the living-room floor.

Mr Starling was saying very little. He was watching Dot, and she was watching him. She never once looked directly at him, but I could tell she was watching him just the same. She laughed a lot, especially when Mrs Bryce made a great show of flirting with Mr Starling. I thought it was very silly of Mrs Bryce to behave like that, but everyone seemed to enjoy it. Mr Bryce finally said they should be getting back, and they all left about quarter to nine.

Mr Starling stopped halfway to the door, and turned towards Dot as though he was about to say something to her, but Dot took his elbow and herded him along with the others, shaking her head as though it wasn't important. It was the kind of gesture you'd make to an old friend, and I began to wonder if I'd been wrong about Mr Starling all along.

Maybe that's all he was – an old friend. Maybe Dot had written to him *as* a friend, hoping he'd help her, and then thought better of burdening him. She wasn't one to burden anybody. Besides, even though my teacher often said it was a great thing to have an imagination, Dad disagreed. 'If you're going to let your imagination run riot, Eleanor, you're bound to get yourself into trouble.' He'd said it more than once.

The more I thought about it, the more dejected I felt. I really, really wanted a grandad. I wanted Mr Starling to be my grandad. But all I'd done was cause a lot of trouble for everyone, and all for nothing. I didn't bother getting washed. Dot said she'd clear up, and I think I heard her moving around, but I was so tired . . .

Dot shook me awake. 'There's someone here to see you.' I knew by her voice who it was.

Hooligan was standing at the bottom of the stairs. I told Dot that he was getting closer to me every day. He'd never come this far into the house.

'He'll miss you right enough,' she agreed. 'We all will.'

When she said that, I realised that it really wouldn't be long before I'd be leaving. I'd always been thinking it, counting the days and all, but . . .

I still *wanted* to go home; I just didn't want to leave Dot and Hooligan behind.

Hooligan laid down as before under Dot's table, and she bent down to examine his leg, but he wouldn't let her near it. I tried to crawl in beside him, but there was something in his eyes that made me back off. It wasn't a threat, he just looked like he wanted to be left alone. I felt he must be getting better though, to have walked out here so early.

Dot said she couldn't have me going home looking like a tink, and gathered up the dirty washing. She seemed a bit quieter than usual, but she laughed when I poured too much soap powder in the water, and we soon had a game going. We tried scooping some of it out, but it turned gooey in our fingers, so it seemed natural to chase each other through the house. Hooligan barked every time Dot caught me and made me scream, but he didn't join in.

Then we made bubbles, and took turns scooshing each other with the water. Dot had a big wringer on her sink, and she let me put the wet clothes through it. It was much better than Mam's twin-tub, except there was still a lot of soap coming out of the clothes. Dot said they might be a bit hard when they dried, but at least they were clean.

We were hanging out the clothes when Rita and Mrs Bryce pulled up. Dot spat the last two pegs out of her mouth as they came round the corner. Rita was limping a bit, which allowed Mrs Bryce to keep up with her.

'For the love o' God, what now?' she sputtered. Rita pulled her inside. I followed them. Rita was pushing Dot down on a chair, and Mrs Bryce was filling the kettle. She turned towards me. 'Get that filthy brute out of the kitchen!' she commanded, leaning backwards away from Hooligan. It was a most insulting thing to say.

Rita hadn't said anything at all – not to me; even though I'd been very important in bringing love to her and Joseph. It had been a great day before they arrived. They'd ruined everything.

I sat on the back step, and Hooligan stretched out between my feet. I tried to lift his leg a little, but he winced and I pulled my hand away so as not to hurt him any more. There was some sticky stuff on it, but it wasn't blood. I wiped it on my skirt. I wasn't going to walk down the lane with him, just so some grown-ups could have a private conversation.

I waited for someone to tell me to move, but nobody did; they were too busy with each other. I was invisible again. As soon as I thought this, Hooligan opened one eye and smiled up at me. It really happened. It wasn't coincidence.

'What're you doing here?' I heard Dot ask. 'Why're yis no' at yir work?'

'He's leaving, Dot. Tomorrow,' Rita said.

I thought she was talking about Joe again.

I was wrong.

CHAPTER 25

I peered back into the kitchen. Rita was almost on top of Dot, and Mrs Bryce had sat down on the other side of her. Mrs Bryce had blocked out most of the light from the living room.

'He's going back to Newcastle,' Rita announced, 'and he's sorry he ever came.' I knew then who she meant.

'So what?' Dot said. The kettle whistled. I heard a chair scrape back. No prizes for guessing whose, I thought.

'Have yis lost leave o' yir senses?' Dot demanded, sounding very cross with them both. 'D'you think that's so important to *me*, that you have to drive out here to tell me? God, Lil, Eckie must think I'm a right head-case, taking you from your work for that! And *you*, Rita, your shop's hardly had its door open since . . .'

'Never mind the shop,' Rita interrupted. 'I can do what I like.' It was Joseph all over. They'd probably be fighting for the rest of their days. 'The point is, Dot, you'll no' get another chance to talk to him.'

'SO WHAT!' Dot said again. She was furious now, and I didn't blame her one bit. She didn't need to waste time talking to someone who was still a stranger, who hadn't even spent a whole week in Inchbrae, and me going home so soon. Mr Starling didn't need Dot. I did.

'Dot.' It was Mrs Bryce's turn. 'Dot, now you just listen to me.' I could hear her clattering the tea-spoon round in the cups. I could smell Dot's coffee. It was a relief to the purple flower. 'All week I was thinking about poor Dodo. The way he was when he came back from the war.'

Somebody sighed. Rita said, 'Listen to her, Dot!' It must have been Dot who sighed.

'They shouldn't send poets to war.'

'He wasn't a poet then.' This was Dot.

'Beside the point,' Mrs Bryce continued. 'Anyway, at least he had a life of sorts.'

'He had a grand life.' Dot again.

'Do I interrupt you? I do not.' Silence. 'Look here, it doesn't take much to see Johnny's no' in the best o' health. He won't say, mind you, but I do believe his time's running out, and he deserves . . .'

What did she mean? Mr Starling didn't look as big and burly as Mr Bryce, but you couldn't say he looked *ill*. It was true, though; if he went back already, I might never find out the truth. Time *was* running out.

'What does he deserve?' Dot asked. 'What in the hell d'you *think* he deserves?'

'DOROTHY!'

'Go on, Lil.' Dot sighed. She sounded fed up.

Mrs Bryce was pleading now. 'Dot, just talk to him . . . give him a chance. He came all this way.'

This was going from bad to worse. Hooligan was chasing something in his sleep. His paws were jumping, and his eyes were flickering like he was going to take a fit. I poked his ribs. I wanted him to wake up. He snarled, and settled back down. I wished he hadn't snarled.

'The long and the short of it is . . .'

'The long of it anyway.' Dot just couldn't keep quiet; couldn't let Mrs Bryce finish whatever it was she was trying to say. Silence again. Deep breaths all round.

Another chair moved. Dot had risen, and was standing with her back to them both. I could have touched her from where I sat. She pulled her cigarette from behind her ear, and lit a match on the wringer handle. Then she looked down, and smiled at me. I wasn't invisible. Dot knew I was there. She leaned forwards and stroked my hair. I held her fingers, and she turned back.

'Could one o' yis get round to telling me what you think I should be doing about it all at this late date?'

'If I could get one minute . . . But do I?' Mrs Bryce seemed cross too now. I wondered how they'd managed to stay friends for so long. 'Dodo had a good life, Dot. And I've had a good life. And Rita's got . . .'

Rita leaned back and folded her arms, waiting to

find out what it was Mrs Bryce thought she had.

'A lot to look forward to. Yes, indeed.' Rita's foot was swinging, but she relaxed slightly. 'But poor Johnny . . . And you, Dot . . .'

Dot thumped her fist on the table. I saw it coming, but I still got a fright. Even Hooligan jumped and looked around him. Then he went back to sleep. He had no sense of drama.

'Don't you DARE feel sorry for me, Lillian Bryce!' Dot fumed. I was glad she was turned away from me. I wouldn't have liked to see her eyes. 'I might not have had the kind of life you'd approve of, but I wouldn't change a day of it. D'you hear me? Not one day!'

'Lil was only saying . . .' Rita ventured, defending Mrs Bryce. 'Och, you're going overboard – as usual!' she grumbled.

Mrs Bryce spoke again. 'He's coming out here this evening, to say cheerio. If you're going to be your usual pain in the arse, I'll tell him no' to bother.' Mrs Bryce hardly ever swore, but she sounded quite casual when she said it. She wasn't in the least frightened of Dot. Not in the least.

'We came to get you ready,' Rita added. 'It's his last night.'

I was still looking at Dot's back. She whirled, throwing her hands in the air. 'Ready for what? He's spent nearly all his time wi' his old cronies in Locheirnan. What in the hell do I have to get ready for?'

'Jeez, Dot, this is important. You can't entertain

him looking like . . . that!' Rita said. 'I could bring you over for a bath, and you could borrow one of my dresses – or skirts. Of course, if you wore a skirt, we'd need to pad out your blouse. You've no bust to speak of.' Rita continued to assess Dot. 'I've enough curlers to set your hair, and *any* make-up would be an improvement. I think I have some Pan-Stik that might be the right shade for you.'

Dot laughed, really laughed. 'Did someone just take a scythe to my heid? D'you honestly think I'm going to do myself up for a man? Any man?'

'He's not any man,' Mrs Bryce said. 'He's . . .'

'Enough!' Dot yelled. It was far too loud, and I got another fright.

'He should have been *your* man,' Mrs Bryce said, very quietly. And then there was complete silence. I wondered if they could hear my heart. Mr Starling *had* been meant for Dot. Mrs Bryce just said so. And suddenly it didn't matter if Mr Starling was my grandad or not. I knew I'd been right in trying to find him, and that it was a good thing he'd come back. Now that he'd met Dot again, he couldn't possibly be lonely. Nobody could be lonely with Dot.

I wanted Hooligan to waken, so I could tell him the good news, and I reached out to stroke him. He rolled on to his side, and opened both eyes, but they weren't seeing anything. He was still dreaming, and his eyes were white in his head.

It was Rita who broke the silence. 'Ellie, how d'you feel about staying at mine? We could get your gran prettified between us, couldn't we? I'm sure you have an idea or two.'

I nodded, but I wasn't convinced it was possible. Dot would take a lot of work, and she wouldn't like us fussing over her. Still, Rita seemed to think I'd be a help.

Dot scratched her head through her turban. 'I must be nuts,' she said.

'No, you're not,' I assured her. 'Nobody's nuts.'

'What time am I to expect him?' Dot asked Mrs Bryce.

'He'll no' be out before seven,' Mrs Bryce answered. She raised her hand for silence. We waited. 'He's booked "dinner"!'

The three of them fell all over each other laughing. Mrs Bryce raised her hand again. 'Mince and tatties!' They got quite hysterical at this. It became annoying.

I went back outside to tell Hooligan we were leaving, but he was gone. When I ran to the front I saw him limping down the lane. I called out to him.

He turned around, once, and shook himself. He seemed to stare at me for a very long time.

'I'll be at Rita's,' I shouted. 'You can come there. You can come there, Hooligan.' He didn't turn back.

We had to take Mrs Bryce back to the Jacobite, as she didn't want to be away too long. Dot and I stayed in the car. Rita ran into Mr Conroy's and was back again in seconds.

'That boy's in his room again. He's an uphill

struggle if ever there was one,' she said. 'Pat'll keep a better eye on him from now on, though.'

Dot was quite fidgety, which wasn't something you'd expect of her. There was a woman outside Rita's shop with her hands up against the window.

'You're losing a customer,' Dot said, pointing.

'She's in the shop every other week. Never buys a damn thing,' Rita answered, driving past the woman and spinning the car round at the corner of the waste-ground. I thought I caught a glimpse of Dreep's body in the old pram, but I couldn't be sure.

By the time we got back to Rita's, Dot had changed her mind. We had an awful job convincing her to stay, but Rita made it seem like a party, which was very clever of her. We had lots of food, and cheese and pineapple on sticks which Dot said was a waste of time. She ate some, though, and also had a couple of glasses of Rita's best whisky.

I helped Rita with everything. We were becoming very close, I thought. She began by bringing out her curlers and all her make-up, and a hair-dryer which had a plastic hood that packed into its own case.

'Let's get to work,' she said. I rolled up my sleeves.

Rita looked at Dot. 'Take your bath first. Then we'll do your hair and pick out a decent outfit for you.'

Dot rose like an obedient child. Rita winked at me, then clutched her cheek, which was still red where Hugh had slapped her, and obviously hurt when she winked. Dot headed off to the bathroom.

'And use the Imperial Leather!' Rita called after her.

Rita let me experiment with her make-up while Dot took her bath. She told me always to remember the magic words, 'cleanse, tone, nourish', and put all her lovely creams on me. I let her do my eyes, as I wasn't sure where to start, but she showed me how to put on my own lipstick – with a brush! The shade was 'Iced Sherbet', and we both agreed it suited me perfectly.

The mascara felt a bit sticky and irritating, but Rita used very little. She said my lashes were one of my best assets. By the time Dot came back, I looked as though I'd just walked through the gates of Hollywood. Dot looked like a drowned rat, but she smelled nice.

She was wearing a red quilted dressing-gown that belonged to Rita. It was quite glamorous and didn't suit her at all. She sat down and lit a cigarette. 'Rita, it's good of you to take the bother, but all this . . . fancy stuff. It's just no' me.' You couldn't help believing her.

'Dot,' Rita said, using her 'Joseph' voice. 'I've seen many a photo of you and Lil when you were young. You were a good-looking dame. You could meet me halfway, you know. It wouldn't kill you!'

'Well . . . my hair maybe' Dot shrugged.

Rita towelled off Dot's hair, and set out her

curlers. They weren't steel, like Mam's. They were all plastic, and she had three different sizes, and a whole box of plastic sticks to keep them in place. She had Dot's hair done in no time. Then we had a fashion show, and that was fun.

Rita brought out lots of different things for Dot to try, but Dot wouldn't put any of them on. She said she couldn't concentrate on anything because of the hair-dryer, and kept trying to pull the hood off. Rita threatened her with electrocution, but ended up giving her another dram instead.

Finally, Dot decided on a straight blue skirt, and a long-sleeved blouse with lemon and blue flowers on it. Rita said it was the oldest thing in her wardrobe and she wouldn't be seen dead in it, but she was getting tired of arguing with Dot. Then she brought out a beautiful set of underwear. It was a creamy pink colour and the slip and knickers and brassière all matched.

'I brought my own knickers, thank you,' Dot said, 'and half that brassière would do me.

'You'll need a slip,' Rita insisted.

Dot sighed and nodded. There was another argument over shoes and stockings. Dot agreed to take a new pair of Rita's stockings home with her, but insisted on wearing garters. She said she had a pair somewhere, and wasn't fastening herself up with suspenders. She chose some navy-blue court shoes which Rita said were 'walking shoes', and would spoil the whole look, but Rita lost that argument too. The shoes were just a bit too big for

Dot, but Rita found a pair of heel-grips which made them fit better.

Then Rita did Dot's make-up. Dot kept swatting Rita's hands away, and there was a lot of wiping off and starting again, but you wouldn't believe how lovely Dot's face looked when Rita had finished. I was kneeling on my chair, watching it all, and I don't know exactly when she changed, but by the time Rita had combed out her hair and got her dressed, you wouldn't have recognised Dot.

I suggested to Rita that she should open a beauty shop like the film stars went to, instead of trying to sell clothes that nobody wanted. She agreed to give it some serious thought.

It was nearly six o'clock by the time we took Dot home. I took in the washing, which was very stiff, and Rita tidied the house, so Dot wouldn't get herself dirty. Dot found her garters while I collected my pyjamas, and I must say that the stockings really finished her off. You hardly noticed the shoes.

'And don't take any more whisky on an empty stomach,' Rita warned, as we got ready to leave.

'My stomach's no' empty,' Dot answered. She seemed quite ungrateful for all of Rita's help.

'You *could* say thanks,' I said.

Dot stared at me. Then she smiled. I caught my breath.

'You look lovely,' I said. It was true.

'Thank you, Ellie – and thank you, Rita.'

Rita gave her a hug, but didn't touch cheeks. 'We'll be over in the morning. I suppose I'll have to go into that damn shop, so I'll bring Ellie by about half-eight. OK?'

Dot sighed. 'Aye, OK.'

Rita took my hand. I didn't want to spoil Dot's make-up either, so I blew her a kiss.

'Tomorrow's ours, Ellie,' she said. She wasn't smiling any more. 'I promise.'

I beamed. Dot always kept her promises.

Rita was quite wound up that evening. She didn't have 'the nerves', though. It was more a happy sort of excitement. It was nice.

We ate some more, and then we cleared everything up. Rita had better records than Dot. She showed me a few different dance steps, and then she let me examine her brassières and roll-ons, so I would know what to look for in foundation garments. When I asked if Mr Conroy and Joe would be coming by, she told me that they had a few things to sort out, and were better left alone for a while.

'I'm glad you told Joe you love him,' I said.

She stopped folding away her underwear, and turned towards me. 'So am I,' she smiled. The she lifted her eyebrows, and shook her head. 'God knows when that happened.'

'I think it's important to him . . . that he's loved.'

'It's important to all of us,' Rita agreed.

'Does Dot love Mr Starling?'

Rita closed the drawer, and sat beside me on the bed. 'I think she did – once.'

'Was it the lilac trees?'

'The what?'

'Dot said something about the scent of the lilac trees. I think she was thinking about Mr Starling when she said it.'

'Really?' Rita said, seeming very interested in this. 'What else did she say?'

'Nothing much. It's just ... well, after I found that letter and got Mr Smith to find Mr Starling, I thought ... I thought ...'

Rita gave me her full attention. 'What letter?'

'The one she wrote ... when she found out she was ... you know.'

'Ellie, are you telling me *you* were the one who got hold of Johnny? He didn't just decide to come here off his own bat?'

'No. I thought everyone knew that.'

Rita shook her head. 'This letter ... ? How did you get hold of it?'

'I found it when I was taking my vanity case out of my bedside cabinet. I ... well, I read it, and Dot had never sent it, but the address was on it, and Mr Smith was here, and he was from Newcastle, so I asked him if he would find Mr Starling for me. I think ... I thought he must be my grandad.'

Rita leaned back and whistled, very quietly. 'My God,' she said. 'My God.'

'Is Mr Starling my grandad?'

Rita got up and opened her underwear drawer again. She folded a couple of slips which were already folded, and then she closed the drawer. It was the kind of thing grown-ups did when they didn't know what to say.

'Have you asked Dot about your grandad?' Rita asked eventually. This was another ploy – answering questions with questions, even though you're always being told by teachers and parents never to do that.

'Rita,' I begged. 'Would *you* tell me? *Is* he my grandad?'

She sat back down beside me. 'Ellie, yir gran's never been a . . . an ordinary sort of woman. She opens her arms to the whole world, but somehow she always manages to keep her own wee corner intact. D'you understand?'

'No.'

Rita rubbed her eyes. 'Well, it's just that she seems very simple and straightforward, but she can be quite complicated with it all. I don't think she'd want me discussing her private affairs with you; not unless she'd . . . well, given us permission. Now, does that make any sense t'you?'

'Aye.' It did. 'Can you tell me about sex then?'

Rita threw herself back on the bed. 'Jeez, you don't waste words. You're a Fairbairn right enough.' She laughed. 'You're too young to be asking that.'

I was truly disappointed. 'You showed me all about underwear!'

'Aye, and just you remember to keep it on,' she said, sitting up and hugging my shoulders. 'Then you'll no have to worry about sex.' It was true then, all the pictures in Marie's book; you would have to take your knickers off to have sex. I'm sure Janet would never do that. I know I wouldn't, not even if I got married.

I had another bath, even though it wasn't Friday yet, and Rita put me to bed. She lay beside me, and we talked about Hollywood and writing. She thought it would be more fun to be a film star, if you didn't mind the competition and the endless auditions. That made me undecided about my career again, but I'd told Dad I'd be a writer, and I didn't think I could go back on it.

Rita said I had plenty of time to make up my mind, and not to worry about it; I would have something to fall back on, if I got an English prize and did well in school.

'I'd also like to be a wonderful mother, and have lots of children,' I confided. This was my third ambition. I'm sure I would move it up my list eventually.

'Don't rush that either,' Rita said. 'If it was that great, men would have found a way to do it.'

CHAPTER 26

Mr Starling's car was at Dot's house when we arrived back on Friday morning. I ran ahead of Rita, who was busy gathering my clothes from the back seat. She shouted at me to wait for her, but I couldn't. Rita had said that Dot hadn't had a real date as long as she'd known her, and I had to find out if it had been as good as we'd hoped.

The house was empty. I called out, but there was no answer. I ran upstairs. I hardly had to hold the banister at all, I was so used to the steps by now. I stopped on the landing. Dot's door was half-closed, and I could hear her snoring. Perhaps Mr Starling had become besotted with Dot's loveliness and had called for another date this morning, only to find her asleep. He had probably gone for a walk until his beloved awoke – although it wasn't usual for her to sleep this late. Not at all.

I pushed the bedroom door wide. Dot opened her eyes. She was an awful sight; her face was black with mascara and all wrinkled on one side where she'd had the blanket scrunched up on her pillow. Her hair looked worse than Dreep's. Mr Starling was sound asleep beside her, his face to the wall. There was a funny smell in the room, like vinegar.

I felt Rita pulling me backwards. I hadn't even heard her on the stairs. Dot sat up and threw off the covers. She was completely, absolutely, bare naked. I had never seen a naked grown-up before. It was horrible.

'For God's sake,' I heard Rita say. 'The bairn, Dot!'

Dot walked over to her basket chair, and pulled on her dressing-gown. 'What of it? She'll look like this herself one day.'

My face was scarlet. I knew they'd been doing S-E-X. I looked up at Rita. Her face was red too, but also from being angry. She whirled me around, and pushed me towards the stairs, rushing along behind me. 'You're the living end, Dot Fairbairn,' she called back. Mr Starling must have been a heavy sleeper. He hadn't stirred.

Rita sat down in the kitchen, and waited for Dot. I inspected Hooligan's bowls, but you couldn't tell if he'd been or not, as they looked the same as when I'd left.

Dot came in. She'd lit a cigarette, and was coughing and smoking at the same time. She'd pulled a brush through her hair, but she still looked far worse with ruined make-up than with none at all. Rita was very disgusted with everything.

'What're you thinking of?' she demanded. 'And the man on his last legs.'

'You'd never know it,' Dot answered, filling the

kettle. She chuckled. I hadn't heard this particular laugh before. Dot was . . . different, and just the same. It was confusing.

Rita narrowed her eyes, glaring at Dot. 'Lil was probably up half the night, worrying about you both. Wait til she hears this . . .' she threatened.

'Lil won't hear anything,' Dot said, 'until *I'm* ready to tell her.'

'I'm taking Ellie into the shop with me,' Rita said, quite defiantly, I thought. 'I'm certainly not leaving her here in this . . . *den*.' Maybe it was because her name had come up, but it struck me that Rita sounded just like Mrs Bryce.

'It's my last day,' I protested. I looked at Dot. Surely she hadn't forgotten that.

'You'll leave her where she is,' Dot retorted. 'And if it's a den she's in, it's no' the only one around here.'

Rita threw her chair back. 'What exactly d'you mean by that? After all the trouble I went to . . .'

'Och, sit down, Rita,' Dot soothed. 'Johnny'll be on his way soon enough. We had a lot to talk about.' Then Dot winked. She looked like a one-eyed panda.

It settled Rita. She glanced at her watch. 'I've time for one cup, I suppose.'

I fetched the cups. I brought four, in case Mr Starling wanted one. Dot looked at it, and smiled at me. I was hoping she wouldn't wink again.

'Did yis . . . go over things?' Rita asked, fiddling with her charm bracelet.

'Over – and over,' Dot answered. Rita threw her another dirty look.

'We did, Rita, go over things,' Dot repeated. She looked solemn for a moment, then she smiled again and touched Rita's arm. 'And I'm grateful to you. Honest.'

Rita warmed to that. 'It's nothing,' she said. Then she swept her eyes over Dot, and shook her head. 'Could y'no' have washed yir face?'

'No time,' Dot answered, lighting another cigarette. The kettle boiled, but Rita reached behind her and turned off the ring. Nobody moved. Dot sat back in her chair, and sighed. 'No time . . .' she said again.

We heard footsteps on the stairs, and Mr Starling came into the room. He was fully dressed, thank goodness. He saluted us. 'Good morning, all.'

Rita stood, and opened her mouth, but I think she forgot what she was going to say. 'Nice to meet you.'

Mr Starling looked puzzled, but he smiled at her anyway. 'We've met.'

'Yes,' Rita said. 'I have to go.' She ran to the door. 'See you later . . .' she mumbled.

'. . . Alligator,' I sang. She turned and pursed her lips at me. 'Don't be singing,' she warned, and left. She was getting more like Mrs Bryce every minute.

Dot turned the kettle back on. 'Coffee?' she asked Mr Starling. He nodded. 'Pour me a cup when it's ready,' she instructed. 'Just as it comes.'

'Where are you off to, Dorothy?' He had a lovely voice.

'I'd better wash my face. Rita's disgusted with me.'

He reached up and touched her cheek. 'I'm not,' he said. He must have been besotted to say that, and I didn't like the way he was looking at her. I closed my eyes for a moment, but I kept seeing her naked. She *was* disgusting.

Dot headed for the stairs. 'Will I pour your coffee?' I asked Mr Starling.

'How about we just sit here and talk till your grandmother gets back?' Mr Starling answered. He was bending down, tying his shoe-laces.

'I call her Dot, even though she *is* my grand-mother. I don't know who my grandad is.' I was so brave, and it was easy.

Mr Starling tied his other shoe. Then he sat up, and looked at me.

'Is it important?'

'Quite.'

He leaned his elbows on the table, and looked at me. 'Have you asked your . . . Dot?'

I nodded. 'She just said he wasn't free to marry her, and he wouldn't have done – marry her, I mean – even if he could.'

Mr Starling shook his head, but he didn't say anything.

'Rita told me you were engaged to Mrs Bryce – and you ran off.' When you started being brave, you couldn't stop.

He nodded. 'That's true. No doubt about it.' He sounded sad. I liked him, and I didn't want to make him sad.

324

'But you're back now,' I smiled. 'Mrs Bryce is very friendly with you. I suppose she doesn't mind any more.'

That cheered him up. 'I'm happy to say that she doesn't.'

'So, did you not love her? Is that why you ran off?'

'I didn't know who I loved, Ellie. And I was too young and ... too much of a coward to hang around long enough to sort it all out.' He took a huge sigh, and another. He seemed to have difficulty with his breathing, and I started to rise. I was going to open the window for him, but then he spoke again.

'So many things would have been different if I'd stayed ... but I suppose you have to go where life takes you. I certainly didn't have any idea what I was leaving behind.'

'Did you find out? Was it Dot you loved all along?'

He laughed, quietly. 'Who knows?' he answered. 'I've a feeling if I'd stayed, she'd have kicked me out anyway.'

'But you never forgot her?'

'You forget a lot of things when you get old.'

'But not Dot?'

He smiled. 'No ... not Dot.'

'Are you my grandad?'

He pursed his lips and thought for a moment. 'Before I could be your grandad, I'd have to be someone's father ...'

At last, at last I would know. I held my breath.

'What's that?' Dot asked. She was wearing her old corduroy trousers and a brown shirt. She'd washed her face, and put on her red turban. She was back to normal.

Mr Starling shrugged. He couldn't be bothered explaining. Dot didn't insist on an answer, and I still hadn't found out if he was my grandad or not. The frustration of it all was killing me.

'Where's my coffee?' she asked, laying an old Clarks shoe-box on the table. Mam would have got very nervous if she'd seen this. It was a fact that you would have bad luck if you put shoes on the table.

Dot turned the ring back on under the kettle, and opened the box. It was full of photos. Some of them must have been very old, because they were brown, like the ones you saw in old people's houses. I couldn't wait to look at them.

I had two glasses of milk, but Dot and Mr Starling must have drunk hundreds of cups of coffee. The kettle was never off the boil. We had a great time with the photos. There were a few of me when I was a baby, but most of them were of Dad when he was wee, and when he was older too. He wasn't smiling in a single one of them.

'He doesn't look too happy,' Mr Starling remarked.

'Och, he's much happier now,' I told him. 'Mam's better, and the house won't be empty when I go home tomorrow – and he's got his holidays, too.'

'Well, who couldn't be happy with all that?' Mr Starling said. I could tell he was relieved.

Dot said Mr Starling could keep some of the photos if he wanted. He picked eight, but only one of them was of me, when I was about three years old. He said I was so grown-up and pretty now that he didn't need a photo to remember me, and he wished he'd got to know me better; so I didn't mind him choosing just one. The other ones he chose were either Dot by herself, or Dot with Dad.

And I think that's what finally convinced me, for surely he was my grandad after all.

When he was ready to leave, he didn't give me a hug. He just held my hand, and looked at me for ages. Dot and I walked out to the car with him. He did hug Dot for quite a long time, and then they kissed, which was awful.

'Do you think you might write, Dot?' Mr Starling asked.

She shook her head. 'I don't know,' she answered. 'If anything changes, though ... I'm thinking on it ...'

I was sure Dot would write. She couldn't let him go away feeling all lonely again.

It was as though she'd read my mind. 'I'm glad you came back,' she told him.

'Me too,' Mr Starling answered. He lifted his hat from the seat, and put it on. 'All these years, and I'm leaving with the same sweet memory.' He was laughing when he said it.

Dot grinned. 'Away wi' you,' she said, pushing

the door closed. Mr Starling turned the car, and waved. I blew him a kiss, and he blew one back to me. He was still smilling. So was Dot. She smiled all the way back into the house. Then she said she had to go to the toilet. She was gone a long time, and I went to the bottom of the stairs and called up to her.

'Coming, Ellie,' she called back. Then I heard the flush and the door opening, but before that, just before I'd called her name, I know I heard her crying.

'Let's get out of here,' Dot said, after we'd eaten. 'We'll go into Inchbrae, and get lots of sweeties and comics – and anything you want for your supper.'

'Grr-eat!'

'We'll phone your mother while we're there,' Dot added, making everything perfect. I could feel the happiness inside me, like when lemonade bubbled inside your stomach; except it wasn't sore.

We went straight into Rita's. Her shop was packed. She was trying to serve three women, and there was another in her fitting-room, so she didn't have time to talk. She seemed just as irritated with having too many customers as having none at all. She asked Dot to look back later, but Dot said we probably wouldn't have the time, and squeezed my hand when she said it.

We crossed the road, and entered the Jacobite. Mrs Bryce was in the lobby. She took one look at Dot, and folded her arms. Then she tutted a few times, and tapped her foot.

'He's left,' she said. 'What were you thinking about?'

Dot shrugged. 'You sound like Rita.' I was thinking the same thing when Mrs Bryce noticed me. I couldn't move fast enough to escape.

'Your mother would die,' she said, squeezing the life out of me. You could tell that Hugh had learned this from his mother. They both had arms of steel.

'I was just going to phone her,' Dot said. 'Would you mind?'

'I'm past minding,' Mrs Bryce answered, letting me go. It was another of those sayings which made no sense, but I was too glad to be free to think about it.

Mam answered on the third ring. Dot handed me the phone right away. 'I'll be wanting a word when you're through,' she said.

'Hello?'

'Mam, it's me, Ellie.'

'Oh, Ellie, it seems like years since I heard you.' Mam sounded like she might cry, so I hurried on.

'I'll be home tomorrow. Is Dad still taking his holidays?'

'Yes, yes, he is. We can't wait to see you.'

'Are you better, Mam?'

Silence. My heart fell.

'Much better, Ellie. I really am. Your father's been a great help.' I let out my breath. 'Of course, he doesn't want us to do anything too ... exciting when he's off. Just a few quiet days at home.' She sounded a bit disappointed, but I knew Dad was

329

concerned with our wellbeing, and wanted Mam to have as much peace and quiet as possible.

'Maybe when you get home, we can persuade him to take us *somewhere* between us,' she urged. I would help her to get round Dad. I knew she wanted me to.

'I'll try, Mam. I can't wait to see you either,' I added, in case she'd forgotten how much I loved her. 'I'll see you tomorrow.'

I'd almost forgotten Dot was standing there. 'Mam, Dot needs to talk to you.'

I heard her take a deep breath as I handed Dot the phone.

'Hello, Sylvia, Dot here.' I giggled – as though Mam wouldn't know that. Dot frowned at me.

'How are you?' She nodded into the phone. 'That's good to hear, Sylvia. I want you both to drive up here tomorrow to collect Ellie.'

I gasped. Dot hadn't even mentioned this to me.

'Wait . . . wait a minute now,' she said, obviously interrupting whatever Mam was trying to say. 'This isn't an option, Sylvia. I need to talk to Adam, and I need him here in person. No . . . no, there's no argument. I'll expect you both about lunchtime.

'If he has anything to say about it, you just tell him I won't take no for an answer. Ellie won't be on that bus tomorrow, Sylvia, so you'll have to come and get her. Goodbye, hen,' and she put down the phone.

'Are they coming?' I asked.

'They'll be here,' Dot assured me.

We didn't stay in Inchbrae too long. Dot said she needed to speak to Mrs Bryce in private, and why didn't I go over to Mrs Alexander's and get my comics. I wanted to spend the rest of my pocket-money, but Mrs Alexander wouldn't hear of it. She gave me the *School Friend* and the *Beano*, but I put back the *Beano* when she wasn't looking, as I didn't want to take advantage. I don't know how she ever made a profit, but when I mentioned this she said they hadn't had such a spate of visitors in a long time, and she was perfectly entitled to spoil anyone she chose.

She'd chosen me.

'So, you're off tomorrow then?'

'Aye,' I answered. 'But I'll be coming back.'

'Certainly,' she said, giving me a hug. She was much gentler than Mrs Bryce. 'I'll see you before you leave.'

I waved at her, and agreed to pop in the next day. When I went into Mr Conroy's he explained that Joseph's friends had arrived home, and that the three of them had headed off on their bikes.

'Maybe he's showing them the tent,' I said, hoping to meet them on our way back.

'There was mention of football,' Mr Conroy answered. 'They might be down at the dump.'

'You don't need his help today?' I asked. He had said Friday was a busy day.

'I'll manage,' he said. 'After all, doesn't the summer go too quick altogether?'

I agreed that it did. 'My dad's got his holidays. We might go somewhere.'

'Won't that be grand?' He smiled. I thought it was a shame Joseph would never be as handsome as Mr Conroy.

'D'you think you'll be getting married before I come back?'

He put down his knife. 'As soon as we can,' he replied. 'I wouldn't be wanting Rita to change her mind now.'

'She's very busy today ... Maybe she should close more often.'

'Isn't it yourself that has the smart ideas!' he exclaimed. He wrapped up some scraps, and a decent-sized bone. 'You'll be wanting to give that animal a treat before you leave. A wee something for him to remember you by.'

I thanked him, and left. Joe and his friends weren't at the dump. Neither was Hooligan. I looked everywhere for him, even down the two lanes behind the shops where I hadn't gone before. Then I heard Dot calling me, so I hurried back. She'd been into the Fishbeins', and her basket was full.

When I told her I couldn't find Hooligan, she whistled for him, but he didn't come. 'It's early,' she said. 'He'll turn up before the day's over.'

Rita saw us leaving from her shop window. She came to the door, and shouted over to Dot. 'Are yis coming for yir baths tonight?'

Dot looked puzzled. 'I had one yesterday,' she answered.

'You'll be needing another one,' Rita said, trying to whisper, which you couldn't do from across the street.

'I'm fine,' Dot laughed. She looked at me. 'Unless . . . ?'

'I'm fine, too,' I assured her.

'We'll see you tomorrow,' Dot called back. Rita went back inside without saying cheerio. She looked disgusted again.

On the way back, I asked Dot if she was sure Dad and Mam would come for me. She laughed. 'They'd better,' she answered.

'But you don't think Dad'll be mad at having to drive up for me?'

'I should think he'll be driving ninety miles an hour just to see your face.'

I couldn't remember feeling so happy in all my life. We were laughing and joking when we turned into the lane – and then I saw him.

CHAPTER 27

He was lying under the lilac trees, and even before I threw my bike down, I knew he was dead. I screamed his name, and ran to him. Dot tried to reach him first and pulled me back, but I struggled free and knelt beside him. I hadn't even felt my tears coming, but my face was wet and my whole body was shaking. He was completely still, his mouth still open and his tongue laying against the grass. I touched him, ran my hand across his ears. They were both flat, and they'd never been like that – never.

'Hooligan … Hooligan, please don't … Oh, please God, please don't . . .' I couldn't see him. My tears were blinding me, and I pushed them away. I had to see him, I had to! He didn't even know I was there. He'd come for me to help him, and I wasn't there.

Inside me, something big and hard cracked open, and I threw myself across his body. It was warm still, so warm. I wanted to shake him and shake him until he opened his eyes, but I knew that he never would. I kissed his poor face and buried my head in his fur. If I could hold him long enough, surely, surely God would let him come back to me. I felt Dot reach for me, but I wouldn't let him go.

'Ellie, Ellie.' I could hear her voice, but from far away. She pulled my arm again and I shouted at her.

'It's *your* fault! You should have mended him. You knew. You KNEW he was hurt. You should have mended him.' My breath left me. I couldn't breathe, couldn't think.

Dot prised my arms from him and lifted me up. She brushed my knees. I could see they were all cut and grazed where I'd been kneeling, but I didn't care. I wanted them to sting and hurt me for ever. I tried to push her away, but she held on to me and I realised that she was crying too.

'We should have saved him,' I sobbed. 'He came for us to help him. It's not fair. It's not fair.'

'I know, hen, I know,' Dot whispered. 'But he's gone, and now we have to bury him. You'll have to be brave, Ellie. You just have to be.'

I stood away from her and gazed down at him. I felt loose and light as though my body might float away, and only this huge ball of hurt inside of me could keep me anchored to the ground. It was as though the world had changed colour. Everything looked red and quivering, and I knew it was the colour of my heart breaking; and I knew I would remember it always – and nothing would ever be the same.

Dot took my hand. 'We'll get the barrow,'

she said, leading me to the shed.

I pulled against her. 'Carry him, Dot. Please . . . please don't put him in the barrow . . .' I sobbed.

She shook her head. 'He's too heavy, Ellie. I'm no strong enough.'

'Between us . . . between us we can carry him. Please, Dot.'

Dot knelt and tried to get her arms underneath him, but she couldn't lift him. I pushed her aside, and she fell against the verge.

'Leave him alone then,' I cried, and lay back down beside him. It seemed like we were there a long time, and at last I stopped shaking, but I thought that I would never, never stop crying in all of my life.

'How will we get him in the barrow?' I asked, at last.

'We can't,' she answered. 'I'll get a blanket. We can wrap it around him, and then we'll just have to pull him along.'

I waited with him while Dot went to the house. I told him how sorry I was, and asked him please to forgive me. I told him all about Mr Starling and how my parents were coming for me, and I'd be going home and that, no matter where I was – even if it was Paris – I would never forget about him. And I told him that, even though my heart was broken, it was still full of my love for him, and that I would love him for ever.

'For ever, Hooligan.' Dot was tapping my shoulder.

'Get up, Ellie. We'll need to wrap him now.'

Dot opened out the tartan plaid across the lane, and lifted his legs very gently and placed them on top of it. Then we pushed on his back until we got him further on to it. He was colder now, and heavier.

When we got all of him on to the blanket, Dot and I took hold of the sides and he sort of slid into the middle. We were both panting with the effort. Dot gathered up the top, and I gathered the bottom, and between us we half-carried, half-pulled him up the lane, and laid him where the sun had cast long shadows at the side of the shed.

Dot looked around. 'The softest dirt's beneath the hedge there,' she said. 'He'll be well protected.'

It took a long time to dig his grave. Dot and I took turns with the spade, but she could work much faster than me. We made it as flat as we could across the bottom, and Dot brought out two of her old turbans to tie up the plaid at each end. Then we laid him in the ground. We couldn't quite hold on to him at the end, and he made a thump as his body fell. I knew he couldn't feel it, but I felt it for him and the pain of it spread all through me.

Dot began the service by reciting the twenty-third psalm, and then I tried to say 'Now I lay me down to sleep', but I kept choking on the words, so Dot finished it for me. We were still crying as we walked back inside.

'Tomorrow I'll lift that,' Dot said as we passed the purple flower. 'We can replant it beside him. A wee bit o' trellis to support it, and he'll feel right at home.' It was kind of her to have thought of it, but I didn't want him smelling that awful flower.

'Maybe not, Dot. If he can't pee on it, he might not want it over him.'

Dot smiled, and I smiled back. I hadn't realised that you could smile and cry at the same time.

'Would you want a wee walk to the river?' Dot asked. 'It might give us an appetite for supper.'

I shook my head. I didn't want to leave Hooligan all alone.

Dot squeezed my hand. 'However you feel,' she said.

I looked up at her clock. Dad would be settled in his chair, recuperating. 'The news should be coming on.'

Dot looked puzzled. We'd never listened to the news all the time I'd been here. 'We can get an idea what the weather's going to do.'

She understood. I didn't want it to rain on Hooligan's grave, and maybe soak through to his blanket. I wanted the weather to stay dry and fine, and for the sun to shine tomorrow. I was sure that it would, as it had shone nearly every day in Inchbrae. I suppose it must have been shining at home too; it wasn't *that* far away. But now, now when I was going back, it seemed to me that all I could remember was the rain.

I was thinking about this when I saw Dot collapse into her chair. I heard the man on the news saying something about Billie Holiday. I tried to listen, but he was handing over to the weather-man. Dot's face was white.

'There's the weather, Dot,' I reminded her. She wasn't hearing me. I pulled her arm. 'Dot . . . it's the weather.' I was frightened. I didn't know what had happened.

She lifted a hand. 'It's all right, Ellie. I'm all right.'

'No you're *not*! What's wrong, Dot? What did he say? Was it Miss Holiday? Please, Dot, please tell me.'

She swallowed and looked at me. 'She died . . . early this morning.' Her face was getting its colour back, but she still didn't look right. 'God, what a waste. It's all such a waste . . .'

I was shivering. I was sorry about Miss Holiday, but she'd had no right to die today. It wasn't fair. We had Hooligan to consider.

'There won't be another like her,' Dot whispered. She began humming. I knew it. It was 'Lady Sings the Blues'.

'Stop it, Dot. Please don't!'

'No more, then. Won't sing the blues no more.'

'Dot . . .' I was crying again. Dot pulled me up on her knee, and rocked me. 'All at once,' she sighed. 'All at once, yis have to leave me.'

'I won't leave, Dot,' I promised. 'I can stay with you. I don't have to go. I don't want to go.' And I didn't. I wanted to stay here, here with Dot and Hooligan . . .

Dot held me away from her, and stared into my

339

eyes. 'Of course you'll go,' she said, wiping my eyes. 'If you don't go, how can I look forward to you coming back?'

We did go to the river that night. Dot lit a cigarette when we got there, and told me to take a good look at the hills. I did, but there wasn't much to see – just mountains and sky, and a few clouds with pink in them.

'They've seen it all,' she said. 'Battles won and lost, lands emptied; people scattered to the four corners.' She pointed her cigarette at me. 'But they endure, Ellie. They endure, and so will we. Wherever you go, keep them in your heart. They know . . .'

I nodded. 'We'll endure,' I repeated. I wasn't sure exactly what that meant, nor what it was that the hills knew, but I didn't ask.

'We should have kept him in the house, Dot . . . until he was better. We should have.'

'It wouldn't have been right,' Dot explained. 'He was never used to closed doors, Ellie. It would have frightened him.'

'No, it wouldn't have. He wasn't frightened of anything. He was so brave, Dot.'

'He was brave in the outside world, hen. Not inside, not cooped up in a house. It would have been like taking his freedom away from him. You canna do that to people, nor to animals either. Don't you remember? When we talked about it?'

'D'you mean like Miss Holiday . . . and Mr

Smith?' I couldn't see how the colour bar could affect dogs. Dogs were already free.

Dot sighed. 'There are different kinds of freedom, hen. We canna always see the traps we set for ourselves, but animals trust us not to do the same to them. Y'see, if Hooligan hadn't felt free to leave when he wanted, then he wouldn't have come here in the first place.'

I hadn't been free to come here. I'd been made to do it. But I knew Dot was willing to let me go, even though she would miss me. And I knew I could always come back. I supposed that was freedom – in a way.

We still weren't hungry when we got back to the house, but we forced ourselves to eat some peaches and cream. When we sat back down by the fireside Dot began telling me some of the things that Hooligan had done over the years, and I began to feel better, as though I was getting to know him all over again. I began to yawn, and Dot pulled me back on to her knee. The next morning I awoke in her chair with a blanket tucked around me. My neck was stiff.

Dot was gathering my clothes and had my case open on the floor. She wasn't making much of a job of packing them and I knew Mam would have them all out and washed again as soon as I got home.

Home. I was finally going home. I yawned.

Dot looked up. 'We'll get you washed and grab a

bite o' something. I thought you'd want to go in and say your goodbyes this morning.'

She was talking faster than usual, as though she was a bit nervous, probably from bending over the case.

Then I remembered. 'Hooligan,' I whispered.

Dot sat back on her heels. 'It didn't rain, Ellie. Look, the sun's shining.'

I didn't have to turn to look out the window. I could see the sun streaming through the back door, and making great shafts of light across the lino. All that sunshine.

'What time will they be here?' I asked.

'I told Sylvia lunchtime. What time d'you have yir dinner at home?'

'One o'clock.'

Dot took a deep breath. 'Knowing your father, that's when they'll be here. One o'clock ... on the dot,' she smiled. She smoothed the last of my clothes and stood up. 'Let's get going, then.'

CHAPTER 28

I wanted to take our bikes, just in case we got delayed in Inchbrae and had to hurry back, but Dot wouldn't hear of it.

'It'll be our last walk for a while,' she said. We smoothed the top of Hooligan's grave again, although it didn't really need it, and set off hand-in-hand.

We didn't get far when we came across Dreep. He was sitting by the roadside, with his head in his hands. My heart sank; I'd forgotten all about him and now we'd have to tell him about Hooligan. Dot bent by him, and spoke first.

'Dreep ... Dreep, what're you doing away out here?'

He raised his head, and I could see dirty tear-tracks all down his face.

'Miss Fairbairn,' he said, gulping, 'I found him ... I found him ...' He began twisting his hands together, and shaking his head.

'Who, Dreep? Who was it you found?'

'Hooligan,' he almost shouted, as though we should know.

Dot shook her head too, as if to clear it. 'Dreep, Hooligan's . . . he's . . .'

'Dead. I know. I know.'

'How d'you know?'

'I *found* him. Can't you listen?' Dot and I looked at each other. Then Dreep began murmuring to himself, and Dot gave him a shove.

'Speak up. I canna hear you.' She was getting impatient with him, and so was I.

He sniffed away his tears, and wiped his nose on his sleeve. 'I found that divine creature here, right here.'

Dot made a loud huffing noise. 'He's no' here, Dreep. Look around you.'

Dreep leapt to his feet, frightening us both. 'HE WAS HERE!' he shouted. Then he clapped his hands to his eyes, and began crying again. 'Yesterday,' he continued, after much snuffling, 'I found him lying here – dead. I brought him to you. I didn't know what else to do.' He sounded bereft.

Dot sighed. 'God save us, Dreep, why didn't you stay? You could have helped us bury him. He's in my garden . . . under the hedge. You should have stayed with him.'

Dreep raised his arms to the heavens. 'He's gone . . . gone. In all the planet the only creature who cared one whit for Leonard Mackleton Mayberry is gone.'

Dot reached out to him. 'You're wrong, Dreep. There's plenty of us care for you. You just don't care enough about yourself.'

344

Dreep stood still, his arms still held aloft. 'You are correct, madam. But allow me to mourn the passing of a dear and faithful companion.' And with that, he set off in the direction from which we'd come.

Above us, a single aeroplane droned into view. Dreep began turning in circles, his arms once more heavenward.

'Wings! Of course . . . wings! Fly, Hooligan. Fly! Fly!' We could hear him quite clearly from where we stood.

'God love him,' Dot said, taking my hand again, and turning toward Inchbrae. I looked back once. It was the last time I saw him.

We went into Mrs Alexander's first. She gave me the *School Friend*, and looked a bit crestfallen when I told her I already had one. 'I'll get you something different,' she said.

'But you just gave me it to me yesterday,' I reminded her. 'I saved it specially.' She was pleased, I could tell. She said she'd look forward to seeing me soon again, and we had another nice hug.

Rita was busy. I asked her if Joseph was about.

'Och, we'll see damn little of him now his friends are back,' she replied. 'Thank God for that though, it'll keep his mind off other things.'

I didn't want to tell her about Hooligan. Somehow, I felt she wouldn't be that hurt by it, and I didn't want to betray his memory. She promised to

345

send me some wedding photos. 'I'll put in a bit o' the cake,' she smiled, 'for luck.'

'Mrs Gilchrist, would you have this in a bigger size?' a woman called, waving a black blouse from between the curtains of the fitting-room.

'She should have taken the bigger size to begin with,' Rita whispered to me. 'She looks like Hattie Jacques.'

I might have giggled at that before, but I just smiled. 'See you later, alligator,' I whispered.

'In a while, crocodile,' she whispered back. Then she grabbed Dot's arm. 'And I'll see *you* tomorrow. I haven't heard the half of it yet.'

Dot pulled her arm free. 'Come over the night . . . if you're not doing anything.' I was glad Dot was having Rita over. I didn't want her to be alone.

Mr Conroy was busy also, so I didn't wait. He waved and told me the sun wouldn't shine on him till I got back.

That just left the Fishbeins and the Bryces. I was getting anxious by now, and afraid that if we went into the Jacobite, Dot might want a dram or two and we'd be late getting back. As usual, she was reading my mind.

'Why don't you say cheerio to the Fishbeins, and I'll tell Lil you're leaving. She won't be wanting Hugh to get in a lather over it.'

I pushed open the grocer's door, and hesitated; I knew I would have to tell them about Hooligan. They had tried to help him more than anyone – more than me.

'Come away in,' Mr Fishbein said. Mrs Fishbein was unpacking some tins of sardines. She put the box down, and came round the counter. She bent down and held out a sugar dummy. I bit my lip, and the tears stung my eyes.

'He didn't get better,' I said. I looked into her sad eyes, and then I was in her arms. She hugged me for a long time, then gently held me away. 'It happens,' she said.

I wiped my eyes. 'I know,' I nodded.

'Ist today you leaving must?'

I nodded again, and she held my shoulders. 'You will come back.' It was perfect English; you couldn't even hear her accent. Then she stood up, and rushed back behind the counter. Mr Fishbein put his arm around her, and kissed her cheek.

'Ve luff you,' he said. I left them together, waving at me from their window, their arms around each other still.

Mrs Bryce came out of the Jacobite with Dot. She had a bottle of tangerine lemonade in her hand. 'That's from Eckie,' she said, her voice low. 'Keep it straight, or it'll burst on you.' I asked her to thank Mr Bryce for me. 'He's keeping an eye on Hugh, or he'd be out himself. He says to hurry back.'

'Is Hugh all right?'

'Aye, hen, he's fine. He's no' very good at saying cheerio, though. It upsets him. We huvna let on about you leaving. I hope you don't mind.'

'No, course not. If he notices I'm gone, you can tell him it's just for a wee while.'

Mrs Bryce wiped at her eyes, and I knew Dot had told her about Hooligan. Mrs Bryce was just too kind to mention it. I was glad. I knew it was coming, and took a deep breath. She hugged me for ever.

'I'd better go in before he comes looking for me,' she said. She rubbed her eyes with her apron, and I thought she was going to grab me again, but she didn't. 'God bless, hen. We'll miss you.'

And then we were alone, me and Dot; just as we were the day I'd arrived.

It didn't last long.

There was the sound of yelling, and Joseph came hurtling along the street on his bicycle. Two other boys raced behind him, one bigger and one smaller. They stopped long before he did, and waited as he skidded to a halt in front of us.

'Are you off?'

I nodded. I couldn't bring myself to talk about Hooligan any more. It hurt too much, and anyway Joseph was going to have to grow up without me. He looked back at his friends, and waved his arm for them to join us, but they wouldn't move.

'They don't like girls.' He grinned. 'When y'coming back?'

'I don't know. I'll write you.'

'Nuht!' he said, screwing his face up. 'Gyudders!'

In the distance, a lorry came trundling along towards Inchbrae. 'Bet we beat it to Locheirnan,' Joe shouted. They all three turned their bikes around.

'You never took me there,' I said. 'We never went to Locheirnan.'

'Take you next time,' he shouted, and they were gone.

All the way back to the house, I tried to look forward to going home, away from everything, away from Inchbrae. I had looked forward to going home almost from the minute I'd arrived, but now I was so confused about everything.

I didn't want to leave Dot alone, with just a grave for company, even though I knew she'd still have her friends coming by. Even my excitement over finding Mr Starling seemed to have evaporated – as though he had never been here. I knew that he had, of course, and that he really was my grandad, and was definitely the reason Dot had asked Mam and Dad to come up to collect me. It just didn't seem important any more.

I was already hearing Mam and Dad in my mind; the quietness of them, the quiet lectures, the quiet tears, the silence in our house – that's what I was hearing most of all. It was the strangest feeling; as though I would have no freedom once I went home.

I think I understood then what Dot had told me about Hooligan. He wasn't the kind of dog who would have put up with *having* to do what he was told, *having* to stay in a house, or anything like that. Hooligan had been free.

We were standing by his grave when I heard

349

Dad's car. For a moment, I forgot everything. My heart leapt with happiness at seeing them again, and I raced round the front of the house. I hurled myself at Dad – he was first out of the car, and he almost had to shake me off him.

'Eleanor,' he gasped. 'Good lord, child.' Then Mam had her arms around me, and I smelled her perfume and looked up into her lovely face. She looked all right; a bit stunned at my welcome, but all right.

Dot was standing at the corner of the house. No hugs from her.

'Come on in,' she said. 'I hope you ate something before you left. I haven't prepared anything.'

Dad just nodded, but Mam smiled – as though she hadn't expected to get anything to eat, and was pleased to be right. It was a real smile, though, it wasn't nasty.

She kept her arm around me all the way to the back door. I didn't want to spoil anything by telling them about Hooligan just yet. Besides, I wasn't sure how Mam might feel about death. She was funny about superstitious stuff like that.

The first thing Dot did was pull out her whisky bottle. I wished she hadn't done that – but then, that was Dot for you.

'You'll no' be having a dram, I suppose?' she asked Dad.

'What's going on, Mother?' he said. I looked at Mam, then I realised he meant Dot. I shivered, for no reason.

'Sit down, the pair of yis. I've something to tell you.' Dot finished her dram in two swallows, and poured another. Then she lit a cigarette. Dad leaned back, and screwed up his face, but she paid him no heed.

'Ellie hasn't been my only visitor this past couple of weeks,' Dot said. She blew the smoke out of her nose. 'Before I go on, it's only fair to ask you, Sylvia, if you're feeling stronger?'

Mam looked confused for a moment. 'I am,' she answered. 'I'm . . . I'm fine, Dot.'

'Good, then. No sense in wasting words, Adam. Your father was here.'

There was a moment of complete silence, and then everything went quite mad. Dad pointed at Dot. 'You're a liar!' he shouted. Dad shouted!

Mam dropped her handbag, and covered her eyes. I could hear her whimpering. Dot threw her chair back, and pushed her hand hard against Dad's chest. 'Don't you raise yir voice to me, Adam Fairbairn!'

Dad caught the back of his knees on his own chair, and grabbed my collar as he stumbled. 'Outside, Eleanor. Outside, *now!*'

Then Dot grabbed me and spun me backwards, behind her. 'Stay where y'are, Ellie. You're no' going anywhere.'

I was dazed, I think, and dizzy too.

'I knew it. I knew it was trouble, Adam,' Mam shrieked. 'God, Dot, is there never any peace with you?'

Dad turned to Mam. 'Quiet, Sylvia,' he commanded. 'Don't start now. Just don't start.' His eyes were wild, and his hair was all ruffled, even though he hadn't touched it. I'd never in all my life seen him like this.

He tried to sweep Mam's handbag off the floor and missed. Then he began marching across the room. 'Get your case. Eleanor. Where *is* your case?'

'For Christ's sake, Adam,' Dot shouted. 'Get a bloody hold of yourself.'

And, as suddenly as it had started, everything went silent.

Mam's face was white, and her mouth was half open, as though she had started to say something, but had forgotten what it was. Dad walked slowly back to his chair, and sat down. He ran his hands through his hair, and straightened his tie. Dot let me go, but I remained behind her, holding on to the old wooden spar of her chair. She sat down too, and stubbed out her cigarette. Then she looked at Dad for a long time.

'Are you ready to listen now?' she asked, at last.

'Is it necessary for the child to be here?' he asked.

'Quite necessary,' Dot replied. 'It was "the child" who brought him here.' I tried to sidle farther behind Dot, but I couldn't escape my father's stare. His eyes were burning into me.

'Eleanor? What *is* this all about?'

'Leave her alone, Adam,' Dot remonstrated. 'She wanted a grandad – rightly enough – and she found one.'

Dad's nostrils flared. I'd never seen him do that before either. I glanced at Mam, but she had shut her mouth, and the colour had come back into her cheeks. In fact, she was looking quite interested in what Dot had to say.

Nobody spoke as Dot told the story. Every once in a while, I caught Mam's eyes, and there was something there ... almost like she was admiring me, but maybe I was imagining that. I was so scared that they would both hate me for causing another 'commotion', and especially now that Dad had just got round to calling me Ellie. I would probably be Eleanor the rest of my days.

Dot left out the bit about Mr Starling staying in the house all night, but then I wouldn't expect her to discuss S-E-X with my parents. I could understand that Dot might feel they had had enough shocks for one day.

'The thing is,' Dot finished, 'he had no idea about any of it, and now ... he's dying, Adam.'

My legs crumpled. It was the last thing I remembered.

CHAPTER 29

Mam was stroking my forehead, and Dad was beside me too, holding my hand. It was a dream.

It wasn't a dream. I sat up. I was in Dot's armchair again.

'Ellie, lie down. Lie down, pet.' Dad! Dad was calling me 'pet'. 'Pet' and 'Ellie', all at once.

Then it came back to me. I searched for Dot's face. She was there too, standing against the door.

'You never said . . .' I whispered.

She shook her head. 'I'm sorry, Ellie. But it's true. We all have to face it. No-one said it was fair.' Her voice was quiet, quiet and calm, and I knew she wasn't lying. She had never lied to me, not once.

'Dad?'

'I don't know, Ellie. It's all . . . a bit much, right now. We need time . . .'

There would be time. When we got home we could call him, call my grandad. Once we were home, Dad would be ready to call him. There would be time. I threw my arms around his neck. 'We can phone him. We have the phone.'

He held me close, and I felt him turn his head

away. I would have to convince him. I knew that I could.

Mam had risen, and was standing with her arm around Dot. She looked just like Rita . . . or Mrs Bryce. She just looked like somebody's friend, like Dot's friend. She looked normal.

I stood up. My head hurt, and my legs were a bit trembly, but I had to show them. 'Will you come outside with me?'

They followed, Mam and Dad. Dot stayed inside, sitting on her chair with her whisky and her cigarettes.

I showed them Hooligan's grave, and told them all about him. Once, Mam sobbed, but then it was over. She was just sorry for me, for me and Hooligan – not for herself. I was very proud of her then, but I couldn't say it, couldn't explain it.

We went back inside, and Dot had my case beside her on the table, my vanity case too. She smiled at me and her eyes were as blue as the sky. 'It's time then,' she said.

I held her hand all the way to the car.

'You'll let me know, Adam?' she said, looking at Dad. 'Whatever you decide?'

'I will,' he answered. 'I'll call . . . and I'll be putting in the phone for you. I'll have it seen to when I get back.'

'You don't have to do that.'

He stared at her, and finally, gave her the briefest of hugs. 'I want to,' he said, getting into the car. Mam and Dot had a longer hug.

'Look after yourself, hen,' Dot said.

'You too,' Mam replied, and she smiled.

'And look after that bairn for me,' Dot added.

I scrambled across the seat, and reached for her hand again. She bent towards me and kissed my cheek, and her eyes were misty.

'There's the tattie-picking holidays . . . in October,' I reminded her. 'Dad? There's the tattie . . .'

'Yes, Ellie, I heard you.' He smiled, and looked up at Dot. 'Why not? It's not that far away.'

She squeezed his arm, and he looked at her again. 'I don't know . . .' he said.

'It's all right, son. It's all right.'

Dad turned the car in a circle and I waved out of the back window all the way to the road, long after I couldn't see her.

I sat back into my seat, and watched Inchbrae disappear behind us. My head was teeming with it all, and I couldn't wait to tell Janet when I got home. I tried to remember it all the way it had happened, but it kept getting jumbled up and out of order. I would write it down in my journal. Then it would make sense. Then I could tell Janet.

I looked at Mam and Dad. He was driving so straight, like he'd always done. And Mam was sitting there beside him, as though it was just an ordinary day. But it wasn't.

'Mam, Dad . . .' I swallowed. 'Could I have a dog for my birthday?'

Dad's eyes met mine in the driving-mirror. He

shook his head. 'A new bicycle would be more appropriate, Ellie. It's what we agreed on.'

'I'd really prefer a dog.' I rushed on, afraid I'd be silenced. 'It'll be good to have one around. I can train it myself, and it'll keep the house guarded when . . .' I'd nearly said 'when Mam goes to work', but I knew Dad had had enough shocks for one day, and Mam might not be ready to go to work just yet. Still, there was plenty of time before the tattie-picking holidays. I could work on it.

'They're noisy, and dirty,' Dad said.

'They can be taught when to be quiet, and you know Mam, you know you wouldn't ever let it get dirty,' I pleaded.

They both laughed at that. It was nice to see them laughing together, especially considering what they'd been through in the last few hours. What *all* of us had been through. It was a great thing, a family.

I was just deciding how important it was to convince them that we'd be even more of a family with a dog, when I realised that I needed the toilet. We were in the middle of the country.

'Can we stop, Dad? I need the toilet.'

This, more than anything, made my father cross. He always insisted we went to the toilet before setting off anywhere, even if we didn't need to go.

'Eleanor,' he protested, 'surely you can wait?' He sounded more tired than angry.

'No, I don't think so.'

Mam was fiddling with her handbag. 'Actually,

Adam, I didn't think about it, but I'm ... well, if you could find somewhere to stop ...'

Dad drove a little distance, and pulled over by some open fields. 'I'm outnumbered,' he sighed.

Mam and I got out. He waved his hand, dismissing us.

'Please be quick. I don't want somebody coming upon us,' he urged.

And together, Mam and I ran laughing through the long grass of summer. And as it swished behind us, I thought I felt his warm breath on my legs. And I knew he was with me somewhere, loping along and grinning – my own beloved Hooligan.

If you enjoyed this book, you might also enjoy *Puppies Are For Life* by Linda Phillips.

Puppies Are For Life

Now that their children have finally flown the nest, Susannah and Paul Harding are looking forward to a trouble-free middle age. Paul is counting down the years to retirement; while Susannah sees a chance to spread her creative wings a little after years of motherhood and a dreary job.

But their nest isn't empty for long. Daughter Katy comes home for comfort having lost her job, closely followed by her brother Simon, licking the wounds of redundancy and a failed relationship – and with a baby and a cat in tow. Finally Susannah's father and stepmother, seeking refuge from a disastrous attempt to settle in the Dordogne, set up camp in the garden.

Paul is delighted to have his family around him once more, but Susannah is horrified at the prospect of a return to domestic drudgery, and seeks solace with her sympathetic neighbour Harvey – who happens to have too much time on his hands . . .

If you would like to order a copy of *Puppies Are For Life*, please turn the page for details.

If you would like to be put on a mailing list to receive regular updates on further new books from Fourth Estate, please send your name and address on a postcard to The Company of Strangers, Press Office, Fourth Estate, 6 Salem Road, London W2 4BU.

To order a copy of *Puppies Are For Life*, price £5.99, please complete the form below. Please allow 75p per book for post and packing in the UK. Overseas customers please allow £1.00 per book for post and packing.

Please send me ... copy/copies (insert number required) of *Puppies Are For Life* by Linda Phillips.

Name ....

Address ....

....

....

Send this page with a cheque/eurocheque/postal order (sterling only), made payable to Book Service by Post, to:

   Fourth Estate Books,
   Book Service By Post,
   PO Box 29, Douglas
   I-O-M, IM99 1BQ

Alternatively you can pay by Access, Visa, or Mastercard: please complete the following details and return this page to the address above.

Card number ....

Expiry date ....

Signature ....

You can also order by phone, tel: 01624 675137; or by fax: 01624 670923

Please allow 28 days for delivery. Please tick box if you do not wish to receive any additional information. ❏

Prices and availability subject to change without notice.